Mission Perilous . . .

Inside the creature several glowing, green bubbles floated. Within those bubbles were a dozen people. Cora could see they were screaming, but could hear nothing through the hull of the submarine.

A bubble drifted nearer and, horrified, Cora recognized the short, dark-skinned man within. He flailed at the film of the bubble, and his eyes were wide and desperate.

As the creature moved away from the viewport, the bubble moved toward the epidermis, then passed through the skin and immediately burst under the tremendous pressure.

The man imploded before he could drown!

Also by Alan Dean Foster
available now from Ballantine Books:

CACHALOT

A NOVEL BY

Alan Dean Foster

A Del Rey Book

BALLANTINE BOOKS • NEW YORK

A Del Rey Book
Published by Ballantine Books

Library of Congress Catalog Card Number: 79-92626

ISBN 0-345-28066-0

Manufactured in the United States of America

First Edition: May 1980

Cover art by Darrell K. Sweet

For Philippe and Jacques Cousteau,
For the men of the *Calypso*,
For the men and women of Greenpeace.

CACHALOT

I

Mustapha Ali sat on the end of Rorqual Towne and was not seasick. There was nothing any save an outsider would have found remarkable in this. Mustapha had lived all his long life on Cachalot, and those who are born to that world know less of seasickness than a worm does of Andromeda. All born on Cachalot rest in two cradles: their nursery, and the greater nursery of the all-encompassing Mother Ocean. Those who arrived on Cachalot from other worlds did not long remain if they proved susceptible to motion sickness.

It was a great change, wrought by history and accident, Mustapha thought as he let his burl-dark legs dangle over the side of the dock. They moved a meter or so above the deep green-black water. His ancestors had come from a high, dry section of Earth, where the sea was only a tale told to wide-eyed children. And here he lived, where most of the land was imported.

His ancestors had been great players of the game. That was his only regret, not being able to carry on the tradition of the game. For where on Cachalot could one find fifty fine horsemen and a dead goat? Mustapha had settled for being a champion water polo player, having mastered that game and its many local variants in his youth. Compared with the game of his forebears, all had been gentle and undemanding.

1

Now he was reduced to experiencing less strenuous pleasures, but he was not unhappy. The old-fashioned fishing pole he extended over the water had been hand-wrought in his spare time from a single piece of broadcast antenna. A line played out through the notch cut in the far end, vanished beneath the surface below the dock. The antenna had once served to seek out invisible words from across the sky and water. Now it helped him find small, tasty fish at far shorter distances.

Mustapha glanced at the clouds writhing overhead, winced when a drop of rain caught him in the eye. The possible storm did not appear heavy. As always, the sky looked more threatening than it would eventually prove to be. Thunder blustered and echoed, but did not dislodge the elderly fisherman from his place.

Behind him the town of Rorqual rested stolidly on the surface. The nearest actual land, the Swinburne Shoals, lay thirty meters beneath. For all that, the town sat motionless on the sea. A vast array of centerboards and crossboards and complex counterjets held it steady against the rising chop. Held it steady so as to provide its inhabitants with a semblance of stability, to provide old Mustapha with a safe place to fish.

The dock was empty now, the catcherboats and gatherers out working. The long stretch of unsinkable gray polymer disappeared beneath a warehouse, the dock being only one of dozens of such supports for the town.

But there was no counterjet or centerboard to hold the dock completely motionless. Four meters wide and equally thick, it bobbed gently to the natural rhythm of the sea. That was why Mustapha chose to fish from the dock's end instead of from one of the more stable outer streets of the town. When he was playing with the ocean and its occupants, he preferred the feel of their environment. It was a cadence, a viscous march that was as much a part of his life as his own heart-beat.

The rain began to pelt him, running down his long white hair. He ignored it. The inhabitants of Cachalot's floating towns had water next to their skin as often as air. Here near the equator the fat drops were warm, almost hot on his bare upper chest. They rolled down from his bald forehead and itched in his drooping mustache.

The pole communicated with his fingers. He lifted it. A small yellow fish wriggled attractively on the hook, its four blue eyes staring dully into the unfamiliar medium in which it now found itself.

Mustapha debated whether to unhook it, decided the fish would serve him better as bait for larger game. He let the fresh catch drop back into the water. An electronic caller would have drawn more food fish than he could have carried, but such a device would have seemed incongruous functioning in tandem with the hook and line. Mustapha enjoyed fishing in the traditional way. He did not fish for food, but for life.

An occasional flash of awkward lightning illuminated the dark underbelly of the storm, forming drainage systems in the sky. The flare made candle flames of the wave crests. He knew there was more heat than fury in the discharges. Their frequency told him the storm would not last long. Nor was it the season of the heavy rains.

Occasional drops continued to wet him. He was alone on the dock. Thirty minutes, he thought, and the sun will be out again. No more than that. Perhaps then I will have more luck.

So he stayed there in his shorts and mustache and waited patiently for a bite. Some thought the pose and activity undignified for the town's computer-planner emeritus, but that did not bother Mustapha. He was wise enough to know that madness and old age excuse a multitude of eccentricities, and he had something of both.

A few deserted gathering ships, sleek vessels wide of

beam, were secured two docks away from him. A couple of magnetically anchored skimmers bobbed off to his right. Their crews would be on their week of off-duty, he reflected, home with family or carousing contentedly in the town's relaxation center.

An affectionate but uncompromising type, Mustapha in his early years had tried life with two different women. They had left more scars on him than all the carnivores he had battled in the name of increasing the town's catch.

His reverie was interrupted by a new, stronger tug at the line. His attention focused on where it intersected the surface. The tug came again, insistent, and the antenna pole curved seaward in a wide arc, its far end pointing like a hunting dog down into the water.

Mustapha held tight to the metal pole, began cranking the homemade reel. There was a lot of line, and it was behaving oddly. It was almost as if something were entangled in the line itself, not fighting the grip of the hook.

A shape was barely visible down in the dark water. Whatever it was, it was moving very quickly. It came nearer, growing until it was altogether too large. The old man's eyes grew wide above the gray mustache. He flung away the pole and the laboriously fashioned reel. The rod bounced once on the end of the bobbing pier before tumbling into the water.

Mustapha ignored it as he ran toward the town. His raised voice was matched by the sudden cry of the town's defense sirens. He did not make it beyond the end of the pier. As it turned out, it would not have made any difference if he had.

Two days later the first of Rorqual Towne's wandering fisherfleet returned, a gatherer loaded several heads high with the magical *Coreen* plant and many crates of sleset-of-the-permanent-spice. The wealth the cargo represented was now rendered meaningless to the men and women of the ship's crew by what they did not find.

Though they crossed and recrossed anxiously and tearfully above Swinburne Shoals, they found no sign of Mustapha Ali. Nor did they find their families or sweethearts, not a single one of the eight hundred inhabitants of Rorqual Towne.

Shattered bits of household goods, a few scraps of clothing, fragments of homes, and pieces of families mixed in with chunks of gray-white eggshell polymer, were all that remained of the town. These, an engima, and the memory of once happy lives.

And for some on the woe-laden boat, the worst of it was the knowledge that this was not the first time . . .

Far, far above the scrap of green sea once occupied by Rorqual Towne, a vast, quiet shape rested silently in a much more diffuse ocean. The occupants of the bulbous metal form were divorced by time and distance from that oceanic tragedy and its cousins.

A comparatively tiny, sharp shadow of the gleaming hulk detached itself from the great stern and dropped like a silver leaf toward the atmospheric sea immediately below. Though it displayed the motions normally indicative of life, the shadow was but a dead thing that served to convoy the living, a shuttlecraft falling from the KK drive transport that dwarfed it like a worker termite leaving its queen.

The argent arrowhead shape turned slightly. Its rear exuded puffs of white, and the craft began to drop more rapidly, more confidently, toward the world below, a world of all adamantine blue-white, a great azurite globe laced with a delicate matrix of cloud.

A full complement of twelve passengers stared out the shuttle's ports as the vessel curved into its approach pattern. Some stared at the nearing surface expectantly, thoughts of incipient fortune percolating through their minds. Others were more relaxed. These were the re-

turning inhabitants, sick of space and land, anxious
once more to be on the waters. A few regarded the
growing sphere with neither anticipation nor greed.
They were full of the tales of the strange life and
beauty that slid tantalizingly through the planetary
ocean.

Only one stared fixedly at the surface with the gaze
of a first-time lover, youthful exhilaration mixing with
the calm detachment of the mature scientist. Cora
Xamantina kept her nose pressed against the port. An
air release below prevented her breath from fogging it.

Intense reflected light from Cachalot's star made her
obsidian skin appear polished behind the glassalloy. It
shone on the high cheekbones that hinted at Amerind
heritage, on the delicate features almost eclipsed by
those protruding structures. Only the vast black eyes,
coins of the night, stood out in that heart-shaped face.
They darted excitedly from one section of the globe to
another. Her hair, tied in a single thick braid that ran
to her waist, swung like a pendulum with her movements.

Physically Cora Xamantina was in her midforties.
Mentally she was somewhat older. Emotionally she
was aged. She was no taller than an average adolescent
and slim to the point of boyishness. A surprisingly deep
voice, coupled with a vivacity that was anything but
matronly, was all that kept her from being mistaken
for a child.

Even when she was quiet, as she was now, her hands
and shoulders seemed always in motion, her body language elegant and personal. She came from stock that
included both slaver and slave, both of whose destinies
had been molded and sacrificed to the recovery of the
sap of a certain tree. Slavers and slaves were part of
history long past now. For the most part, sadly, so
were the trees.

She commented frequently on the beauty of the
world they were steadily approaching. Her descriptions

were intended for the younger woman seated next to her. For the most part, they were accepted with an air of helpless resignation by the taller, far more voluptuous shadow of herself. Where Cora's movements were frequent and full of nervous energy, those of the younger woman were all languorous stretchings and physical sighs. She cradled a peculiar and very special musical instrument in her arms and made no attempt to appear anything other than bored.

"Isn't it beautiful, Rachael?" Cora leaned back in her deceleration lounge. "Here—lean over and you can see, too." The enervated siren made no move to peer outward. "Don't you want to see? We're going to be living down there, you know."

"Only temporarily." She sighed tiredly. "I know what Cachalot looks like, Mother. God knows how many tapes of it you've made me study since you found out we were being assigned there. Maybe I have got a year's work left to finish at the Institute, but I still know how to do homework." Her eyes turned to study the narrow aisle running down the center of the shuttle. "The sooner we get this over with, the sooner we can get back to Terra and the better I'll like it!"

"Is that all you can think of to say, girl? We're not even down yet and already you can't wait to leave?"

"Mother . . . please!" It was a warning.

"All right." Cora made calming gestures with mannequin hands, the long fingers fluttering restrainingly. "I'm not asking for commitment until we've been down there for a while. You're only my special assistant on this assignment, just as it says in the directive. The fact that you're also my daughter is incidental."

"Fine. Suits me fine."

"Just try to keep an open mind, that's all."

"I'll try, Mother. I've said that for six years now. Another few months seems fair."

"Good. That's all I ask." Cora turned her attention

back to the port, the view drawing her insistently, soothing her, massaging away the concern she felt for her daughter's future. And the guilt.

She had been pushing, cajoling, Rachael for three years of advanced work in extramarine biology. The girl's reports were good, her work was good—dammit, she *was* good! She has all the tools, Cora thought. More than I do, and without bragging, that's saying something. She lacks only one thing, a single ingredient that keeps her from embarking on a brilliant career in the same field as mine: enthusiasm.

Cora had gotten that from Silvio. Ah, Silvio . . . "Keep an open mind, Cora," he had always told her. And she had kept an open mind. She had kept it so open that she lost him to another woman. To a string of other women. And then he had died, his enthusiasm for life and loving having proved incapable of finally saving him.

No, she told herself firmly. He lost me. Not the other way around. She still missed him, from time to time. Brilliant he had not been. Nor had he been especially handsome, or rich, or a sexual magician. What he had been, she thought, startled at the sudden knot that had formed in her chest, was enthusiastic. About everything. And comfortable. He had been oh so comfortable. Like her battered old Nymph underwater camera, the fraying *Elatridez Encyclopedia of Commonwealth Marine Life,* the voodoo necklace her great-grandmother had given her on her second birthday—which she still wore, incongruously, around her neck—Silvio had been comfortable.

She missed having him around, just as she would have missed the encyclopedia or the necklace. Lots of other women probably missed him also. She had kept an open mind, though. Each time. Until after Rachael was born. The funny thing was, Silvio never truly understood the reason behind her fury. He liked everyone and everything—too much. But then he had died. The hurt had died with him. Now she was only occasionally plagued by a hurt of a different kind.

As it kissed the outer fringe of atmosphere, the shuttle lurched slightly. Below was the culmination of a dream, of twenty years' hard work. She had performed well for the various companies that had employed her, even better when the government services called on her expertise. Twenty years of choosing exploitable salt domes. A year on the anthology of poisonous Riviera system marine life. Four years of arduous work among the seallike natives of Largesse, then back to still more dull, boring government research. Always she had kept up with the latest techniques, the latest developments and discoveries. Always wishing for something that could carry her to the mecca of all marine biologists: Cachalot.

Now that goal had been realized. The ocean world lay close beneath her, shining with nacreous beauty, awaiting her with promises of wonder and a mystery yet to be solved. If anything could ignite the genius that Cora knew lay hidden inside her daughter's head, it would be Cachalot.

Though she continued to press against the port and search hard with those huge and sensitive eyes, she could not locate any of the widely scattered islands that were the only land on Cachalot. Nor were the isolated islands formed of rock or stone. On Cachalot, the eternal war of wave and cliff had long ago been decided in favor of the wave. Tiny creatures called hexalates left behind their hard exoskeletons, building atolls and reefs much like the corals of Earth.

There was nothing that could be called a continent, though in places the oceans were quite shallow, if never for any great extent. All that showed above water from Cora's present position were the bright mirror-white patches at opposite poles, ice packs tense on the water. They were far smaller than those of Earth.

Cora pointed them out to Rachael, who responded by picking indifferently at the strings of her neurophon.

"Stop that." Cora frowned at her. "You know better than that."

Rachael wrinkled her brow. "Oh, Mother . . . I've got the projection matrix turned off and the power way down. I can't possibly bother the shuttle."

But Cora had experienced a telltale if faint tingle along her spine. "Your axonics are lit. I felt it. You might disturb the other passengers."

"I haven't heard any complaints," Rachael said softly. But she touched several contact points on the chordal dendritics, cut final power. She plucked petulantly at one string. It produced a normal musical tone that drifted through the cabin. Several passengers turned back to look at her.

Cora's nerves did not respond. Satisfied, she returned her gaze to the port.

Rachael was sharp enough to find nonverbal ways to show her unhappiness. Cora told herself that her daughter knew damn well that playing a neurophon in an unsealed room on board any craft was against all flight rules. It would have been bad enough on board the liner-transport they had just left. In a shuttle, where the descent was a matter of delicate, critical adjustments by pilot and machine, it could have placed them in deep trouble. Rachael was fooling with her damnable toy only to irritate her mother, Cora knew. It would be so much better for her if she would simply disown the instrument. It occupied far too much of her study time. Cora had tried to persuade her to abandon the device. She had tried only once. It had become an obsession with her daughter, and more than that, a surrogate larynx. Rachael knew she couldn't battle her mother with words, so she would sometimes counter an argument by sulking and speaking only with the nerve music. Her daughter was turning into a tonal ventriloquist.

A polite, slightly tense voice came from the cabin speaker. "Brace for heavy atmosphere, ladies and gentlemen. Thank you."

Cora made certain her harness was properly secured. She gripped the arms of her lounge and leaned back. For a few minutes there was nothing of note, then a sharp bump. A second, a stomach-queasing drop, and then they were coasting gently through clear blue sky. She eased her grip on the lounge arms and looked out the port.

The whirlpool of a small cyclone appeared beneath them, raced past and behind. Clouds of all shapes and sizes flew by, and once, only once, she thought she saw a bright flash that might have hidden an island. She hunted through her memory for the details of Cachalot's topography she had force-fed herself, finally decided the brightness had been a low cumulus cloud and not land.

Commonwealth headquarters were located on Mou'-anui, one of several enormous lagoons enclosed by land sufficiently stable to permit the establishment of permanent, nonfloating installations. Cora was hunting the sea for it when a voice sounded from behind them. "Excuse me."

The harness sign was off. She unbuckled, looked over the back of her reclined lounge. The speaker sat across the aisle, one row behind their seats, a stocky, coffee-colored gentleman about her own age. His hair and eyes were as black as her own. The hair hung to his shoulders, was combed straight back, and exhibited not even an echo of a curl or kink. He had a wide mouth, almost lost beneath a sharp, hooked nose like the beak of a predatory bird.

"That's a neurophon, isn't it? I thought I felt something picking at me a little while ago." He smiled explosively, changing suddenly from nondescript to swarthily good-looking.

"Yes, it is." Rachael spoke coolly, and Cora thought, Good for you, girl.

"It's a Chalcopyritic finish, Twelve Plank model, isn't it? Made on Amropolus? With the Yhu Hive tuner?"

"That's right." Rachael brightened, turned in her seat. "Do you play?"

"No." The man sounded apologetic. "Wish I did. I'm afraid my musical abilities are pretty nonexistent. But I know enough to be able to appreciate a skilled performer when I hear one. However briefly." Again the lustrous grin.

"Is that so?" Rachael's tone was turning from cool to coy. "I can understand when you say you know talent when you hear it, but it seems to me you're doing more looking than listening."

"I can't see talent, no," the man replied. He seemed uncomfortable, shy, yet unwilling to retreat into silence. "But sensitivity and emotional flexibility, those I think I can see."

"Really?" Rachael responded, flattered and pleased. "Are you trying to flatter me?"

"I am flattering you, aren't I?" he said with disarming directness. It was honestly a question.

Rachael controlled herself a few seconds longer, then broke into a high, girlish giggle that contrasted strikingly with her normal husky speaking voice.

"All right, I suppose you are." She eyed him interestedly. "Next you're going to ask me to please come over to your place and play something for you."

"That would be nice, yes," the man replied openly. Just in time he added, "But I'm afraid I can't. I don't even know where I'm going to be staying on Cachalot."

Rachael stared at him. "I think you mean it. About just wanting to listen to the music."

"That's what I said, wasn't it? If we do meet again, my name is Merced. Pucara Merced."

"Rachael Xamantina."

"Tell me," he said, shifting in his seat as they skipped a light bump in the atmosphere, "on directional projections, can you change keys and limbs simultaneously?"

"Sometimes," She sounded enthusiastic. Cora stared resolutely out the port. "It's hard, though, when you're concentrating on the music and trying to produce the matching neurologic responses in your audience. It's so difficult just to execute those properly, without trying to worry about physiological orientation, too. There's so damn much to concentrate on."

"I know."

"Would you like me to play something for you now, maybe?" She swung the lyre-shaped instrument into playing position, her left hand caressing the strings, the right poised over the power controls and projector sensors. "In spite of what my mother says, I don't think the pilot would mind."

"It's not a question of the pilot's minding," he said. thoughtfully. "I know you can keep the level down. But it wouldn't be courteous to our fellow passengers. They might not all be music lovers. Besides," and he smiled slightly again, "you might accidentally put out the lights, or drop the temperature thirty degrees."

"All right. But when we get down, if you don't disappear on me too fast, I promise I'll play something for you. Tell me," she went on excitedly, leaning farther into the aisle, "do you know anything about the new cerebral excluder? That's the one that's supposed to allow you to add another forty watts' neuronic power."

"I've heard of it," he admitted pleasantly. "They say that it can . . ."

They rambled on enthusiastically, the discussion shifting from matters musical to the latest developments in instrumental electronics.

It was all somewhat beyond Cora. A top-flight neurophon player had to be musician, physicist, and physiologist all in one. She still refused to give her daughter credit for attempting to master the extraordinarily difficult device. To her it represented a three-fold waste of energy.

Of one thing she was certain. For all that he was a head shorter than Rachael and apparently shy to boot, Merced was interested in more than just her daughter's aesthetic abilities. Not that that made him anything out of the ordinary. Any man not intrigued by Rachael did not deserve the gender. That was the nature of men, and it was intensified by her daughter's nonmental assets.

But there was nothing she could do about it. If she tried to order Rachael not to speak to him, it would produce exactly the opposite result. And there was the possibility she was wrong about him. Certainly he did not have the look of a collector of bedrooms.

Better, she told herself, to put the best light on the situation. Let Rachael remain interested in him instead of, say, being drawn to the more conventionally handsome pilot of our shuttle. Once we are down and settled in our quarters, it will no longer matter anyway.

She stole another glance at Merced. He was listening quietly while Rachael expounded on the virtues of Amropolous-made neurophons as opposed to those manufactured on Willow-Wane. He had the look of a fisherman returning home, or perhaps a financial expert shipped out by an investment firm to explore the earnings of one or two of its floating farms. His skin was properly dark, but his facial features and small bone structure did not jibe with those of the dominant Polynesian-descended settlers of the water world. He was an off-worlder for sure.

Well, she would keep an eye on him. A lifetime of experience made that automatic. Thoughts of unhappy past experiences led her to the dim possibility of future ones. She mused on the problem that had brought her to Cachalot. It involved more than the destruction of property or fisheries. There had been, it seemed, many deaths. She had been sent off with only enough information to tease her. Someone was going to great efforts to keep whatever was happening on Cachalot from the general public.

No matter. She would learn soon enough. The possibility of work on Cachalot had been sufficient to persuade her to accept the assignment. When offered choice of her own assistant, Cora had been able to choose Rachael. Now, if she could only convince her daughter to junk that bizarre instrument, one of the two major problems Cora had come to solve would have a happy resolution.

There had been some trouble. Rachael was still technically a student, and a few howls had been heard when it was declared she had been appointed Cora's assistant. Hundreds would have taken the job. Very few scientists made it to Cachalot, despite its wealth of unusual marine life. That was part of the agreement that had been struck with the original settlers of the blue planet, who had been studied so long they were sick of it. They did not object to the presence of a very limited number of fishers and gatherers and even some light industry, but they put a strict quota on the number of researchers resident on the planet at any one time. Hence the rarity of the opportunity granted to Cora and Rachael. It was a chance Cora would not waste, would not permit Rachael to waste.

"That's an interesting name." Rachael spoke as the shuttle skimmed low now over an endless expanse of gently rolling sea. Cachalot had no moon, therefore very little in the way of tides. Severe storms like the cyclone they had recently passed over were common, but predictable. It was altogether a far more benign world than most.

"It's an amalgam of words from two ancient human languages," he was explaining to her. "Pucara means 'shining' in a tongue called Quechua, which was the principal language of my ancestors who lived on the continent of South America."

"I'm sorry," Rachael said. "I'm afraid I don't know Terran geography very well. I've lived there only for a few years, while I've been in school."

"No matter. Merced means 'river' in the language of my other ancestors, who conquered my principal ones."

" 'Shining river.' Very pretty."

"What about yours? Does it mean anything?"

"Damned if I know." A hand reached back, touched Cora. "Hey, Mother, what does 'Xamantina' mean?"

"I don't know, Rachael." She looked again at the earnest little man behind them. "It's an Amerind name, also derived from South America. A different region, though, I think."

Merced looked intrigued. "Perhaps our ancestors were neighbors, then."

"Possibly." Cora spoke softly. "No doubt they fought and killed one another with great vigor." She turned away, looked back out the port.

"Mother," Rachael whispered at her angrily, "you have a talent for displaying the most exquisite rudeness."

"Calm down, dear. We'll be landing soon. You wouldn't want your toy scattered all over the cabin, would you?"

Rachael huffily snuggled down into her seat, though Cora could still feel her daughter's eyes on the back of her neck as she stared out the port. She chuckled to herself, thankful that Merced had given her the chance to let him know how she felt without her having to intrude on the conversation.

"Four minutes to touchdown," the speaker voice said. "Refasten harnessing, please."

Cora did so mechanically. Mou'anui should be straight ahead of them. She should be able to see at least part of it immediately prior to touchdown. They would approach the oval lagoon from one end. It was sixty kilometers long in places, and surely they—yes, there!

A brilliant flash stung her eyes through the port, from where direct sunlight impacted on the hexalate sands. She stared at the kaleidoscope of color until her eyes filled with tears.

A dull thunk sounded as the long, solid pontoons were lowered. Seconds before contact, the light had become so strong Cora had to turn from the port. The brief impression she had had of Mou'anui would never leave her, however. It was as if they were touching down inside a diamond.

Another, louder thump was heard as they touched water. The rear engines roared. Cora struggled to clear her vision, but occasional lances of reflected light shot through the port, blinding her. She was aware of a different motion, one that was at once familiar and yet strange.

They were floating now, adrift on an alien sea.

II

"We will be debarking shortly, ladies and gentlemen," the voice from the speaker said. "Welcome to Cachalot."

Passengers were unslipping their flight harnesses, organizing luggage and tapecases and personal effects. Cora tried to single out those who might be natives, settled on the man and woman in the first two portside seats. They were not of Polynesian ancestry, but boasted skin tanned the color of light chocolate. They wore only fishnet tops over swim shorts.

The shuttlecraft slowly taxied across the lagoon. Through the windows, which had automatically darkened in response to the reflected light, she could see down into the limpid transparency that was the surface. Gradually the darkness gave way to lighter, brighter colors as the water grew shallower.

Now Cora could make out shapes moving through the water. So excited was she at these first signs of Cachalot life that she almost forgot to breathe. The forms darted in and around the peculiar branchlike growths formed by the hexalates.

None of the crystalline growths possessed the gentle curves or smooth surfaces of the corals of Earth. Large or small, the formations universally displayed straight, angular architecture, a crystallographer's nightmare. The tiny creatures whose decomposed skeletons formed the sand that filled the lagoon's bottom and comprised its shores created their exoskeletons from silicon, whereas the corals of Earth utilized lime. The beaches of Cachalot were made of glass. Multicolored glass at that, for minute quantities of different minerals were enough to produce hexalates of every color of the spectrum. The tridee solidos Cora had seen of Cachalot's islands reminded her of vast heaps of gemstones.

She could see buildings now, built on the nearest outer island. Scattered here and there around the structures were long, low green plants. They were sealanges, varieties of local plant life that had developed the ability to take oxygen from the air instead of from the water. Their roots were anchored deep within the body of the reef.

More familiar vegetation had been used to landscape the complex. Cora recognized numerous varieties of off-world, salt-tolerant plant life, including several from Earth. Outstanding among the latter were the prosaic, arching shapes of coconut palms. Probably the plants and the soil they survived in were imported.

Several small docks came into view. Men and women worked on or near them, engaged in unknown tasks. All were clad in the barest essentials. Wide-brimmed dark hats seemed popular among many. The instrument belts several wore contained more material than the rest of their clothing.

Turning right, the shuttle slid toward several large, two-storied structures. Traveling in the opposite direction, a small skimmer roared past. Its crew waved cheerily at the shuttle's occupants.

The once reverberant thunder of the shuttle's engines had been reduced to a chemical snore. They coughed once or twice more as the pilot altered the shuttle's heading slightly. Then it was sitting silently alongside a floating dock of brown polymer. The dock bobbed between thin posts of green glass.

Cora wondered if the glass was composed of hexal-ate sands, decided that most likely it was. Any out-post world had to make the most of its own resources. Self-sufficiency was the goal of every colony. She expected to find a great many of Cachalot's everyday items constructed of glass. A small suprafoil was linked to the far side of the dock.

The forward door between the pilot's compartment and the passengers' was opened. A gust of warm air filled the cabin, replacing the stale canned atmosphere with dampness and the strong, pungent aroma of the sea. Cora inhaled, her eyes closing in pleasure. Perfume, pure perfume.

"Why is it," Rachael was grumbling, "that all the oceans of all the planets have to stink?"

They had been through such arguments before. Cora did not comment on her daughter's insensitivity to one of the most wonderful smells in the universe.

Abruptly, the doorway was filled by a large, bearish form. It squeezed into the cabin, ducking its head to clear the entryway, and surveyed the human contents.

The massive man was clad only in a trylon pareu, patterned with blue nebulae and pink flowers, loosely draped around his waist down to his ankles. Chest and chin were hairless, though the huge round skull was thickly overgrown with black ringlets that might have been combed once in the past dozen years.

While the man was only a few centimeters taller than Rachael, his physique was that of a giant. Or a granite massif. He was in his early forties, Cora guessed, but with the roundness of a child in his features. Most prominent among the latter was a consider-able belly that curved out and away from beneath his chest but had no fat ripples. The structure was a smooth, slick curve of solid muscle that arced back to vanish beneath the almost hidden waistband of the pareu.

The face was also rounded, giving Cora the eerie

feeling she was looking not at a mature man but at a seven-year-old giant. Besides his size, all that marked him as a knowledgable adult was the instrument-laden belt he wore around hips and waist, tucked more under the belly than across it. She studied the array, recognized the emergency underwater breathing unit that could give a diver twenty minutes of air, an underwater lumar, several instruments of uncertain purpose, and, on his left side, a small rectangle of metal with a constantly changing digital readout. She had a similar rectangle in her own gear. On command it could provide time, depth, direction and speed of current, water temperature, and numerous other factors of vital interest to anyone working underwater. It was expensive, not the sort of device that would be carried by, for example, a common fisherman. Possibly he was attached to the local science station? She would find out soon enough.

The massive amount of flesh he revealed did not disturb her. Of necessity the citizens of the Commonweatlh who lived on its oceans wore less than their landlocked counterparts. Partly this was related to convention, partly to reasons of comfort, and partly, she often suspected, to man's having risen from the sea and his secret wish to return to it. The closer man got to the sea, the greater the number of civilization's artifacts he seemed to shuck.

Cora was dressed only in a simple one-piece bit of shipboard fluff that ended above her knees. Even so, now that she was on Cachalot, she felt unbearably overdressed. Once they were assigned quarters, she would change into a suit. She couldn't wait.

It would be nicer still to be able to go about only in skin, but even a world as casual as Cachalot would likely be affected by universal conventions. Sadly, these included the wearing of at least minimal clothing. Not all the inhabitants, let alone visitors and temporary workers, would willingly trade false morality for

sensibility and comfort. And there was always the awkward problem of the desires and proximity of men.
Those she would be working with would be fellow scientists, but experience had shown that scientific detachment had a disarming way of dissolving in her
presence. Not to mention in Rachael's.

"Sam Mataroreva." The man was looking down at
her. His voice was gentle as a cat's, as easy and open
as he seemed to be. He was ambling down the aisle,
squeezing his bulk lithely between the lounges. Despite
his size, he was physically less intimidating to her than
men half as large. Perhaps it was the baby-smooth,
hairless visage. Perhaps simply the charming smile.

"You're Cora Xamantina?" His palm enfolded hers.

She pulled it away defensively. "Pardon?" Now, why
did you do that? she asked herself. Why that instinctive
pulling away? Looks and deceitfulness did not necessarily go together. That was Silvio's fault. Scientifi-
cally, there was no basis for such an assumption.

Mataroreva appeared not to notice her defensive-
ness. He was already shaking Rachael's hand. "And
you are Rachael, e'?"

"Yes." She shied away slightly when that huge mass
of flesh leaned over her.

Some official sent out to greet them, Cora thought.
Well, that was only to be expected. She stood, prepared
to ask those same but necessary questions all visitors to
a new place must ask, when Mataroreva shocked her
by moving farther down the aisle and addressing a third
passenger.

"And Mr. Merced, of course."

"That's right."

Cora stared open-mouthed at the little man.

"You're from Commissioner Hwoshien's office?"
Merced asked.

Mataroreva smiled, ran thick fingers through the
kelp-bed on his head. "Sort of a liaison between the
government and the private companies chartered to

operate here. That gives me the best and the worst of both sectors."

Cora continued to stare at Merced, who looked like a dark splinter fallen from the flank of the huge Polynesian. Merced noticed her stare, appeared more embarrassed than ever.

"I'm terribly sorry. I suppose I should have introduced myself before." He stepped out into the aisle. "I was just so fascinated by your daughter's instrument. They're very rare, you know, and . . ." He stopped, flustered, and extended a hand. "I'm Professor of Advanced Oceanographic Research at the University of Toleamia on Repler."

"Toleamia?" She wasn't ready to believe this irritating person was a representative of so prestigious an institution.

"That's right." He sounded apologetic. "Please excuse me. I really was interested in the neurophon."

"And in its operator?"

"Mother . . ." Rachael said warningly.

"I'd be lying if I said no." Merced seemed nothing if not truthful.

Mataroreva's smile had faded somewhat as he listened to the exchange. "Am I missing something?"

"No." Cora turned, forced herself to smile up at him. "Nothing important. We're very glad to be here, Mr. Mataroreva. I just hope that we can be of some help." She noted that they were the only passengers still aboard the shuttle. "If I seem confused, it's only because I was led to believe that my daughter and I were the only experts called in for consultation, to consider your problem." She looked at Merced. "I don't suppose your presence here and your being greeted by Mr. Mataroreva could mean you're going to work on something else?"

"We're all here for the same reason, I'm afraid." Merced shifted his feet. "For what it's worth, I was as ignorant of your involvement until you boarded the shuttle as you were of mine. The difference was that I knew something of you by reputation and sight, and you did not know me." He forced a smile. "I shouldn't think we'd have any trouble working together."

"Assuming that we do indeed end up working together." Cora was conceding nothing.

Matatoreva was growing distinctly uncomfortable. She decided he deserved some reassurance.

"I'm not usually this testy. It's been a long, difficult journey."

"I understand." He relaxed a little. "Call me Sam, please."

"Okay . . . Sam it is." She was too tired to debate protocol with anyone. Besides, "Sam" was a lot easier to say than "Matatoreva."

"Good." He beamed. "Your large luggage should already be on its way to your rooms. Anything else?"

They all shook their heads. Each had his or her instrument belt comfortably stocked and settled around the waist.

"We can leave for Administration, then. But first . . ." Reaching into a large waterproof packet clipped to his Christmas-treelike belt, Matatoreva withdrew a handful of goggles made entirely of some supple, transparent material, the headband of the same stuff as the lenses. He slipped another pair over his own face. "They're completely self-adjusting," he said as the others slipped on their own. "I suggest you don't take them off until you're inside a building. You don't need them out on the open sea, either. All our buildings have windows formed from the same material."

"Can't you grow used to the glare?" Cora asked.

Matatoreva shook his head. "There's simply too much of it. You'd go blind eventually. You can take it early in the morning," and he stared into Cora's eyes in a way she didn't like, "or late at night when the sun's almost down. But while the local star is up, it's simply too much." He turned and exited the shuttle.

Cora followed him, then Rachael with her precious neurophon, and lastly Merced.

Then they were standing on the narrow, motionless pier. Clouds and sky appeared sunset dark because of the goggles. The lagoon itself stretched some twenty kilometers to the north, another thirty to the south. Transplanted off-world trees, water-anchored scrub growth, and additional piers all appeared dark from behind the special plastic. There was a dim reflection from the buildings scattered along the wide spit of sand.

Cora raised her right hand and slipped a finger beneath the lower rim of the goggles. She lifted it slightly, glanced down and across at where the pier was slotted into the shore. Instantly something stabbed at the back of her eyes; crimson, emerald, blue, and yellow knives battered her outraged optic nerves. The light seemed as intense if not as pure as a cluster of tiny lasers. Hurriedly she let the goggles slip back into place, blinking away tears. Now the sand ahead merely twinkled at her through the lenses, did not blind.

They were preparing to leave the pier when she felt a gentle tingle in her lower legs. The tingle traveled up her thighs, ran like an acrobatic arachnid up her spine. Simultaneously a plaintive melody sounded in her ears, counterpointing the delicate rippling active inside her.

Apparently the subdued beauty was inspiring Rachael. Her daughter's hands caressed the neurophon. One strummed the dual sets of circular strings that lay in the center of the instrument, the other fluttered over the contact controls set in the instrument's handle and base. The coupling of aural music with the subsonic vibrations affecting her skin and nerves produced a relaxing sensation throughout Cora's body, as if she had just spent an hour beneath a fine-spray shower.

Merced appeared similarly affected, but Mataroreva's reaction was quite different. The smile vanished from his face and he turned so abruptly he almost knocked Cora down.

"What's the matter?" She tried to make the wide grin return. "I'm no music lover myself, but . . ."

"It's not that." He was looking nervously beyond her. "It has nothing to do with the music. I like the music and the neuronics. It's just that . . . I think she'd better stop." He was standing on the edge of the pier, across from the shuttle, staring down into the muted crystalline water. Elongated bands of light, reflections of the sun on water ripples, flashed up at him.

Rachael paused when he made a quieting gesture in her direction. "But you said you liked it," she protested. "I can play something else if you want."

"Just turn off the dendritic resonators."

"Not *again*." She petulantly ran her hand across a long series of contacts. Cora felt something combing her nerves. "I keep trying to explain it's all of one piece, the aural and the neuronics. If I can't conjoin them properly, I might as well give it up and take up the violin."

"Just for now," Mataroreva said.

Merced was also staring over the side of the pier. "I do believe there is something under the sand."

Rachael ignored them both, her hands flicking angrily over the neurophon's controls, generating a last discordant dual projection before shutting the instrument off.

Cora's nerves jumped a little under the sharp stimulation. Then she discovered herself bewilderedly stumbling backward. Seawater geysered in front of her. Draped by the water like a maiden in a blue-green suit was a four-meter-high orange body, flattened like a flounder's and encrusted with rough protrusions like a chunk of pumice. Several thick pink pseudopods waved at the air. Cora did not see any eyes but received the distinct impression that the creature perceived her clearly.

Mataroreva fell flat. From his cluttered equipment belt he withdrew a very compact beamer. The underwater weapon functioned well on dry land; a beam of bright blue struck the apparition in its midsection, or what Cora assumed to be its midsection. She could see it a bit more clearly now. Only seconds had passed. It looked like a cross between an obese squid and a starfish with delusions of grandeur. The blue fire struck between a pair of tentacles, pierced clean through the orange flesh. One thick, bristly appendage slapped wetly on the pier, only centimeters from Cora's ankles. The blue beam struck the creature again and it slid back into the water. It had not made a sound.

Most would have lain quietly, panting and fearful. There was too much of the scientist in Cora to permit that. As soon as the creature vanished beneath the water she crawled quickly but cautiously to the edge. Large bubbles were making blemishes on the clear surface. She could barely make out a hint of thick bristles breaking the sand as the creature receded beneath it. Soon the bottom appeared undisturbed, as if nothing had slept there in the first place.

Several figures were running toward them from the nearest of the low-lying buildings. A few were armed. Mataroreva got to his feet. Carefully he clipped the beamer back onto his belt.

A hint of polished blue metal disappeared as Pucara Merced slid something indistinct into an inside compartment of his own belt. No one noticed. Cora's attention was still on the sea floor, as was Mataroreva's. Only the still-motionless Rachael, arms wrapped protectively around her instrument, had the faintest glimpse of the object, and she was too stunned by the suddenness of the attack for the tiny shape to register immediately on her mind.

A couple from the building reached them, panting heavily. As soon as they saw that Mataroreva had re-clipped his beamer, they put away their own. He was leaning over the side of the pier.

"What happened, Sam?"

"Toglut."

Now the man joined Mataroreva in inspecting the sand below. "It must've gone crazy." His brow was creased and he sounded confused. "I don't understand."

The big Polynesian gestured toward Rachael. The woman who had joined them nodded understandingly. "She was playing that?"

"I—I'm sorry." Rachael stared at them dumbly. "I didn't know. I mean, I know that a neurophon's vibrations can affect certain animals. It's just . . . the water here is so shallow, and we're in a protected lagoon near human habitation and I—I didn't see . . ."

Mataroreva stared grimly at her, seemed about to say something, and then he was smiling broadly as before, as if nothing had happened.

"Forget it. It's over and no one was hurt. Not even the toglut, I think. I suppose that from a biological standpoint your assumptions were accurate. You couldn't have known there would be something within range of your instrument *under* the sand. Actually, your thinking was mostly correct. There are very few dangerous creatures living inside the reef, and most of them stay out in the center, where the water's deep." He pointed downward, over the side of the pier. "The toglut's big, but normally it's about as offensive as a kitten. I guess," he joked, "it wasn't much of a music lover, either." He grinned at Cora. "Anyway, you've had an introduction to the real Cachalot. This is a poorly explored, little-researched colony world. Paradise orbits a different star.

"Come on." He looked over at the two newcomers who had joined them so hurriedly. "We'll manage, Terii," he told the woman. She nodded, turned to leave, but not before giving Rachael a disapproving glare.

Mataroreva started to follow, but when he saw Cora still on hands and knees, staring over the side of the pier, he walked over to her and extended a massive brown paw. "Ms. Xamantina? Cora?"

She glanced up at him. "A toglut, you called it?"

"That's right. They spend *most* of their time under the sand. They can tear up a boat without working hard, but normally one would rather run than fight something half its size."

"I wish I'd had a better look." She took his hand and he helped her to her feet. She continued to gaze down into the water. "Fascinating. I've never seen a cephalopod like that."

"It's not a cephalopod."

"Echinoderm?"

He shook his head. "Polydermata. If I remember right. A new class, native to Cachalot. We have a lot of them, I'm told. You'll learn the reason for the name if you ever get the chance to dissect one. The cephalopodian characteristics are coincidental. Or mimicry."

"That's marvelous. Really marvelous." She grew aware he was still holding her hand and pulled free.

"Rachael—"

"Please, Mother. No lectures, huh? I explained myself. Nobody's as sorry as I am."

Cora sighed deeply. "You and that toy. I'm surprised at you, ascribing Earthly characteristics to an alien world. But I suppose I myself would have said, if asked, that it was probably safe to play that thing here." She started for the buildings, chatting with Mataroreva.

Merced moved to walk alongside Rachael. "Anyone would have made the same assumption, just as your mother said. Besides," he added softly, "I thought what you were playing was beautiful."

She looked down at him. "Flattery will get you nowhere, Mr. Merced."

"Pucara, please. We are going to be working together."

"Maybe," she replied cautiously. "We don't know the nature of the trouble, so I think it's a little premature to say we'll be working together." He looked away, lapsed into silence. "However," she added, "I hope that we will." She smiled enigmatically.

"It's my hope also, Rachael. Maybe you'd be willing to play for me another time, as you said you would. When we're a bit farther away from the water where your instrument's projections won't, uh, irritate the local life."

"That'll have to include my mother. She tends to react like that toglut thing did." She chuckled.

They were mounting a slight slope now, climbing the firmly packed sand. Occasional shafts of brightly colored light made her blink even through the protective haze created by the goggles.

"She's protective of you," Merced ventured. "You can't blame her."

"Protective of me?"

Rachael laughed, the rhythmic trill so different from her husky speaking voice. "I can take care of myself. Besides, what does she have to be so protective of me for? What's there to protect me from?" And she smiled at Merced in what could only be called a challenging way. He simply smiled slightly and looked away.

Intriguing character, she thought to herself. He acts so shy and tentative, yet some of his comments and questions are damned direct. She slid the neurophon around on its straps so that it snuggled beneath her left arm, made certain the power was off.

Two mysteries for her to explore: Cachalot and Pucara Merced. Two mysteries to inspire music. She ran three fingers over the steel strings of her soul.

III

Having reached the top of the gentle slope, they found themselves among a complex of buildings. All displayed windows formed of the same phototropic material as their goggles. Some of the structures looked like housing, others were clearly used as offices and labs. Far to the south were the outlines of much larger buildings. Warehousing, perhaps, or processing facilities.

The shuttle that had brought them in was now docked near one of the other, larger structures. Small human shapes could be seen using floaters to shift containers from building to shuttlebay and vice versa.

They were approaching a two-story building larger than any they had yet passed. It occupied the crest of the hill. A flag, hanging limply from a post in front of the entrance, displayed four circles arranged in a square: two blue, representing Terra; two green, standing for Hivehom. A fifth circle occupied the center, tangent to the other four. It was marked with a Maltese cross, half blue and half green on a crimson field. Were this a Church facility, the field would have been aquamarine. Flag and post were sufficient to indicate they were nearing the center of humanx activity on Cachalot.

From what Rachael had learned of the ocean world, she knew it was not developed enough to qualify for even associate status in the Commonwealth. It was listed as a mere class nine, a general colony with no direct representation in the Council. Instead, it operated under the direction of a Resident Commissioner, like any other world without full membership. Its inhabitants would have true franchise only through their home-worlds. Those with multigenerational ancestry on Cachalot would be represented through the Commissioner.

They halted before the entrance, and she and Merced slowed behind her mother and their guide.

"I don't understand," Cora was saying, gesturing first at the Administration Building and then at the others nearby. "Don't you have a fusion plant?"

"Sure," Sam told her. "For backup purposes. We hardly ever use it. Why do you find the photovoltaic paneling so unusual? It may not generate as much power as fast as a fusion reactor, but we have excellent storage systems and a year with ninety-five percent of the days sunny. In the long run it's much more efficient."

"Meaning cheaper?"

"Exactly. Generating a fusion reaction isn't that expensive. Containing and channeling it are."

They passed the flagpole and encountered a small sign attached to a post made of coconut palm. Cora glanced expectantly at Mataroreva, who grinned at her.

"That marks the highest point of land yet measured on Cachalot. Thirty-two meters above sea level." His grin grew wider and he gestured at the atoll. "The name 'Mou'anui' is itself a joke. It's the name this atoll was given by the first workers who settled here. My ancestors were among them. It means 'big mountain' in the ancient Tahitian tongue."

"Everything's relative," Merced said from behind him.

"Very true."

"I would think you'd be swamped here." Cora

looked back at the calm water of the lagoon. "We passed over a pretty good-sized storm on our way down."

"That's why most of the people on Cachalot would choose to live on the floating towns even if there was more land. It's safer, easier to ride with a storm rather than fight against it." Mataroreva shrugged. "But for an administrative center, for a central distribution and product collection and processing point, it was decided that a truly permanent installation was required. There are larger atolls, but none with this much stable land, so it was decided to place the fixed buildings on Mou'anui.

"The foundations of these buildings go many meters down into the solid rock of the sea mount on which the reef stands. The reef follows the contour of the crest of an ancient volcanic caldera. The mountain comes very close to the surface here. Even if the sand were to be completely washed away, most of the buildings would remain. We're safe. The majority of big storms strike the atoll on the far side anyway."

"Is there any place," Rachael asked, "where real land actually projects above the water?"

Mataroreva thought a moment. "Not that I've heard of. Sea mounts like the one below us come within a couple dozen meters of the surface. But wherever you see dry land projecting above the water, it's there because the little hexalates have worked to make it so for millions of years."

They passed through the tinted plastic doors of the Administration Building. "Most of the people I've seen so far have retained much of their Polynesian ancestry in their faces and physiques," Cora said.

"Oh, you know how it is," Mataroreva replied casually. "The Commonwealth's not so ancient that pockets of settlers on nonurbanized worlds haven't retained their ethnicity. That's not to say you won't find ancient Northern Europeans or Central American farmstockers or Mongols working here on Cachalot. Not to mention a very few thranx, despite their natural hatred of large bodies of water. But the permanent residents, the ones who aren't here simply to try to get rich quick in pharmaceuticals, say, derive mostly from Polynesian or Melanesian ocean-going ancestors. I'm sure there's no genetic reason for it. But tradition dies as hard in certain ethnic groupings as it does in families."

Down a hall, than around a corner. "Here we are."

But the door before them refused admittance. "Commissioner Hwoshien is not here," it politely informed them. "He is working elsewhere at the moment."

"Where is he, then?" Mataroreva did not try to conceal his exasperation at the delay.

The door hesitated briefly, then replied, "I believe Commissioner Hwoshien is in Storage and Packing Number Two."

"Oh, terrific," their guide mumbled. Then his frustration vanished, as all such upsets seemed to after an instant. "Nothing for it but to go find him, I suppose." He turned, began retracing their steps.

A rich roaring greeted them when they exited the building. The shuttle, having completed its exchanges, was departing. It thundered down the lagoon on its pontoons. Then the nose tipped up. Engines boiled the sea behind as the craft arced sharply into a sky polka-dotted with white.

The noise and violence startled a flock of creatures just below the surface. Flapping membranous wings, they soared aloft, circled several times, and glided over the Administration Building.

"Ichthyorniths!" Cora shouted delightedly, clapping her hands together like a little girl. "Those I was able to study prior to leaving Earth. How wonderful!"

"Mother, what are they—birds?" Rachael was staring curiously at the distant flock.

"Didn't you read anything before you left home?"

"Yeah, I did," her daughter snapped, and she rattled off a list of popular fiction.

Cora looked resigned. "They're flying fish. Real flying fish." She stared upward, enraptured by yet another of the sea's miraculous examples of protective adaptation. Each ichthyornith had a transparent, gelatinous membrane surrounding the rear portion of its streamlined body. Within those membranes they carried oxygen-rich water, enabling them to stay airborne and clear of the water for substantial periods of time.

There were no land animals native to Cachalot. So there were no reptiles or mammals for true birds to evolve from. In the absence of true birds or flying snakes or their relatives, the ichthyorniths, with their water-carrying body sacs, had adapted to a partial aerial existence, spending as little time in the water as possible, breeding and living in a mostly predator-free niche left to them by a nonwasteful nature.

Their long silvery forms shone in the sun, light bouncing from wide wet wings and the full water sacs. They returned to the lagoon and skimmed low, searching for a place to set down.

As Cora watched, one of the winged shapes suddenly fell from formation, splashed into the water.

"Koolyanif," Matatoreva explained. "It floats just below the surface, changing color to match the sand or deep water below it. It has an arsenal of stinging spines which it can blow outward, like arrows, through a kind of internal air compression system. That's what brought down the ichthyornith."

Even in the air, life is not safe on Cachalot, Cora told herself. This is not the friendly, familiar ocean of Earth. She found herself longing for the sight of something as predictable as a shark.

Around her the plants waved lazily in the faint breeze. All seemed peaceful and quiet. But they had been on this world only a short time and had seen togluts and koolyanifs. The sea and the peacefulness were deceptive.

She wondered how the original settlers of Cachalot had coped with the inhabitants native to the world-ocean. Not being human, they had possessed other advantages. She was intensely curious to find out for herself if they had done as well as all the histories and infrequent reports indicated they had.

It seemed that would have to wait until she had confronted this Hwoshien person. She had dealt with bureaucratic demagogues before. She could handle this one, even if he could intimidate as impressive a specimen as Sam Mataroreva.

She eyed the big Polynesian as he led them down the slope toward another pier. Maybe she was overrating him. He was so relaxed, so easygoing. Perhaps it wasn't that he was intimidated so much as overly respectful of authority. He was certainly gentle enough with everyone, like an oversized teddy bear.

She resolutely turned her thoughts away from such trivialities. More important was the matter of their still unspecified assignment and her anger at being bounced around like a servant ever since they had set foot on this globe. She would straighten out both as soon as they confronted Hwoshien.

A number of craft were docked at the pier. Mataroreva directed them to a small, waterstained skimmer. They boarded and he activated controls. Immediately the little ship lifted a meter off the water. It could go considerably higher, but there was no need to expend the power. A touch on another switch and they found themselves racing across the broad lagoon toward its southernmost end.

Cora leaned back, marveled at the faceted hexalate formations speeding past beneath the rapidly moving craft. She could hardly wait to get into the water here, to see at first hand the marine marvels she had studied. Reefs a thousand meters and more in depth were not unknown, for the hexalates had been building on Cachalot for millions of years, long before the land had all been worn away or had subsided.

Mataroreva looked back from the controls, watched her watching. "You love the sea, don't you, Cora?"

"All my life," she told him quietly. "Ever since I was old enough to realize the difference between ocean and bathtub."

"I know how you feel," he replied. "To me, Cachalot the planet is one vast, perfect ozmidine, cut and polished by the hand of God. If I could," he said in the same voice, "I would make a bracelet of it so you could wear it on your wrist."

"Thanks for the thought, Sam. But I've been given similar gifts and promises in the past. The bracelets were fake, and the promises broke, too."

"I understand." Mataroreva turned back to his controls but continued to speak. "Bracelets, gems, can be like that sometimes; bright and flashy instead of solid, well crafted, and made with care . . . like promises."

Cora felt ashamed. Why couldn't she be more open, like Rachael? Age had nothing to do with her way of looking at people. It was a question of experience.

Take Mataroreva, for example. Why assume his deference toward Hwoshien was owing to a lack of backbone? He was only an employee here, without her off-world independence. And he was charming.

Ah, but Silvio had been charming. Oh, how charming! As charming, as bright, as the crystal formations they were skimming over. But Mataroreva was not Silvio. Why condemn him for being pleasant? The two had nothing in common save gender. Wasn't it time she ceased condemning all because of one? She was so tired of acting tough.

Downright delightful, this Mataroreva—Sam. Mentally he was still a mystery. But he shared her love of the sea, and the warmth of holiday and the sense of eternal vacation that hung over this world were beginning to weaken her.

Mataroreva shattered the reverie. "You know, another town was destroyed last week. Rorqual."

This brought her brusquely back to reality. She was all business again. "Destroyed—an entire town? I know we were being brought in on this because people were being killed, but no one mentioned anything about the destruction of an entire town. And you said 'another.' "

"There have been several such incidents."

"How many?" Merced asked patiently.

"Four."

"Four deaths?" Rachael was staring at Mataroreva now.

He shook his head. His expression had become solemn. "Four towns. The entire populations, completely wiped out. Not a trace of them left behind, and we've no idea what's causing it. Twenty-five hundred men, women, and children. All gone. *'Ati.'*

"Similarities?" Cora wanted to know. "What were the similarities, the links tying these incidents together?"

Sam smiled patiently at her. "Hard at work already? Take your time, Cora Xamantina. We have already eliminated the obvious." He glanced back at Rachael and Merced. "You all may as well take your time. We haven't just been swimming in circles here, so don't expect to find any quick answers. Twenty-five hundred people." He returned his full attention to the skimmer controls.

"We'll determine the cause," Cora said finally, after a long silence in the craft, "and put a stop to it."

He smiled affectionately at her, not boyish at all now. "Maybe you will, Cora Xamantina. Maybe you will. I hope so, because the thought of you becoming a new addendum to the obituary disturbs me. You've seen only a bare fraction of the hostile life-forms of

Cachalot, and what they are capable of. Remember that most of the Cachalot world-ocean has not been explored, nor any of the great deeps. We don't know what's out there. Maybe something that can take a floating town apart piece by piece."

"Well said." Cora grinned back at him. "We're all suitably intimidated. Now—what are the similarities?"

Mataroreva chuckled. "If stubbornness were a cure, this world would be healthy in a day. Hwoshien will want to explain himself."

"I'd rather you tell me, Sam."

"Don't condemn Yu until you've met him. He's been through a lot this past month."

"Isn't it permissible?"

"Well," he said thoughtfully, "I haven't been instructed *not* to tell you.

"I suppose the most obvious link is the impossibility of this happening to a single town, much less to four. The towns themselves are supposed to be impossible to sink. Hell, they *are* impossible to sink! They are not solid structures. Each town is a vast raft composed of thick slabs of buoyant polymer, like the piers we just left. The town slabs are as much as ten meters thick in places, beneath some of the larger buildings. They can be broken, but the individual fragments will continue to float.

"The varied shapes of the polymer slabs—triangles, trapezoids, and so forth—give the raft tremendous structural strength while still leaving sufficient flexibility for it to glide over the waves."

"Even so," Rachael pointed out from the rear of the thrumming skimmer, "couldn't a storm, a really big storm, take a town apart?"

"No. At least, it hasn't happened yet. Even the largest waves slip under the raft sections. Those that break atop the town sift down through the drain places between the sections, or slide off. The polymer actually rejects water, in addition being a hundred percent non-porous. And the hinges that link the sections together are magnetic or chemical, not affected by brute mechanical wave action.

"Also, each town has several means of further stabilizing itself—centerboards, special fluids which can inhibit wave action, and so on. No, storms are out of the question. Except for," and he glanced back at them helplessly, "one awkward contradiction."

"What's that?" Cora wondered.

"The fact that each town has disappeared during a storm."

"I'd call that more than an awkward contradiction."

Mataroreva adjusted the heading of the skimmer, angling it slightly to starboard. "But some of the storms have been too light to damage a sensitive flower, let alone an entire town. The storm that covered Warmouth when it was lost was measured by a weather satellite almost directly above it. Our weather system is even more advanced than our cross-planet communications system. It recorded the winds at the height of the storm at less than forty kilometers per hour. There's no potential for destruction in that."

"Sounds like something is using the storms for cover," Merced murmured. Mataroreva nodded.

Cora wasn't ready to rule out natural causes. "What about seismic disturbances?"

"All the towns, though drifting near fishing reefs or sea mounts, were in essentially open ocean. The biggest quake on this world might shatter someplace stable like Mou'anui, but it would send only a swell rippling under the floating towns. They're immune to quakes."

"You said you found pieces of the polymer sections?"

"Yes. Shattered and torn. Not only sections of the town foundations but buildings, equipment, structures; but not a single body. Not one corpse. Either the cause of the destruction has a ghoulish nature, or it's a red herring. True, corpses will eventually sink, or be taken by the numerous scavenger species, but it does seem unlikely that not one out of twenty-five hundred has been found."

"Did all the wreckage show similar damage, the effect of identical forces?" Merced was making notes on a recorder.

"Everything was just—splintered." Mataroreva shrugged enormous shoulders.

"You've been out to the sites?" Rachael asked the question respectfully.

"No, but I've seen the tridee tapes that were brought back."

"There was no sign of melt-down in the debris?"

Mataroreva looked approvingly back at Merced. "I know what you're thinking. No, no meltage. No indication of the use of energy weapons. The polymer sections would show that for sure. We discarded that possibility long ago."

"Then you've discarded weaponry as a cause?"

"No, of course not. We have our own specialists working on sections of broken buildings and raft, on the chance that a more exotic variety of weapon might have been used. But the molecular structure of the polymer fragments is unaltered. That rules out, for example, the use of supercryogenics, which could freeze the material and cause it to fragment."

"What about ultrasonics? That could produce a similar effect without affecting structure."

Mataroreva threw him a peculiar look. "I thought you were all just oceanographers."

"Physics is only a hobby." Merced sounded apologetic.

"Sure. Yes, I suppose that's a possible explanation. But I've been told by our local peaceforcer computer that in order for ultrasonics to produce that kind of universal destruction, a different frequency setting would have to be used for each element of the town.

One for the polymers, one for the stelamic walls, another for seacane furniture, and so on. Practically every object of any size that was recovered was in pieces. It seems incredible that an attacker could have enough weaponry or could adjust frequencies rapidly enough to obliterate everything before counteraction could be taken."

"They wouldn't have to destroy everything," Merced argued. "All they'd have to do is jam or eliminate a town's communications. Then they could proceed with methodical annihilation under cover of the storm. You said your satellite system was sophisticated. Can't it monitor the towns through a few clouds?"

"Certain energy weapons, yes, they'd be detected if used. That's one of the things that has contributed to the frustration. Our satellites have given us nothing in the way of explanatory information. It seems self-evident that there are weapons which can operate without being detected."

Merced nodded. "I know of a couple which probably could, no matter how advanced the orbital scanning system."

"For example?"

Merced squirmed uncomfortably, aware he was very much the center of attention. "As I said, it's a hobby. Now, I'm not positive about this, but I've heard that the Commonwealth armed forces have access to devices which can affect the interatomic bonds of elements. The explosive result would be very much like the destruction you've described, Sam. The device could be adjusted far more rapidly than a subsonic projector and would be unlikely to set off a town's warning system, which, I presume, would be directed to keep an eye out for much more conventional weaponry."

"Some of them aren't even equipped to detect that," their pilot admitted. "Our primary source of danger on Cachalot has always been inimical local life-forms, not other people." He looked unhappy. "By this world's nature, by the way the population is concentrated yet dispersed, we have to maintain a peaceful society.

"Oh, we have our occasional troublemakers, but we've never, never experienced anything on this scale of mass murder. The local peaceforcers have always been able to cope. Our problems run more along the line of drunken brawls or jealous husbands. And there are some who become frustrated because they're unable to adapt to our world and our ways. But frustrated enough to organize and commit wholesale slaughter? I doubt it."

"If we rule out human or off-world attack," Cora declared in measured tones, "that leaves something from the sea."

"That's your department. That's why you've been brought in. Human or other intelligent assailants will be dealt with by the peaceforcers, but . . . well, the Commonwealth has had people on Cachalot for over four hundred years and the original settlers for four or five hundred years before that, and we're still comparatively ignorant about the local denizens."

"That's nothing new," Cora said. "There's still much we don't know about life in Earth's oceans. You needn't apologize."

"I wasn't apologizing," Sam said matter-of-factly. "I'm not the apologetic type."

"Well, we can rule out the storms as direct causes," Merced allowed. "I don't know about you ladies, but I personally am not ready to deal with human attackers. All we could do is determine that they were the likely cause of the trouble."

"That would be sufficient," Mataroreva told him. "You're not here to provide final solutions. Only to determine causes."

Odd thing for him to say, Cora mused. Oddly definitive. "Sam, you've never told us exactly what it is that *you* do."

"That's true," Merced agreed. "Are you attached to the scientific community here, or are you independent, or what?"

"Neither," Sam finally confessed, with that same easy smile. "I'm a government employee."

"Communications." Cora snapped her fingers. "That why you were sent to greet us."

"Not exactly, Cora. Communications is only a part of my job. All that talk about less-than-benign human agencies at work on this world is taken quite seriously by the government as well as by local authorities. I gave you my name, but not my title." He used his free left hand to turn down a blank section of his belt. Cora saw a radiant olive branch glowing on a circular blue field. Beneath the olive branch was a pair of tiny, glowing gold bars.

"It's Captain Sam Matatoreva, actually. I'm the commander of the peaceforcer contingent on this world. My primary task wasn't to greet you. It was to protect you."

IV

This news upset Cora even more than she showed. "So we're to suffer a bodyguard." She tried to make light of it. "So the powers that be are afraid someone might try to—what was it you and Pucara were talking about?—explosively debond my molecular structure or something."

Mataroreva did not smile. "If there are groups or individuals who are preying on the floating towns, and if they are already responsible for the deaths of twenty-five hundred people, it's unlikely they'd balk at assassinating a few imported specialists if they felt that action would continue to keep their operations secret and unimpaired."

She had no reply for that, fumed silently at the lack of specific information. Perhaps the original settlers could provide some information, despite all she had heard about their famous (or infamous) insistence on privacy. They were the real, secret reason for her leaving her comfortable post on Earth and coming all this way, regardless of the potential danger of the assignment. She found herself trying to see over the enclosing reef, out beyond the garland of glass that surrounded the lagoon, to the open ocean beyond.

"I want to meet the whales, Sam." He continued to steer the skimmer, listening. "I *need* to meet some of them. Ever since I was a little girl I've read about the whales of Cachalot. Every adult oceanographer's dream is to come here and perhaps be granted one of those extremely rare opportunities to study them, if only briefly. To wangle the chance to come here, to observe what many consider to be the greatest experiment in Terran sociohistory . . . I couldn't return, couldn't leave, without doing that."

"I'd like to see some of them, too." Rachael was peering over the side of the skimmer, studying the rising bottom.

"Well, you won't see any of them here," Cora chided her. "It's unlikely they'd come into the lagoon."

"As a matter of fact," Sam countered, "there *are* a couple of passages through the reef large enough to admit them. The lagoon is big enough and deep enough to accommodate some. Many, I understand, like to calve in the larger lagoons. But not in Mou'-anui."

"Why not?" Cora asked.

Sam told her, his words touched with something beyond his usual carefree self. "They could explain in words, but they don't wish to. It's simple enough to guess. They came to Cachalot to get away from people, remember."

"I would think that by this time," she murmured, "on an alien world, having come from a common planet of origin, all mammals together—"

Sam interrupted her gently. "You'll understand better if you do meet any of them."

"What do you mean 'if'? I know it's difficult, but surely it can be arranged. It's unthinkable to come all this way and—"

"Mother," Rachael said admonishingly, "we weren't sent here to study whales. We were sent to find a solution, or at least a causative factor, for a very dangerous situation."

"I know, I know. But to come to Cachalot and not study the cetaceans . . ."

"Remember that they don't wish to be studied," Sam told her. "Part of the Agreement of Transfer is that they can't be studied or bothered unless they specifically ask to be. There are certain species who are friendlier than others, of course. You know about the porpoises and their relatives. But the great whales shy away from any human contact. They find us . . . well, irritating. Their privacy is their right. The details of the Agreement of Transfer go back to before the Amalgamation and the formation of the Commonwealth. No one would even think of violating it."

"What about individuals?"

"We don't know that they think individually. That's one of the mysteries. They may have evolved a collective consciousness by now. And it's not a matter merely of irritating them. They can be downright hostile at times. That right is reserved to them as well."

"Six, seven hundred years or more," Cora whispered. "I would've thought they'd gotten over *that* by now."

"They'll never get over it," Sam replied, disturbed by his own certainty. "At least, they haven't as yet. It's been seven hundred and thirty years exactly, if I remember the histories right, since the serum was discovered that enabled the Cetacea to utilize all of their enormous brains. That's when it was decided to settle some of the pitiful survivors of the second holocaust on a world of their own. No, they haven't gotten over it."

Cora knew that Sam was right, though it was hard to feel guilty for the actions of an ignorant and primitive humanity. She insisted she should not feel guilt for the repugnant and idiotic actions of her distant ancestors.

Sending the whales to Cachalot had been hailed as a magnificent experiment, a gigantic fleet of huge transports working for two decades to accomplish the Transfer. It had been done, so the politicians claimed, to see what kind of civilization the cetaceans might create on a world of their own.

In actuality, it had been done as penance, a racial apology for nearly exterminating the only other intelligent life ever to evolve on Earth. The Cetacea had possessed cognitive abilities for nearly eight hundred years now. From all the reports she had eagerly devoured, as keenly anticipated as they were infrequent, she knew they were still growing mentally.

Part of the Agreement of Transfer stated that they would be left alone, to develop as they wished, in their own fashion. Intensive monitoring of their progress, or lack of it, was expressly forbidden by the Agreement. But the idea that they would resist such study to the point of open hostility was new to her, and surprising.

"I would think by now they'd enjoy contact," she said. "When you're building a society, conversation with others is helpful and psychologically soothing. Our experiences with other space-going races has shown that."

"Other space-going races didn't have the racial trauma that the Cetacea did," Sam reminded her. "And the society they're constructing, slowly and painfully, is different from any we've yet encountered. Maybe it's a reflection of their size, but I think they have a slower and yet greater perspective than we do. Their outlook, their view of societies as well as of the universe, is totally different from ours.

"When they were first settled here, they were offered, for example, aid in developing devices with which they could manipulate the physical world. Tools for creatures without hands or tentacles. They refused. They're not developing as a larger offshoot of mankind. They're going their own way.

"Sure, it seems slow, but as I said, their outlook is different from ours. A few experts do study them a little, and depart discouraged in the belief that in the past half a millennium the Cetacea haven't made any progress." There was a twinkle in his eye.

"Then there are some of us on Cachalot who think they *are* making progress. Not progress as we would consider it. See, I don't think they care much for what we call civilization. They're content to swim, calve, eat, and think. It's the last of those that's critical. We really know very little about how they think, or even what they think about. But some of us think that maybe our original colonists are progressing a little faster than anyone realizes."

"All the reports I've read are fascinating in that respect, Sam. I understand they've developed and discarded dozens of new religions."

"You'd know more about that than I," Mataroreva confessed. "I'm just a peaceforcer. My interest in the Cetacea is personal, not professional. I only know as much about them as I do because I live on their world.

"As to whether we'll encounter any of them, that I can't say. They've multiplied and done well on this world, but it's still incomprehensibly vast. We are duty-bound not to seek them out."

"Don't you think that under the present circumstances we might make an exception?"

Sam considered the matter, spoke cautiously. "If it's vital to your research, well, we might try locating a herd or two. But only if it's absolutely necessary."

"Whom do I have to clear it with?"

"With the cetaceans, of course. No arguing permitted, by the way." He spoke sternly. "If we do happen to run into a pod and they don't want to stop and chat, there must be no disappointed tantrums. If we pester them beyond a certain point, they're fully within their rights to smash the boat—and its inhabitants."

They were approaching the southern tip of the atoll. Curving beaches reached out and around to embrace their arrival. The buildings here were larger than any they had seen up close, larger even than the central

Administration Building back by the shuttle dock.
Some were circular, others massive and foursquare
to the sand. All were coated with photovoltaic paneling. Much plastic and metal tubing ran between the
buildings. Bulky structures running up each end of
the atoll looked like warehouses. And far more activity was visible than they had encountered at Administration. The Commonwealth is present on Cachalot because of this, Cora told herself, and not the other
way around.

"South Terminus," Mataroreva announced. "The
clearing area for the produce of Cachalot's ocean."

"What about the processing?" Rachael inquired.

"The basics are performed on the floating towns
themselves—sizing and grading *corbyianver,* for example. Concentrating and precrating are mostly done
right here. The final refining takes place," and he
waved at the sky, "out there. There are a number of
fairly large orbital factories set in synchronous orbits
above us."

Cora nodded. "We saw one on our way down, I
think."

"That's where the final work takes place." He angled
toward the beach. "All of the more valuable products
are completed up there: pharmaceuticals, perfumes
and other cosmetics, foodstuffs, minerals. It's cheaper
than trying to build a floating factory down here. Also,
most of the raw materials take acceleration better
than the finished products would."

"I wouldn't think an orbital factory would be
cheaper," Cora protested.

"Consider that everything you see on Mou'anui
was built with imported materials. Undersea mining
is prohibitively expensive, not to mention refining.
Cachalot's population doesn't call for an extensive
manufacturing base. It's cheaper to import."

He slowed, edged the craft up against one of several
empty piers. Switches were flipped and the engine

died. Another switch locked the craft to the pier. They followed their guide into a complex of buildings that were as modern as any Cora had seen. Ferrocrete covered the sand. It sounded harsh and alien against her sandals.

Around them strolled technicians whose accents she traced to many worlds. The atmosphere was radically different from the casual aura that enveloped the Administration Center. "Hustle" was the word here, commerce the constant reaction. This realization killed some of the charm Cora had come to associate with the new world. She had to remind herself that the human presence on Cachalot existed because of cold economic figures.

Mataroreva left them to chat with a lanky lady who looked rather like one of the imported coconut palms. She held an electronic notepad as she inspected man-high rows of opaque plastic containers.

"He's inside," Cora heard her say, "near the conveyors. He's checking potential extract yield himself. Seychelles Town brought in a large batch of formicary foam."

"Thanks, Kina." As she turned to resume her counting, he gave her a fond pat on the derriere. Cora took note of this, along with the ambient temperature and the time of day.

As they penetrated farther into the complex, Mataroreva pointed out the functions of various structures. Eventually they entered a long, cavernous edifice that seemed to stretch onward forever. The clank and hum of machinery grinding out credits for distant, uncaring proprietors further deepened Cora's melancholy. The last vestiges of paradise were being drowned around her. An ancient bit of music by Mossolov echoed in her head.

Clearly Cora had arrived on Cachalot with a brace of misconceptions, which she was rapidly shedding. No wonder the cetacean settlers wanted nothing to do with the local humanity. The same self-centered, acquisitive drives that had goosed mankind across a thousand parsecs in six directions were functioning round the clock on Cachalot.

She noticed a few thranx working some of the more intricate machinery. No doubt they were more comfortable here, inside, well away from the threatening water.

Occasionally Mataroreva would wave at this worker or another. Some were human, some not. Of the former, the majority was female.

They turned a corner and a gust of fresh salt air swept over them. They had completely crossed the reef and were now in a huge chamber, the far end of which lay open to the ocean. Gentle waves slapped metallically against the duralloy seawall. Two large suprafoils bobbed queasily against the broad metal platform. Both were portside-up to the wall. Their foils lay beneath the water. Stabilizers kept them from rolling farther.

Conveyors were moving large bulk crates from the holds of both vessels, stacking them neatly in a far corner of the chamber. The crates were pink, marked with blue stripes and black lettering. A small group of people were gathered by the nearest conveyor. Dwarfed by the mechanical arms and large crates, they seemed to be arguing politely. Mataroreva headed toward them.

Two men and one woman were chatting with four others. They wore pareus similar to Mataroreva's. One was a strikingly handsome blond youth of late adolescence who stood over two meters tall. Of the four they confronted physically and verbally, two were clad in suits and the popular net overshirts. One man wore standard trousers and a casual shirt. The last was clad collar to toe as if he were about to attend an inaugural ball. His shirt was long-sleeved, of jet-black satiny material that blended into crimson metal fiber at wrists and waist. The trousers were identical in material and cut. The high collar buttoned beneath the chin was also of woven metal. The soft plastic sandals he stood in seemed strikingly out of place.

It was to him alone the three pareu-clad visitors spoke, while the other three deferred to him in voice and manner. Cora studied Yu Hwoshien. He was no taller than she, but seemed so because of his posture, as stiff as any antenna. When he spoke only his mouth moved. He did not gesture with hand or face. His hair was pure white, thinning in the front. Though he was at least thirty years older than she, there was nothing shaky about him. His eyes, small and deep-sunk, were the rich blue of daydreams.

Mataroreva did not interrupt to announce their arrival, so they were compelled to listen in on the conversation, which had something to do with formicary foam. Cora knew nothing about that, but when the words "exene extract" were mentioned, she perked up quickly.

Exene was not quite a miracle drug, and its application was specialized and limited. However, anything Commonwealth chemistry had been unable to synthesize was extremely valuable. Of such substances, exene was among the most desired.

As safe as cerebral surgery had become over the last several centuries, there was always a certain degree of danger whenever one tampered with the human brain. Microxerography could detect even the smallest embolisms, but such dangers still had to be excised. No longer, though. Not since the discovery of formicary foam, which could be reduced to produce exene. A small dose injected into the bloodstream would dissolve any arterial buildup or blockage. It was nontoxic and had no side effects. The enzyme literally scoured clean the patient's circulatory system. The ancient scourge colloquially known as a "stroke" had been banished forever.

So, the famous drug was made from something called formicary foam. Cora could neither see nor smell the stuff, encased as it was in the airtight crates. It seemed as if quite a lot of foam was required to produce a small amount of exene. She wondered what the antlike creatures which secreted it looked like.

During the conversation Hwoshien spoke less than any of his companions. He was apparently content to let his subordinates do most of the talking. He remained motionless, arms folded across his chest. When he did speak, the arms didn't move.

For a wild instant Cora suspected his extraordinary rigidity was a result of some physical infirmity. But when the discussion ended and he shook hands with each of the visitors, she saw there was nothing wrong with him. His movements were just extremely spare. He was as economical of gesture as of word.

As he turned toward them she noted a few wrinkles in the long, impassive face, but not nearly as many as one would expect in someone of his apparent age. Those startling blue eyes seemed to stare not through her but past her.

Hwoshien spoke to Mataroreva. His voice was soft but not gentle, each word loaded with irresistible commitment. Then he again eyed them each in turn, stopping on Cora. To her surprise she discovered she was fidgeting. It was not that Hwoshien intimidated her. No one intimidated her. But he somehow managed to convey the inescapable feeling that he was just a bit smarter than anyone else in the room.

He extended a hand and smiled. The smile seemed to say, "This is my official greeting smile. It's genuine and friendly, but not warm." There doesn't seem to be much warmth in him, she thought as she shook the hand. Not that he was cold, just distant. Here was a man impossible to get to know. Whatever Yu Hwoshien was made of was sealed behind many layers of professionalism.

You could live, work, with such a person, she thought, but you could never be his friend. Associate, yes; companion, yes; but not his friend. She decided that somehow, somewhere in the past, a part of his humanity had been killed off.

"Welcome to Cachalot." The smile did not change. His tone was cordial. Just not warm.

"I've already told them about the towns, sir," Mataroreva hastened to put in. That eliminated any worry Cora had about whether Sam had said more than he was supposed to. Though why should she care how Hwoshien dealt with their guide? My mind, she told herself angrily, is filling up with extraneous material. Cotton-candy thoughts. She tried to shove aside all considerations except the reason for their presence here and gave her full attention to Hwoshien. That was easy to do. He still had not unbent, remained perpendicular to the center of the planet.

His smile disappeared, was replaced by a neutral expression that was neither grin nor frown but a carefully controlled in-between. But at least he unfolded his arms. He locked his fingers together, gestured with the combination as if praying while he talked. He seemed to have trouble deciding what to do with his limbs.

"I have very little to add to what Sam has already told you, save that we recently lost another town and several hundreds of citizens to the same unknown cause, with all the grief that implies. On our side of the ledger we have learned nothing new. Our ignorance only justifies my request for outside assistance. I am glad you have finally arrived." Just a hint of irritation showed through the mask.

"It was suggested by some of our local specialists, after Warmouth was annihilated, that they would eventually identify the cause of all the destruction. I gave them one additional day. I was rewarded only with an elaboration of the possibles that I am sure Sam has already mentioned to you. Any one of them could be correct, or there might be something we have overlooked. Regardless, at that point I was determined to bring in outside help.

"I do not think," he said casually, indifferent to how his words might affect them personally, "that just because the three of you are new to Cachalot, you are any more intelligent or better versed in such matters than our local experts. Quite the contrary, in fact. But they have all lived here for many years. As I'm sure you are aware, one's approach to problems, one's way of thinking, is often colored by one's environment. I saw no harm in trying a new approach."

He took a small scent-stick from a pocket, put it between his lips, and ignited it by flicking off the protective tip. It burned cleanly as soon as it came in contact with the air. As he continued speaking he puffed lightly on the stick. Mildly narcotic smoke began to tickle Cora's nose.

"It is my own personal feeling that your off-world approach will be productive within a month or not at all. Either you will hit on a cause within that time or you will not. Four towns, twenty-five hundred citizens. It's my responsibility to see that no inexplicable fifth disaster occurs. If it must be, I will tolerate a fifth *ex*plicable disaster, but a solution *must* be found—you are all marine biospecialists."

"That's right." Cora became aware that she had listened to him as a student would a professor. She steadied herself. That was not an accurate reflection of their relationship.

"I'm sure Sam has already mentioned the theory that intelligent forces could be behind all this?"

"The possibility was alluded to," Merced admitted.

"They may be local, they may be off-world," Hwoshien said. "Sam's people are already working on that." Behind him, the huge doors to the sea were beginning to slide downward. The jet engines on the suprafoils

were revving up, filling the huge chamber with an
ostinato thunder.

"That is not your concern; though of course, if you
find anything indicative of such a cause, you will so
inform Sam. Your job is to find out if some as yet
unidentified variety of local marine life could be responsible.

"Being well aware of what certain claimants to the
name 'humanity' are capable of, I suspect that our
search will lead us eventually to causes of a two-legged
nature. As we presently dwell in ignorance, we can
ill afford to neglect any possibility.

"Many of those specialists I mentioned have local
tasks they have long neglected to work on this major
problem. I cannot insist they continue to do so. Most
of them are under contract to the large companies that
finance Cachalot's commerce. Those concerns have
expressed their wish that their expensive people return to their expensive jobs. I can't require otherwise
without declaring martial law." He looked slightly
unhappy. "I would rather not do that. The panic that
might result could be devastating to business."

"I would think that the destruction of the floating
towns would be a damnsight more devastating,"
Rachael said indignantly.

"I'm afraid you don't understand the situation—Ms.
Xamantina the younger, isn't it? You see, the floating
towns are not owned directly by any of the large companies. They are variously leased, sublet, or otherwise
rented to the citizens who live and work on them. In
return for supplies and salaries, the bulk of their
catches is turned over to the large plants here on Mou-
'anui or on the other permanent atoll installations and
is credited against a town's general account.

"So if a town is destroyed," he said easily, as if he
were talking only about equipment and structures
and not about people, "it is the company that bears the
financial loss, not the inhabitants."

"They only lose their lives," Rachael muttered. But Hwoshien did not hear her, or chose to ignore the comment.

"Without any huge investment in the towns, the citizens are free to pick up and leave if they so desire. If a major panic arose, the companies would be left with the expensive floating towns, no one to run them, and no raw materials for their equally expensive orbital factories. The repercussions would be felt throughout the Commonwealth. And ordinary citizens would feel the loss of such irreplaceable substances as exene. We simply cannot afford a panic."

"So you shield the commercial interests involved," Cora commented quietly.

"As I said, in addition to other things, yes." The Commissioner seemed not the least perturbed by her veiled accusation.

"Of course," Merced agreed. "Death is a fiscally irresponsible policy."

V

Hwoshien looked over at the little scientist, finally replied in a different tone, a touch less formal than the one he had been employing thus far.

"I had friends on those lost towns myself. Kindly keep in mind that I'm in a very difficult personal position here. I do not expect you to sympathize. I do expect you to understand. I am trapped between the average citizen, who cares nothing as long as he or she is protected, and the commercial interests, which don't care what happens as long as the flow of produce is not interrupted. In addition, I am responsible first to a third party, the Commonwealth government itself.

"My sympathies lie with the first group, my thoughts with the second, and my allegiance with the last. This is a problem none of you must face. You will have everything in the way of material assistance you request, though I would ask you to be circumspect. Large, new concentrations of scientific instrumentation could attract the attention of our as yet hypothetical human killers.

"You will have complete working freedom. I sincerely hope you won't disappoint me."

Despite his formality, a formality that bordered on hostility, Cora found herself wanting to please Hwoshien. He inspired in others the desire to please him, as one would try to please a distant but concerned parent.

Could he be a mechanism, a robot? On rare occasions the Commonwealth was known to make such substitutions for organic personnel. No, she decided. He could not be a machine. A robot assigned to such a position already would have displayed far more warmth and affection. Hwoshien was too mechanical to be mechanical.

"We'll do our best." Rachael was becoming irritable, and it showed in her tone. Cora knew that her daughter was unable to remain interested in anything besides her neurophon for anything longer than half an hour at a time.

Hwoshien gazed at her a moment, then turned sharply and gestured them to follow. "Come over here."

Cora and the others followed him towards the docks. He walks like a thranx, she reflected. Stiffly and from the joints.

The doors had stopped descending, leaving a three-meter gap between floor and door bottom. They mounted a slight rampway. Then they were standing on the edge of a brown wall of burnished duralloy against which the waves beat ceaselessly. The suprafoils had long since departed, their faint whines swallowed by distance.

Hwoshien put his left foot up on the low flange that edged the dock, his left hand on his hip, and pointed with his right.

"Look out there, visitors." His finger traced the horizon. "Stretch your eyes. Travel any direction you choose and you will likely circumnavigate this world without ever seeing land. Cachalot's land lies beneath its waters, beneath a fluid, unstable atmosphere we have only just begun to understand. Man is still more at home in interstellar space than in the medium of his birth.

"This is home to the creatures that have evolved here, home also to the cetacean settlers, but it can never be that to those of us here on Mou'anui or to those out on the floating towns. We live here on sufferance. For all that we staggered out of the seas of Earth, they are still only places that we visit." He stepped off the flange, stared hard at each of them in turn.

"Thirty-six years I've lived on Cachalot. Still I feel like an alien. I am comfortable in my living arrangements, secure in my chosen profession. Were I not, I would never have been appointed Resident Commissioner. But at 'home'?" He shook his head, a small, controlled movement. "That is something I can never be. Though there are those who claim to feel otherwise. They say I do not think in the 'Cachalot' manner. Sam here is one."

The officer looked uncomfortable.

"That's all right, Sam. In no way am I being critical of you. You know what I mean."

Mataroreva nodded. Again Cora had that sugary sensation in her brain that something very important was being said, and she could not understand.

"Even Sam cannot be at home here. He can only *try* to be."

"Respectfully, sir, I do feel at home here."

"I know." Something shifted in Hwoshien's head and he was suddenly downright cordial. "I know how tired you must be. Would you join me for dinner tonight, please? We're very informal about such things here. We can talk further then. You'll have an opportunity to sample the unique cuisine of our kitchen . . . we sometimes even use human chefs to prepare our food. Again, I apologize for rushing you so abruptly from your long journey to this meeting, but I wanted everything spelled out quickly . . . and to meet you myself."

"We'd be happy to join you," Cora said. "Anything—as long as we can shower first."

"Of course. Surely the humidity is no worse than you expected?"

"I think we're all prepared for everything we might encounter," she said significantly.

"Good. At nineteen hundred, then?" He added a last comment that was so atypical, Cora had to reassure herself that he had actually spoken. "It will be a distinct pleasure to work with two such beautiful ladies."

The cafeteria-style dining area was separate from their quarters. Sam had to escort the three newcomers from their rooms. He and the two women waited in the small lobby for Merced, who arrived late, puffing slightly, tucking his net shirt into his shorts.

Cora wore a drape-weave that swirled around her body from right shoulder to left calf in alternating rows of fluorescent pink and yellow, dotted with deadcolor black flowers. Maybe everyone else on this world dressed informally when they ate together, but she still retained a number of civilized virtues. Besides, this would probably be the last time she would be able to dress decently before they got out into the field.

Rachael had opted for a seemingly simpler summer drape, in pale green. The simplicity was deceptive. Several fish were inlaid in silver thread along the hem. They breathed bubbles that appeared to flow up the dress. At certain wavelengths, depending on the illumination, the sizable bubbles were transparent. The motile peekaboo effect that resulted turned a number of heads as they entered the mess.

One corner was deserted save for Hwoshien. He wore the same stiff, utilitarian dark suit he had worn earlier in the day. Cora looked at his chest for the expected crimson insignia of a Commissioner. There wasn't one. His lack of pretentiousness is the most humanizing thing about him, she mused.

There was some small talk and some absolutely magnificent local food. Matatoreva had managed to slip quickly into the chair next to Cora. Merced and Rachael sat on the other side. Occasionally Merced would lean over and hesitantly whisper something to her and she would giggle. Then he would turn rapidly away, as if embarrassed by his own temerity in talking to her, and shovel his food.

The interchanges troubled Cora, but she was too busy talking with Hwoshien to pay much attention. Not that she could have done anything to prevent them.

"What would human agents have to gain by destroying the towns?" she asked. "Surely you must have some suspects?"

"Were that only the case." Hwoshien caressed his tall drinking glass. "Cachalot's oceans hold many riches. You saw a tiny sample of them today. Some small, independent operators would be happy to see their better-organized competition obliterated.

"For example, there are the people of the ships. They live and work on old-fashioned ocean-going boats. Not suprafoils, but real ships in the ancient floating sense. They own their vessels, unlike the people of the towns, who only lease their homes and equipment from the larger companies. They also refine some of their own produce right on board.

"The quantity is small, but it still cuts into the profits of the large concerns by bypassing the expensive orbital factories. So there has always been dislike between the people of the ships and the citizens who inhabit the floating towns."

Cora speared a forkful of a delicate white meat, chewed as she spoke. "Wouldn't they be easily discovered? Wouldn't a sudden rise in some ship's production be noticed?"

Mataroreva shook his head. "They don't *have* to ship off-world via Mou'anui or any of the other atoll bases. A shuttle could put down anywhere on Cachalot and take off fully loaded with refined goods or raw materials."

"Expensive," Hwoshien commented, "but with the produce and booty of an entire town to pay for it, such an operation would be immediately profitable. Eliminating the populations involved would be the best way of covering such piracy.

"Economically it is feasible. One would think the inherent danger would override such potential profits, but there are people who do not think such things through very clearly, to whom murder and destruction require little in the way of rationalization.

"Actually, we have been questioning the ship folk intensively. But you must understand that the existing rivalry precludes our making any overt accusations without irrefutable facts to back them up. We can't afford to alienate a large segment of the populace by accusing it of something none of its number may be responsible for. Off-world agencies may be involved. The AAnn, for instance, would enjoy watching and abetting chaos on any Commonwealth world.

"But as I have said, that is not your problem. Specify what equipment you wish, and Sam will have it drawn from government stores or billed to the local Commonwealth account. The question of personal financial recompense was settled, I believe, prior to your departure for Cachalot."

"You say you want to try to keep our purpose here a secret?" Rachael asked.

"You will be treated as visiting specialists engaged in typical commercial exploration. Escorts for such visitors are not uncommon, so Sam's presence among you should not be remarked on." He stared down at his plate. "This destruction *must* stop. It is bad for living, and bad for business."

They ate on in silence, finished with a dessert that Mataroreva informed them had been produced from the jellied insides of a round creature about the size of his fist. The substance was coated with poisonous spines and had to be properly treated prior to serving or it could kill instantly. The treatment was effective, however, and there were no known deaths attributable to comsumption of the delicacy. If he was trying to tease Cora, he had picked the wrong person. She had eaten far more bizarre products from several oceans. The transparent gelatin was cool and had a flavor like pomegranate.

The graphic description made Rachael queasy, though. Cora finished her daughter's plate as well as her own. She was just downing the last spoonful of her second helping when Merced asked quietly, "What about the whales?"

"What *about* the whales, Mr. Merced?" Hwoshien was puffing contentedly on another scent-stick.

"They're intelligent, they have no love of mankind. Couldn't they destroy a town?"

"Sure they could," Mataroreva yelled, "but why should they!" Aware of the effect of his violent reaction on Cora and Rachael, he lapsed into his usual boyish tone. But what the announcement of his profession had begun, his unexpected violence concluded. For better or worse, the mantle of innocence Cora had bestowed on him had vanished forever.

"They could," he said more calmly, "if they had a reason to, and if they could organize sufficiently. Remember that every floating town is protected against inimical local life-forms. Each has sophisticated warning systems and large underwater needlers which operate automatically in tandem when anything comes too close.

"There are leviathans in Cachalot's ocean larger than the largest whale that ever lived. The town needlers are quite capable of frying even a mallost.

"What's a mallost?"

"Something I hope you never see, Rachael." Hwoshien answered with such intensity that she subsided. "As Sam says, one could make short work of a whale, but it couldn't get within tentacle-throwing range of even a small town.

"A whole pod of whales working in perfect unison might destroy a town, but they do not think that way. For one thing, nothing like competition exists between the cetaceans and the towns. By and large, the townspeople are after varieties of local life the whales have no interest in. The plankton the towns take and strain for a few types doesn't make a dent in the copepod population. There is more plankton on this world than a million times as many baleen whales could ever consume. The baleens are the largest of the Cetacea, and also the dumbest. The toothed whales, which are more capable of considering such an attack, don't eat plankton."

"And they're either openly friendly," Matareva continued, "or indifferent to us, as I explained before. Unless they're bothered, and then their reactions have always been direct and personal. They've shown no interest one way or the other in the towns. They go after the togluts and the large teleosts.

"While they travel in herds, the catodons, largest of the toothed whales, have nothing resembling military guile. They've no experience in organized warfare—there are simply too many factors against it." He added an afterthought, "I suppose you have to consider every possibility. That's what you're here for. I just don't think the whales fit the requirements we've established for our mysterious cause."

He leaned back in his chair and toyed with his own second helping of dessert, uncomfortably aware of the reaction his initial outburst had produced.

Cora pushed back her chair, delicately dabbed at her lips with a napkin, and forced a smile as she spoke to Hwoshien. "Thanks for the delicious meal. We'll start work in a couple of days, as soon as we've had a chance to become a bit more acclimated."

"Very well." Hwoshien rose and shook hands with her. "I bid you all a good evening."

Mataroreva escorted them out of the mess.

"Isn't there some other way to return to our quarters without going through all these corridors?" Cora asked.

"You mean, Cora-doors?" She winced. They turned right, exited the structure.

The door deposited them onto a path paved with jewels, wilder in hue, richer in extent, than any ancient prince from Haroun al-Rashid on down could have dreamed of. They had started dinner before sundown. Now the stars shone on glass sands, making of them an echo of the distant Milky Way.

They trod cold fires. Buildings and trees became mere cutouts from a child's games, toy silhouettes against the night. Merced and Rachael had fallen well behind.

"How did you happen to get into peaceforcer work?" Cora asked Sam curiously. "You don't strike me as the type."

"Meaning I fit the mold physically but not mentally?" He grinned at her discomfort.

"I didn't mean . . ."

"Forget it. I'm used to it. I just drifted into it, I guess. Why *do* people become what they become? Life twists and turns on picayune events."

"Well, I always wanted to be a marine biologist."

"And I always wanted to have it easy and be happy," he countered. "Not very elevated career goals, but satisfying ones. I was born and raised here on Cachalot. Didn't have the aptitude for science, and fishing, gathering, and mining were too much work. That left some kind of administrative post.

"I wasn't much good with tapework, so when the

request was made for local peaceforcers, I joined up. Hwoshien believes strongly in compromise. Well, if I have any talent, it seems to be the ability to get others to do just that. Which is another way of saying I'm very good at stopping fights before they get started.

"I guess I've reached my present position because I did my job, didn't offend anyone or make too many mistakes. I also happen to be good at what's necessary after compromise has failed."

"I know," Cora said. "I could tell that from the way you reacted to that toglut by the pier."

"Oh, a toglut is nothing." He spoke in an off-handed way that indicated he wasn't boasting. "As I explained, they're slow and generally inoffensive. Wait till we're out on the open ocean. Away from Mou'anui. Cachalot's predators have evolved in the most extensive oceanic environment in the Commonwealth. A mallost would have togluts for breakfast."

"I can't wait," she told him honestly.

They had almost reached the looming shadow of the administrative dormitory. A few lights were visible within the structure, moth-eyes in the night. Somewhere the somnolent hum of storage batteries taking over from the now useless photovoltaics sounded a counterpoint to the steady slapping of small waves against the distant beach.

"Wait a second," Sam said.

Oh, oh . . . Cora readied herself. What sort of line would he try? She doubted it would be very original. Bless his gentle boyish soul, Sam didn't seem the type. But it would be a line nonetheless. Years had enabled her to assemble a formidable arsenal of disarming responses. Because she liked him, she would opt for one of the milder disclaimers.

Instead of reaching for her with words or hands he knelt. One hand held a palmful of sand, the other worked at his utility belt. "Have a look." A small light winked on, ultraviolet. He thumbed a switch on the side of the generator. The beam broadened slightly. He turned it on the sand he held.

It was as if he had dipped his hand into the treasure chest of some ancient mogul or pirate. Under the ultra-violet beam the hexalate grains fluoresced brilliantly in a hundred shades, sawdust shaved from a rainbow. The glow did not have the blinding prismatic harshness created by sunlight. Instead, the colors were soft and rich, gentle on the eyes.

The light winked out, but to her delight the colors remained. The phosphorescence faded slowly, reluctantly. As it did so, he turned his hand and let the ribbon of tiny suns dribble from his palm.

"Oh, how beautiful, Sam! I expected a fairyland world, but not in such variety."

"Remember the predators." He chuckled. "Some of those 'fairies' will gobble you down quick."

They moved on, stopped outside the dormitory. She turned, looked up at him. "I enjoyed walking back with you."

"Thanks for letting me. You really couldn't have gotten lost. You can't do that on land on Cachalot."

She was waiting for the kiss, wondering if she would object, wondering if she would let him and like it, when he startled her by touching her on the nose with one finger.

"Good night, Cora Xamantina. See you *ananahi 'ia po'ipo'i*. Tomorrow morning."

More puzzled than disappointed, she watched him lumber off into the night. Unlike the sands, he did not glow in the dark, though she felt that with the right kind of stimulus, he might.

Thoughts drifting, she made two wrong turns in the building before finding her room.

Her chamber was Spartan but impeccably clean, although bits of hexalate sand glittered in spots. She suspected one could be completely free of that substance only on the open sea. The room contained a

bed, a small clothes closet, a couple of chairs woven
from some local sea plant, and a matching mat of
emerald-green growth and intricate handwork: off to
one side was a small sanitary annex with amenities
for cleaning and washing.

In one corner were three neatly placed cases, two
large and one small. The seamless plastic responded
to her electronically encoded key when she pressed it
to the exterior of the seal-lock. From the second case
she carefully removed her diving suit. Her second
skin, really, considering the amount of time she had
spent inside it. It consisted of a double layer of vir-
tually untearable plastic alloy colored a watery blue-
green. Between the two incredibly thin layers was a
special thermosensitive gel that would keep the body
warm to a depth of a hundred meters at one gravity.

She laid the suit neatly across one of the chairs.
It was unharmed, as always, but that never prevented
her from going through the ritual check.

Next she withdrew the special face mask that
covered her entire head and sealed itself to the body
of the suit. In addition to examining the curved glassalloy faceplate that permitted excellent peripheral
vision, she checked the regulator on the gillsystem.
The backpack unit took oxygen directly from the
water and mixed it in proper proportion with nitro-
helium from a second small tank.

The tiny container of concentrated liquid rations
that would rest behind her left ear was full. She hooked
it to the head mask, made sure the spigot feed inside
the faceplate was clear. A spigot entering from the
other side provided desalinated seawater for drinking.

Weighing very little, the complete ensemble permitted a human to exist underwater for several weeks
without having to surface for food, water, or air. She
set the mask alongside the suit, brought out the last
item, which was not vital for survival but which made
working underwater considerably more enjoyable.

The belt contained packets that held a pressure-sensitive, liquid metal alloy. It was at its heaviest now, out of water, at one atmosphere. But as the diver wearing it descended, the weight of the metal decreased until, at a depth of ninety meters, well below normal diving limits, it achieved negative buoyancy. The diver could not descend farther without dropping the belt.

The check completed, Cora walked into the sanitary chamber and took a rapid shower. Then she retired, fell almost instantly into a dreamless sleep as soon as she decided what had been troubling her. There were no wave sounds.

VI

Cora had neutralized the window glass so that when the sun rose, it would not automatically be compensated for. The light woke her.

Joints aching, she crawled from the bed. Her neck hurt from having slept in a single position too long. She wondered why she hadn't slept more easily.

Rachael was in the hallway, greeted her with a cheery "Good morning, Mother."

"Morning. Got everything?" Rachael displayed a case dangling from each hand. Cora carried only a single container. "Don't forget to put on your goggles."

The photosensitive lenses could not completely dampen the electrifying brilliance of sunrise on Mou'anui. It took a few minutes for their eyes to adjust before they left the confines of the dormitory.

Anchored at the end of the main pier was a much larger vessel than the skimmer Core had expected to see. It was a broad-beamed, aerodynamic shape of gray metal with a crimson stripe running around it just above the waterline and with the imprint of the Commonwealth stamped on each side of the bow. Two small beams emerged from the side of the craft facing them and disappeared into the water. A four-foil craft, she reflected.

There was a single, large, above-deck cabin and an enclosed bridge near the bow. The entire craft was coated with photovoltaic elements, which would produce plenty of power for the electric engine.

No need to wonder why Sam had chosen such a vessel over a large skimmer. It would be slower, but they were likely to be out on Cachalot's ocean for some time. A skimmer could not hover forever, because it required a type of engine more powerful than anything the sun could fuel. The suprafoil could sit powerless on the water and act like a boat, whereas a skimmer would be helpless, or worse, would sink. Cora knew from experience that even large skimmers had trouble maneuvering in rough weather. A powerless foil could ride out a storm that would sink a skimmer in a minute. And on a long journey a foil's spaciousness would be more than welcome; it would be vital. No aircraft could provide such comfort, even if Cachalot could afford such expensive luxuries, which it could not.

Mataroreva appeared from below, moved to the dock to help them with their luggage. *"E aha te huru* —how y'all doing?"

Cora mumbled something about their being ready to go.

"Not a bad ship," he said buoyantly. "I angled for the largest one possible."

"It's more than big enough," Cora agreed, stepping aboard.

"We each have a private cabin," he went on. "Nothing like research in style. They let the requisition pass because this is such important business. And because I told them that you work better when relaxed." He chuckled. "So they let us have the *Caribe* without so much as a question."

"How nice." Cora noticed that Rachel was bent over one of her cases. It was open. Without surprise she saw that her daughter was carefully inspecting her neurophon.

"Don't worry. I'm not going to play anything."

"Then we're ready to leave—except," she said to Mataroreva, "for Merced." She tugged at the bodice of her suit netting, studied the shore. "Here he comes."

Looking awkward with his burden of cases, the little oceanographer was jogging hurriedly toward them. He ran down the dock, tossed the containers up to the waiting Mataroreva with evident disregard for their contents. Cora winced, preferred to think they held no delicate apparatus.

In a second he had clambered monkeylike over the side and was standing on deck clad only in a thin swimsuit. His muscular body was slightly darker than Sam's, though nowhere near the deep chocolate of her own or Rachael's. A thick mat of black hair covered his chest.

"That's all of us, then," Rachael said brightly.

"Not quite," Mataroreva corrected her. "There'll be two more joining us."

Cora frowned at him. "I thought that we three constituted all the imported help."

"You do, but we'll be assisted by a couple of local specialists."

Cora was so upset she failed to notice his wink. "What is this? Hwoshien told us they were all tied up with other projects and didn't have any more time to devote to this problem, or that they'd exhausted their own ideas."

"Not these two." He grinned at her. "Don't worry, Cora. They won't intrude on your work. They're coming along more to help me than to help you."

More security people, she thought. Yet Hwoshien had told them Sam would be their only escort. She looked down the gangway into the bowels of the ship.

"Where are they, then?"

"Waiting for us outside the reef." Before she could question him further, he had turned and bounded up toward the bridge.

"Nice day, Ms. Xamantina." Merced was standing next to her.

"So far," she replied noncommittally. "Listen, you might as well call me Cora. We're going to be living and working in first-name proximity to each other, so we might as well identify each other the same way."

No point in offending this man, she was thinking. After all, he was a colleague, though of unproven ability. Like it or not, she was going to be working with him.

"Sure thing . . . Cora." He strolled over to Rachael.

Cora moved forward, away from them. If she remained she would overhear their conversation, something she preferred to avoid.

A waking noise was coming from inside the stern. The suprafoil slipped free of the anchorage. Once out in the lagoon, they turned to port. The waking sound became a steady, rich growl. The wind blew Cora's hair back free of her shoulders and the salt air commenced its gentle massage.

Raised out of the water on four foils, the *Caribe* was skating across the surface at sixty kilometers an hour, heading northwest. Cora walked to within a couple of meters of the bow, enjoying the smooth ride while at the same time mentally decrying the wastefulness. They could have managed efficiently with a ship half the size. She had to admit, though, that having her own cabin would be nice.

The foil was traveling too fast for her to make out anything beneath the blurred surface. A small cloud of icthyorniths, their water-holding sacs fully distended, shot out of the water ahead and curved away to starboard. Following them, her gaze was intercepted by the sight of Sam standing alone up in the enclosed bridge, his huge shoulders blocking out any view of the overhead instruments, pareu rippling in the slight breeze, eyes straight ahead.

For the first time since she had touched down on

Cachalot, she felt the cold kiss of fear. It occurred to her that whatever had obliterated four entire towns could probably dispose of a single boat and its occupants as easily as she could stifle a sneeze. She forced the worry aside. There was no point in wasting her time thinking about such a possibility. Death was merely a physiochronological abstraction she would have to deal with sooner or later.

Even at the *Caribe*'s speed, it was many minutes before they had crossed the gigantic lagoon of Mou'anui and the first of the small outlying motus, or islands, came into view. No tall transplanted palms waved acknowledgment of their presence. They were almost on top of the low, sandy piles when she finally noticed them.

Mataroreva had slowed their pace. While the passage through the reef was reasonably wide, he took his time guiding the *Caribe* through. A thick accumulation of transparent hexalate could not harm the duralloy hull but might do damage to the more delicate, flexible foils.

Only a slightly increased swell met the craft as it slipped free of the lagoon. No thunderous breakers to ride out here, except during a storm.

They were well clear of the exterior motus, and Mataroreva still held their speed down as he turned farther to the west. Cora watched interestedly as they approached a small atoll, a miniature version of Mou'anui complete with two glassy islets whose crowns barely broke the surface. Sam was leaning out of the bridge enclosure, hunting for something even the slight distortion caused by the transparent glassalloy chamber might hide.

Cora looked in the same direction, but strain as she did, she could not find a boat, a raft, or anyone on the islets. If they were supposed to meet their additional assistants here, she couldn't . . . What she did finally espy, and what broke her train of thought, were two huge dorsal fins moving straight for the *Caribe*. They were black with white markings. Orcas—killer whales!

"Rachael—Rachael!"

Her daughter joined her, her expression anxious. "Mother, what's.? . . ."

Cora was pointing excitedly over the side. Rachael and then Merced noticed the approaching fins of a pair of Cachalot's true colonists.

Cora called up to the bridge. "Sam!" He glanced down at her. "Can't you pull over for a better look?"

"Not necessary," he shouted down to her. "You'll meet them in a moment. They're the two other experts I told you about."

He pressed several switches inside the transparent bridge, climbed down to join the others. In one hand he held several ear-and-mouthpiece sets. The other held a thick black box—the heart of the ship, with which he could control most of the *Caribe*'s movements and actions.

"Here," he said, handing the headsets around. "These are analogs of the speaker-receiver units in your gelsuits. If you want to listen in or join the conversation, you'll need one of these." He was wearing one already.

Like two racing spacecraft in a blue-green void, the orcas drew alongside the bobbing suprafoil. Cora studied the black and white coloring through the clear water. The sandy bottom was still only some fourteen meters below them, and the orcas hung within that medium, floating as if suspended in air.

Whistles and squeaks came from Sam, and she hurriedly adjusted her own headset. His voice was distorted by the electronic diaphragm, but the words were now understandable.

"These are our lookouts and helpfriends," he was saying. "I've known them both for a long time. The big male is Wenkoseemansa. In orca that translates roughly as Double-White-Death-Scar-Over-Right-Eye.

You can see it when he rolls to port. Got it when a calf in a fight with a sunmori fish. His mate is Latehoht—She-Who-Rises-Above-The-World."

"What is the origin of?—" Merced started to ask. Before Matatoreva could reply, the question was answered by action.

Cora stumbled backward in spite of herself, in spite of all her supposed scientific preparedness, and fell to the deck. Rachael gave a scream and ran into Merced, nearly knocking him over. Only Matororeva wasn't affected. He ducked, bent over as much from expectation as from laughter.

All seven meters and nine tons of Latehoht had exploded in a geyser of salt spray. Cora lay on her back, staring in horror and fascination as the enormous body flew completely over the low bow of the *Caribe,* to land with a tremendous splash on the starboard side.

She fought the wildly rocking deck as she scrambled back to her feet, dripping water and shouting angrily at Matororeva. "Why the hell didn't you warn us?" He was laughing too hard to reply. She had to admit she was more embarrassed than frightened. "Why didn't you!—"

"Awwwoman—awwwoman!" She was so startled by the unexpected, mellifluous voice that suddenly sounded in her ears that she forgot her embarrassment and Sam completely. In a daze she turned and walked to the starboard railing. She had studied many tapes of cetacean talk, both in the natural state and translated into terranglo. But it was one thing to hear such an alien yet warm voice on tape, quite another to experience it in reality.

A massive blunt head protruded above the water. Two tiny, almost imperceptible eyes of vitreous black were staring up at her as the head moved slowly from side to side. The mouth was open, showing startlingly white, sharp teeth. The sounds uttered from within reached Cora not as squirps and squeals but as rich, clean terranglo.

"You drop in fear. You worrry and wince with your body and soullll. She-Who-Rises-Above-The-World intimidates and does not pleasse you in herr greeting-time." Then, more quietly, "I do not kноww if I like this one-she, Sammm."

"I'm sorry," Cora said automatically. "Really I am." She ignored the whistles and yelps that blasted from her headset speaker, concentrated on forming the words with her lips. "I was startled, that's all. Probably," she continued more confidently, "I could do some things which would startle you."

"She of surprise, she of mystery haunts my dayyy. Unknowwwn neww quality. Can it be that a female human has such capability, Samm?"

"I don't know," he said. "But in the case of this one, it is possible-thing." He grinned at Cora, then spoke again to the distraught orca. "You should not be upset, little one."

A second, more massive head emerged from the water next to Latehoht's, rose to the railing, and turned one eye on Cora. She did not pull back. White teeth were centimeters from her face.

"She did not mean to upset or displease," Wenkoseemansa rumbled. He sank back toward the water, no longer treading on his tail. "But onlyy to greeeet."

"I wasn't upset," Cora replied a bit defensively. She leaned over the railing. "It was a glorious jump, Latehoht. I've swum many of the oceans of the universe and encountered much in them that amazes and delights me, but none that truly displeases."

"Know we fast ones nothingg of the otherrr oceans, though Samm tells us sometimes of them." Wenkoseemansa did a neat little pirouette on his tail. "Know we much of the universe that isss this ocean. We will protect you frommm it. We sufferr you to live upon and within it. We will watch over you for our friend Sammm, for such is whatt we wish to do."

"Whatt we wish to do," Latehoht echoed.

Another fountain of water spurted as Wenkoseemansa rolled onto his side and slapped the surface with his flukes. "Timmme to swim, time to go. Time to kill a little more the parasite impatience, the gerrrm of boredom, beneath a fairr upper sky. Where go we to, friend Sam?"

"To where I told you seven days ago," Mataroreva replied. "To the place of my people last dying, to the town on the waters that is no more. Toward the nonscarred side of the sun."

"To the placcce of deathhh," Latehoht said somberly. "To the where of sudden screamming and the realms of the vanished men, to therrre we go." The great head ducked out of sight as she and her mate turned to the northwest.

"Wait!" Cora yelled, the high-pitched screech from her headset speaker almost deafening her. The two whales paused. "Do you know what caused the death place? Do you have any idea what might be responsible for the vanished men?"

"Would that we knew," Wenkoseemansa bemoaned. "Would that we had the rhyme or reason of it, so that youu would not havve to be herre. Would thatt it had not happened."

"Swim with uss, Samm!" Latehoht cried in an entirely different voice.

"Yes, swwim with us!" her mate added.

"I can't," he told them, looking over the railing. "I have to guide the boat."

"Poorr humans," Wenkoseemansa observed sadly. "Poorr people of the airr. A thin environment makes for narroww people. Narroww people make forr narroww thoughts. And narroww thoughts make for too much worryy to the nonscarred side of the sunn." He ducked his massive head and started westward.

"Nonscarred side of the sunn." Latehoht performed one final prodigious leap, again drenching the unprepared passengers on the foil, then joined her mate, vanishing to the west. In a moment even the two towering dorsal fins had disappeared and nothing could be seen breaking the gentle blue swells ahead.

"You'll lose them, Sam!" Cora called to him.

He shook his head. "We're headed in the same direction, for the same destination. They'll always know where we are."

"They'll stay within range?" she asked uncertainly.

"Of our sonar as well as theirs, yes." He started back up toward the bridge as the *Caribe* began to accelerate.

Cora knew that, of all the cetaceans, the orcas were the ones who found the company of mankind congenial and that they thought more like humans than did any of their relatives. But she suspected from what she had just observed that these two had a more than merely tolerant relationship with Sam. They were more than assistants and advisers; they were friends.

Spray stung her cheek and eyes. In the absence of hexalate sands they had no need of the protective goggles. The glare off the water was no worse than on the seas of other worlds.

She leaned over the railing and looked sternward. Distant flashes of light, green and pink and yellow, were fading behind their rear horizon. They were the last signals of Mou'anui's sands and the subsidiary motus that surrounded the great atoll.

Then there was just ocean. Ocean, air, and sun. They were surrounded by Cachalot. She decided she was hungry.

There was no rocking motion to the *Caribe,* only the steady, soft vibration which transferred itself from the foils to the hull. From the hull to the mattress of her bed the vibration dimmed still more. It was too much sleep that finally awakened her, groggy and cotton-mouthed.

The small port was covered, shutting out any exterior light. A glance at the chronometer indicated she had been asleep for nearly twelve hours. She hadn't thought she was particularly tired, but in this case it seemed her body had disagreed with her brain.

She put her face back together; then, feeling no less than fifty percent human, she made her way up to the deck.

They were cruising at a slightly slower speed now. So as not, she suspected, to exhaust even the muscular orcas. Rachael was sunbathing on the rear deck. Merced was nowhere to be seen this new morning, and Sam was on the deck above the central cabin, behind the bridge.

The master control lay nearby. To her surprise Sam was reading a book. A real book, not a tape or disc.

"Ia ora na—morning," he greeted her. "It's not often I have the pleasure of meeting someone who lives in reverse."

"I'm still half asleep, Sam," she told him with only a touch of irritation. "Don't play games. What are you talking about?"

"Only that you get younger and more beautiful each day."

"That's nice." She turned, scanned the endless ocean, the view no different from the day before, that she knew would be no different tomorrow. "When I regress all the way back to an egg, I'm yours."

"Fried, poached, scrambled, diced, or in an omelet?"

"Hard-boiled," she responded, not missing a beat. She eyed the empty bridge. "Master remote or no, shouldn't you be up there checking other instruments?"

"For instance? You worry too much, Cora." He eased back into the lounge. The material cooled his back, kept him from perspiring too much. "The Commonwealth's been overtechnologized for centuries. If anything goes wrong, the ship will stop. If nothing stops, there's no reason for me to hover over the instruments. You're still thinking in terms of the oceans of more developed worlds.

"There isn't an island or reef within kilometers. This section of sea, this close to Mou'anui, has been fairly well mapped. The chance of our encountering another ship, let alone running into one, is about one in several million. A true passenger passages and lets his ship take care of itself. That's what it's designed to do. In the unlikely event we do encounter something, it will warn us in plenty of time. You don't think any vessel as smart as this one is going to bash itself up simply because it has a few dumb humans aboard, do you?"

"Okay—let up on me, will you?"

Several high whistles and squeaks joined the conversation. She looked to starboard. Sam put down his book, frowned intently. "That's Latehoht. She's talking to you."

"How do you know, and why to me?"

"I know a little orca. As to the second"—he smiled at her—"ask her yourself. You'll need your headset. And hurry." He glanced upward. "Soon it will be hot noon and they'll slide beneath the ship. They like to travel in the shade of the hull."

She started to leave. "It's down in my cabin. I'll go get it."

"Never mind. Use mine." He pointed.

She located the translator unit, donned it, and adjusted the controls. Then she was leaning over the side and shouting, "Good morning."

"Haill and good hunttingg, grreetings to thhe sssun!" the joyful response came. For an instant the magnificently streamlined black and white body disappeared, only to break the surface seconds later. "A ggood dayy to beee alivve, to swwim and to eatt and to thhinkkkk."

"Haill and morrrning," a slightly deeper echo

sounded. Wenkoseemansa greeted her nearby. Cora
noted that when traveling, one had to adopt a pause-
and-wait style of conversation to match the whales
arcing in and out of the water. But the male did not
reappear.

"What's wrong with Wenkoseemansa?" Cora asked
Sam, moving the headset pickup aside so the unit
would not translate her question into orca. "Doesn't
he like me?"

"What makes you think Latehoht likes you?" he
teased. "Don't mind Wenkoseemansa. He's the strong,
silent type."

"Awwwoman, off anothher wworrrld!" a new cry
sounded. Cora turned her attention back to the waters. From her position high on the overdeck she
could see the entire powerful body. It cut through the
water like a ship through vacuum, sometimes playing
only centimeters from the sharp, flexible metal of the
fore starboard foil.

"Lissten to a tale, lissten to a tale!"

Wenkoseemansa reappeared but did not speak. He
cut under his more loquacious mate, raced just ahead
of the dangerous foil, and let it kiss his tail flukes.

"I could listen to you all day," Cora replied honestly.

"Nottt sso longg," Latehoht corrected her quickly.

Cora heard a noise, raised her earphones, and heard
in terranglo, "The translator has a difficult time with
metaphors," Sam was telling her. "Try to be as literal
as possible, even if Latehoht is not. And pay attention,
or you'll miss something good." He turned onto his
side, his huge stomach shifting to cover completely the
instrument belt encircling his waist.

"Latehoht's a fine storyteller. Orcas love to tell
stories. They all think they're poets. Sometimes I think
they stay around men just to have someone new to
listen to them. So be a good audience."

With pauses while she was beneath the surface,

Latehoht proceeded to tell the story of Poleetat, an ancestral orca and one of the first to reach Cachalot. It seemed that Poleetat, in exploring his new home, encountered a megalichthyian, one of the largest creatures inhabiting Cachalot's ocean. The megalichthyian was four times Poleetat's mass. Its teeth were sharp and small and many, and it boasted an enormous single tusk protruding from its lower jaw like a sword.

Unlike some of the younger orcas, Poleetat did not try to bite the megalichthyian. Instead, it remained out of range of that murderous, sharp-edged tusk and harried its wielder, teased and tired and tempted it. All the while the furious megalichthyian, which had already killed or severely wounded several less circumspect orcas, slashed and thrust at its tormentor.

Eventually, all the other orcas either had been wounded or had fled in confusion, not knowing how to deal with this alien enemy. And this was no ordinary megalichthyian, Latehoht explained, but an enchanted one. It would not tire or give up the fight.

Yet Poleetat, though his strength waned, refused to flee or pause to eat lest this dangerous monster harm others of the pod. So they dueled a dance of death, the enchanted megalichthyian twisting and stabbing, having only to make a single strike with its great tusk to kill, while Poleetat spiraled and spun around the great spotted brown bulk, snapping at its fins and tail and trying to get in a bite at one of the monster's several eyes.

They danced their way all around the world, changed direction, and fought from pole to pole, fighting even beneath the ice packs. Still the megalichthyian did not tire. But Poleetat, though the strongest of the orcas, was nearing the end of his strength and saw that something radically new in the way of fighting would be needed to end this war.

So he faked exhaustion, letting the spear of his opponent pass close, so close to his belly that blood was drawn. Then he turned to swim limply away. Smelling death and triumph, the megalichthyian rushed in pursuit, growing nearer and nearer, ready to run Poleetat through from fluke to nose.

With his apparent last bit of strength Poleetat gave a final burst of speed and soared out of the water as if to escape. Contemptuously the megalichthyian followed.

Ah, but Poleetat had judged well his distance. He shot through the air and passed over the thick ice, to land an incredible distance away—and drop cleanly through the far hole he had perceived.

But the megalichthyian could no more fit through that comparatively tiny hole than the waltzing sea worms of the lagoon floors could slip through the breathing duct of a clam. It landed hard on the ice pack, which cracked slightly but did not give.

It lay flopping there, helpless beneath the pressure of its own great weight. Poleetat swam back up to the open sea, stuck his head out of the water to inspect his beached enemy. The convulsions faded and the monster soon died, for it could not breathe air, as could orcas and men.

With his remaining strength the dying Poleetat summoned orcas from wherever they had scattered to, and told them they could swim safely with their calves now, for this particularly dangerous enemy had been vanquished. Then he died, and there was much mourning in the sea that day. The orcas managed to grasp the tail of the megalichthyian where it lay on the edge of the ice. They pulled it back into the sea and feasted on it for days, and made this song-story so that Poleetat would not remain dead, but would be ever reborn in the tales parents tell to their calves on the long hunts for food.

"That's a wonderful story," Cora finally told her. "There's an incredibly ancient human tale similar to it, involving a man named Hercules and a wrestler named

Antaeus, who lost his strength when he was held away
from his mother, the Earth, the solid ground."

"You'll have to tell me the tale sometimme," Latehoht said.

"Yes!" Wenkoseemansa might not talk, but he apparently listened well. "Sometimme you will have to
tell uss the story and we will listen, will listenn." He
sounded interested now.

"Don't you have any stories remembered from times
before you came to Cachalot?" Cora asked. "Times
and stories from Earth, from Terra?"

"Tales from the past," Latehoht murmured. "Tales
from the time of mourning."

"We do nott go back to the pasts," Wenkoseemansa
said sternly. "To the times of troubles, to the timmes
of terror." He sounded upset. "We go *noww* to the
place of recent passing of menn." In tandem they
shot forward past the bow.

"Wait! I didn't mean . . ."

She took off the headset, explained to Sam what had
happened. "I've offended them, haven't I? Are
they sorry because they have no such stories?"

"Oh, they remember." He spoke very quietly.
"Many of them hold the stories sent down through the
generations raised on this world. They have no mechanical memories, but those huge brains of theirs can
retain much more than we can. It just bothers them
to have to do the remembering.

"Earth is remembered as a paradise, you see. Until the rise of 'intelligence' among men. Then paradise
was transformed into purgatory."

"I know the history of ancient whaling." She found
the word hard to pronounce. "I would have thought
all that had been—"

"Forgotten by now?" he finished for her. "I just told
you, they don't forget. There are scattered citizens of
the Commonwealth who trace their ethnic ancestry
back to a people known as the Jews. They have a par-

ticular abhorrence, I understand, for a period of
Terran history known as the midtwentieth, old calen-
dar. A thing called the Holocaust in the old records.
The cetaceans know of it. Their own holocaust over-
lapped that same period, though it lasted far longer.
For centuries. They regard the gift of Cachalot as
mankind's attempt at an apologia for that time."

She looked stricken.

"They're not offended by your asking. Don't look so
distraught, Cora. They simply prefer not to talk about
it. Earth isn't their true home any more, though some
cetaceans still exist there. Cachalot is their world now.

"But I'm sure they'll appreciate it if you don't mention it again."

VII

A beeper sounded from the bridge. He put aside the book and moved to investigate. She joined him, studied the instrumentation professionally.

"Reef?"

"No, porpoises. They're not quite paralleling us, should cut our course in a little while. Maybe they'll stay with us for a bit."

"Won't Wenkoseemansa and Latehoht scare them off?"

He smiled, tried not to sound patronizing. "Didn't you study anything before coming here?"

"There's practically nothing on intercetacean relationships," she countered testily. "You know that. I didn't have the advantage of being raised with them."

"Hey, easy—they don't hunt each other any more. With all the food available on this world, the orcas don't bother with blood relatives. Even if all the local life vanished, I think Wenkoseemansa and Latehoht would starve to death before eating a cousin." He studied the small screen nearby. "Call your daughter and Pucara. It's a fair-sized school. They should enjoy the sight."

Merced had been reading below decks, in his cabin. He joined the other three at the starboard railing. Rachael cradled her neurophon, hoping perhaps for melodic inspiration.

At first only tiny glints could be made out here and there, sun sparkling off thrown water or gray backs. The reflections became brighter and more frequent, resolved themselves eventually into slim shapes.

Then they were surrounded, engulfed by lean, perpetually grinning gray forms that broke the water in repeated leaps of breathtaking symmetry. Wenkoseemansa and Latehoht remained close to the hull.

"Thousands, there must be thousands of them!" Rachael finally gasped into the awed silence. The sea was alive around the suprafoil, from horizon to horizon.

"No one can say how many thousands," Matatoreva agreed. "Ten, twenty—herds of thirty and more have been reported by aerial transports. The porpoises have done well on Cachalot, too." He was slipping on his headset, and now Cora had to rush below to locate her own.

"Want to talk to them?" he asked when she had rejoined him at the rail.

"I—I don't know. How do you pick one out?"

"You don't. Just switch on and shout 'Howdy.' "

She adjusted her speaker, called aloud, "Greetings to the gray friends of man!"

"Greetings—hello—how are you—good day—cheers!—" Her earphones rang as the barrage of replies nearly overloaded the headset. There was also a great deal of whistling and piping that came through unaltered. She fiddled with the tuner, but the sounds did not resolve into words.

"I'm getting something that's not being translated."

Sam described it back to her, nodded. "There's no way *to* translate it," he told her amusedly. "It's laughter."

"Foolishh wasteful of time!" Latehoht muttered.

"Foolish wasteful of life," Wenkoseemansa added.

"Just because they no longer hunt porpoises doesn't

mean they've become particularly fond of them," Sam noted.

"Why not?" Cora had given up trying to estimate the size of the herd. "They're close relatives." She leaned over the railing. "Why don't you like the gray ones?"

"Flighty, silly, useless creatures!" Latehoht replied at the top of a jump.

"No direction . . . no purpose," Wenkoseemansa agreed. "Their lives are all frivolity and playy. They think not seriously on any matterr. They knoww only howw to enjoy themselves and fritter away their living-time."

"That's not so bad."

"Are there menn who do that wayy?" Latehoht sounded curious.

"Some," Cora admitted.

Without slowing, the female orca indicated her displeasure by slapping angrily at the surface with her tail flukes. She came up, inquired, "Whatt think you of such of your own people?"

"Yes, of your owwn people, what do you thinkk?" her mate wondered.

Cora hesitated a moment, then smiled as she told them, "I think they're lazy, frivolous, and useless!"

At that the two orcas commenced to spiral about a common axis as they continued to parallel the *Caribe,* as if rifling an unseen gun barrel.

"Ah, she sees wisdomm, this she!" Wenkoseemansa said.

"The wisdom she sees," Latehoht added. "In manyy ways are orca and man truly closerr to each other than orca and porpoise."

Twenty-five minutes went by before the enormous herd of flashing, silver-sided animals passed from view to the northeast of the cruising suprafoil.

"I thought porpoises were supposed to be as smart

as orcas." Rachael was still composing a silent song to the departed herd.

"They are," her mother told her. "Almost. They didn't try to talk to us, though."

"Too busy having fun," Sam told her. "You can argue with that kind of lotus-eating existence, as do the orcas, but there's much to be said for it. They love to perform tricks on us poor air-bound humans. Hereditary delight of theirs, I'm told. Handed—or finned—down from their domesticated ancestors.

"I was called outside Mou'anui one day by a harried local guide. Seems a small herd of porps had joined his tourist party and wouldn't let any of them out of the water. They were pushing them around like toys, but the tourists didn't know what was going on, and some of them were panicking.

"Then there's the story of a couple of males who encountered some visiting teachers from . . . from Horseye, I think it was. They put on a display that the helpless guide—he was afraid to interfere—later described as 'elegantly obscene.' The porps were just having fun, but the young ladies were a little worried about just what their intent was. Scared them some, I'm afraid.

"The porps apologized when they learned their antics weren't taken in the spirit of casual friendliness. They made amends with a voluntary display of aquatic acrobatics few visitors ever see."

"Lazy, good-for-nothings!" Latehoht bawled over the earphones. "Unrepentent calves!"

Cora switched her speaker back on. "Tell me, Latehoht, why shouldn't they spend all their lives playing? What purpose is there other than to eat and live and enjoy oneself? Since you don't desire to explore other worlds as mankind does, what do you do with your time when you aren't at play?" She held her breath, remembering what she had been told about cetacean sensitivity to interference in their lives.

But Latehoht replied immediately, without rancor. "We do explorre the universe. The ends we seekk are closerr to uss than yours to you, yet no less reall to us for thatt. You said we 'don't desirre to explore other worlds as mankind does.' Why should we have to explorre 'as mankind does'? We leavve it to man to look upwardd. We wishh to spend many thousands of years looking inwardd."

The orcas put on a momentary burst of speed, continued cruising several meters ahead of each fore foil, riding the slight bow waves from each side.

Cora slipped free of her headset. "So they're all philosophers?"

"Many see themselves that way," Sam told her, "except for the porpoises and a few others, like the belugas. The orcas are a little confused. They think sometimes like the great whales and sometimes like the porpoises—and sometimes, as Latehoht hinted, like us.

"I don't pretend to be able to make sense of everything Latehoht and Wenkoseemansa say, but some of the finest alien psychologists in the Commonwealth have listened to tapes of their conversations and haven't been able to follow their multilevel semantics, either. So I don't feel I'm missing much." He shrugged. "Who knows? Give them another few thousand years and they might be building spaceships of their own, though I can't imagine how. We know a little about how they think. We don't know much about what they're thinking of."

Several days passed before Latehoht and her mate raced back to circle the *Caribe* excitedly. It was early evening, and the sun was bequeathing the world-ocean its last hours of light.

Everyone was finishing the evening meal when the monitors began to squawk with orca cries. Sam led the rush for the deck, fumbling with his own headset as he waddled explosively up the stairs.

"What is it, Wenkoseemansa?" he asked the first massive black and white head he saw.

"You wish to know of the cauuse of destruction. Of what has caused the deathh and disappearancces, of the absencing of peoplle."

"Of the vanishhment of your friends," Latehoht added, breaking the surface nearby.

Cora found herself nodding, not sure whether the orcas knew what the gesture meant. Surely, as long as they had been around humans like Sam, they would understand so simple a movement.

In any case, Latehoht rambled on. "Those comme who might be best to answwer." There was a slight touch of awe in her voice.

"Thosse come who would be besst to ask," Wenko-seemansa declared somberly, "butt they will not an-swwer."

"Likely will they nott answer," Latehoht concurred, "but if you wishh it, we will askk them if they will deign to be askked."

"Yes, do so," Sam urged, "and hurry—before they get too far away. We won't intrude on their course, but will wait here if they swerve."

He raised the master control, cut the ship's speed to a crawl, though he did not, Cora noticed, completely shut down the engines.

"Who's coming?" she asked. "Whom were they talking about?"

"Exactly whom they indicated, Cora. Those who would be in the best position to give us information on the destruction of the towns. As I said before, the Cetacea no longer fight among themselves, haven't for a thousand years. They have nothing here on Cachalot like a formal hierarchy or caste system or pecking order as we know it. But there is such a thing as respect—we humans occasionally practice it ourselves—

and we're going to meet some of those whom the orcas and their brethren respect most of all.''

She was nodding understanding. "I know whom you mean now. This is one of those 'exceptions' you told me we might make."

"Yes." He shifted his stance uncomfortably. "Pardon me if I'm a little nervous. I've never talked to any of them before. Very few humans have."

"Who's he talking about?" Rachael had her headset resting on her forehead.

"What creature has the largest brain of any animal that ever lived on the Earth?"

"Sperm whale," her daughter said promptly. "They're going to talk to us?"

Cora looked back to Sam, ignored Rachael's wide-eyed expression. "I'll get the cameras. Think they'll mind?"

"If they do," he replied in a no-nonsense tone, "they'll let us know."

Time passed. They remained together, leaning against the rail and staring to the west. There was no sign of the orcas, nor yet of those they would try to question.

Sam studied the miniature grid on the master control. "Pretty far-sized pod, according to the sonarizer. I'd guess between two and three hundred." He felt a hesitant hand on his arm, saw in surprise that it was Cora's.

"No, I'm not all that worried," he told her. "The catodons aren't openly hostile toward humanity. None of the great whales are. They just don't like our company. They're more indifferent than anything else, I believe. We annoy them. They're the most suspicious of the Cetacea, as well as the smartest.

"However, Latehoht and Wenkoseemansa can be persuasive. As to whether they can turn the pod to speak to us, that will depend largely on the mood the pod leaders are in. If they *do* consent to talk with us, it will likely be only to insure that we won't chase them in hopes of getting them to talk at some future date. They may try to get rid of us now, as soon as possible."

"Not worried, then, but still nervous. I can sense it."

"You know me that well already?" he asked gently.

She pulled her hand from his arm. "I can tell when anybody's nervous. You learn."

"They're just so damned unpredictable," Sam said after several minutes had passed in silence. "I said they're not overtly hostile, but that doesn't mean this bunch couldn't be covertly hostile. Without witnesses, they could do whatever they pleased to us without fear of retribution. The law here favors them every step of the way."

"Why take the chance, then?" Rachael wondered.

"Because what Wenkoseemansa said happens to be true. If any among the native cetaceans knows anything about what happened to the four lost towns and their inhabitants, it would be the catodons."

"Because they have morbid interests?"

"Because they're interested in everything, young lady—except maintaining a relationship with mankind. I think it's a chance we have to take at least once, and we'll never have a better opportunity or meet a more likely placed pod than now." He studied the increasing darkness.

"Anyway, I trust Latehoht and Wenkoseemansa. If the pod appears irritated or cantankerous, if there's any significant mating taking place, they'll stay clear and not make the request."

"Shouldn't you be up in the bridge?" Merced wondered.

"What for? To run our puny weapons system?" He waved the master control at the horizon. "There's two to three hundred catodons out there. If they do join us, they'll surround us in a minute. Most of them are likely bigger than this ship. If they're friendly, all's

well. If they take it into their heads to get nasty . . .
well, we'll be up against twelve to twenty thousand
tons of intelligent, carnivorous mass. Might as well
pray."

It was almost dark and still no sign of any visitors.
Cora had believed herself well prepared, but she forgot all her preparations, fell back against the wall of
the cabin. She let out a loud "Oh!" of surprise.
Rachael actually comported herself better because
she was too stunned to move or speak. Even Sam took
an involuntary step or two backward. Knowledge
never eliminates all the old racial fears man retains for
something bigger and stronger than he is. Knowledge
can sometimes vitiate that fear, but on a strange
world, in near night, it was hoping for more than mere
fact could supply.

The head that loomed against the night was a good
six meters long and weighed no less than twenty tons,
probably more. A long, narrow lower jaw hung open
beneath it, showing sharp ivory teeth bigger than a
fist. An absurdly tiny eye, close enough to touch,
glared over the railing and twitched as it regarded
them with an unmistakable air of contemptuous boredom.

The catodon, or sperm whale, was balancing on its
tail. Most of the gigantic, spermaceti-filled skull was
thrust vertically from the water. The head itself
weighed more than the entire suprafoil.

It slid leisurely back into the water, having had its
look at the tiny humans on the ship. Gradual as the
slippage was, it still threw enough water on deck to
drench the dazed watchers.

Sam wiped back his hair, reminded Cora, "Switch
on your headset."

"What?" she mumbled, still stunned by the proximity of so much flesh.

"Your translator unit—switch it on."

She moved slowly to the railing, wondering if she had imagined the apparition. Her hands were shaking. Stop that, she ordered herself. You're dealing with intelligence here, and a mammalian intelligence at that. Not gross brute strength. She switched on her unit, stared over the side.

Around them the dark water was no longer flat and smooth. It had grown an instant topography, a field of brown hills. The hills moved slowly, filling the evening air with explosive hisses and puffs, the exhalations of a colossal cetacean calliope. Dead breath made music in the night.

It was a relief to see two familiar black and white forms drifting lazily alongside the slowly moving hull. The once intimidating torpedo shapes were dwarfed by the great bulks lolling around them.

"They've comme," Wenkoseemansa announced anticlimactically.

"They havve come." Latehoht breathed easily. "Come to talkk to the people from off this worrld. To listen to their words and taste of their thoughts. That is the reasson they havve come."

"I guess we should feel flattered." Cora giggled, nervously self-conscious.

They waited. The two orcas fluttered toward the bow. To make room. "One of the podd leaders commes," Latehoht said. "Onne of the Thinkers, whosse thoughts are rich as milkk."

I will not, Cora told herself, act like a schoolgirl this time! Both small hands clenched tightly around the railing. I won't back up. I will not allow myself to be shamed.

But it was not easy. A new head rose out of the sea. It was half again as big as the first, deeply lined and dotted here and there with thick clumps of parasites. It was streaked with long white scars, inflicted by some unimaginable adversary of the Cachalot Deeps. Cora wondered what could do such damage to an intelligent catodon, larger and leagues smarter than its ancient Terran progenitor who had warred eternally with the giant kraken.

Like the rest of the Cetacea, the catodonia had prospered on this world, growing to sizes unmatched by its persecuted and intellectually stunted ancestors. Evidently there was ample local food to support the population, although, as evidenced by the terrible scars this individual boasted, that food did not quietly accept its place in Cachalot's newly revised food chain.

There was also a curious growth, a thickening of the lower jaw at the front end. It resembled a burl on a tree. The eye, small in comparison to the rest of the gigantic body, viewed Cora appraisingly. She did not have time to wonder at the herculean strength that kept the great head above water, because a voice reverberated in her headphones. It was slower than that of the orcas, almost as if its orginator found the mere process of speaking boring beyond belief.

"My Little Cousins Say That Thou Wouldst Have Converse With Us."

"Yes." Cora spoke without hesitation now. "We thank you."

"Do Not Thank Us." The huge mammal continued to tread water, unbearably graceful for something so massive. "We Did It Not To Please Thee, But To Please Our Cousins, For They Were Most Insistent.

"Now Say What Thou Wilt. Already Is The Talk Wearying To Us, And We Would Be On Our Way."

"What do you—but we haven't even started yet."

The head commenced a slow slide surfaceward. Around them sounded a vast, explosive heaving as the herd expelled bad air preparatory to sounding.

"That Ends It," the whale said.

"Wait, wait!" Cora was waving frantically at the receding eye. "I didn't mean to insult you. I—"

"You can't be subtle or dilatory with His kind." Sam spoke curtly, angry not at her but at Them. "They understand neither." He raised the volume on his translator.

"Four floating towns. Four of the off-bottom islands on which our people lived have vanished in the past three months! All the people on them also disappeared. Nothing has been heard of them; no trace of their passing has been found. Have you any idea what might have happened?"

The head paused, the eye now just above water. "We Do Not."

"But how can you say that?" Rachael left off programming her instrument to interrupt undiplomatically. This did not upset Cora. At least her daughter was becoming involved. "You haven't even asked the other members of your pod!"

The great eye swiveled to stare dispassionately up at her. "I Am Called," and the translator fought with whistles and squeaks to announce finally, "Lumpjaw. Lumpjaw Speaks For The Pod. If Thou Hast Anything More To Say To Lumpjaw, Then He Bids Thou Sayest It. If Thou Hast Anything More To Say To The Pod, Then Say It To Lumpjaw. If Not . . ."

"No, we do. At least I do." Cora took a cautious breath. "Why are you so hostile?" Her curiosity had the better of her now. "We haven't done anything to you. Why can't you wait?"

From the water rose the great head. It eased toward her, barely touched the railing. Even so, the *Caribe* slid slightly sideways and listed several degrees to starboard.

"Nothing To Us? How Many Whales Did Thy Ancestors Slay? How Near To Completion Came Man's Policy Of Genocide?"

"That was a thousand years ago," she said indignantly. "I will not be held accountable for the transgressions of my distant ancestors. Nor should you identify so intensely with your equally ancient ones."

The whale pulled away. The railing groaned, unbent

in the middle. "The Little Female Hath Spirit. We Do Care. We Do Remember. The Diaspora Came Almost Too Late. But What Mankind Hath Done He May Do Again.'

"Mankind has changed." She moved tentatively to the bent rail, looked down. "Just as radically as have the Cetacea."

"Words!" Lumpjaw rumbled, though with seemingly less conviction. "And Worse, They Are Words of Mankind, Who Is Not To Be Believed."

"What about Wenkoseemansa and Latehoht?" Cora argued. "And their cousins the porpoises? They trust."

"The Little Ones Who-Leap-All-The-Time Are But Children, Locked Into A Degraded, Permanent Infancy Of Their Own Choosing. As For The Mottled Brave Who Are Also Our Cousins; They Have For Reasons Of Their Own Chosen Friendliness And Association With Thy Kind. We Do Not."

"Unhappy to you," a new voice said, "Ponderous Swimmer." Latehoht had appeared nearby.

"Perhaps So." Lumpjaw sounded philosophical, not angry with the orca. "We Cannot Judge Eventuality, Only The Present. Perhaps Thy Course May Be The True One, Little Mottled Cousin. But We Of The Catodonia Have Not Yet Forgotten Nor Forgiven. We Only Hope For Thy Sake That Thy Trust Is Never Betrayed."

"It won't be," Sam insisted.

"May It Be So." The head turned slightly, bringing huge ivory teeth within Cora's reach. She did not flinch. "There Are Men, And There Are Men. They May Differ As Much As The Colors Of The Fish Who School In The Millions, And Their Feelings And Beliefs And Desires May Be Equally Diverse. That Be The Difference Between Us. We Strive For A Singularity Of Thought, A Unity. Not Diversity."

"Mankind has its own form of unity," Cora pointed out.

"Aye, But 'Tis Not A Unity of Soul." The whale waxed poetic: "Thy Unity Springs From A Drive For Survival. We Of The Catodonia Have No Such Need And Find Our Strength In Individual Independence Joined To A Unity Of Thought.

"In That Unity There Is As Yet," he added almost as an afterthought, "No Room For Trusting Mankind. I Have Seen Nothing Of Man As Yet To Convince Me Otherwise And I Have Made The Great Migration Yea, Twenty Times."

"Five years of adolescence," Sam murmured, "give or take a little, and four years per migration. That would make him eight-five years old, or more."

"How can you be so sure of man if you remain aloof from him?" Cora wanted to know.

"I Would Debate Philosophy With Thee Longer, Little Female," Lumpjaw said, "But There Are Those In The Pod Who Grow Anxious. We Have Distances To Travel And Thoughts To Think. Thou Hast Interrupted Both."

"Are you sure," Merced interrupted, speaking for the first time, "that in all your travels you've seen or learned nothing from other whales that could give us a hint of what might have caused the obliteration of the four towns? The destruction occurred over a wide area. Surely some of the cetaceans must have been nearby. With your ability to sense and hear over considerable distances, it seems inconceivable that—"

"Why Should We Trouble Ourselves?" Lumpjaw muttered the question with alarming indifference. "We Care Not What Happens To Humans." The eye turned back up to Cora. "We Do Not Oppose Thee. We Do Not Support Thee. We Tolerate. Cachalot Is Our World. As Long As Man Realizes That, We Will Coexist Here Better Than Ever We Did A Millennium Ago On Earth. The Loss Of A Few Human Lives Is of No Concern To Us. Less So Than Was The Loss Of Thousands Of Cetacean Lives To Thy Ancestors."

"I wish you'd stop going on about people long since turned to dust!" Cora shouted, more out of frustration than from anger. "I told you, I won't assume the guilt of a thousand years."

"Perhaps Not, Little Female. But Remember Always That Somewhere, At Sometime In Thy Past, One Of Thy Ancestors Ate, Or Read A Book By The Light Of, Or Dressed In Part Of The Corpse Of, A Whale. We Cannot Forgive Thee, For Thou Knew What Thee Were About."

Merced had more courage than sense, because he finally asked the unaskable question. "You say you've no idea what happened to the towns or their missing inhabitants." Cora and Rachael turned to him in surprise. Sam was making urgent silencing motions. But Merced ignored him. "Just for the sake of conversation, wouldn't it be possible for a large, well-organized group of like-thinking cetaceans—yourselves, for example—to commit that kind of destruction?"

Rachael stared at him in horror, held her breath. Sam's fingers tensed on the master control, ready to give full throttle to the engines if a probably futile attempt at flight became necessary.

But Lumpjaw's reaction was no more and no less hostile than his previous statements. "Of Course Such A Thing Would Be Possible." He considered the question dispassionately. "But Why Would We Do Such A Thing?"

"To force humans off Cachalot," Merced offered.

Another gray-brown wall rose into the starlight. A third suddenly loomed over the rear deck of the ship. Two more huge eyes stared down at the puny inhabitants. The three catodons could have demolished the *Caribe* merely by nodding. They did not. The newcomers, however, were less controlled than Lumpjaw. One, whose voice was translated with a distinctly feminine tone by the head unit, said in outrage, "What A Bizarre Conception!"

"How Typically Human," the other new arrival agreed. "Dost Thou Believe That Because We Have Gained Intelligence We Are Doomed To Repeat The Mistakes Of Mankind?"

"We Have Heard Tales Of Things Like 'War,' " the female said. " 'Tis Difficult Enough For Us Merely To Imagine Such An Obscenity. The Idea Of Practicing It Is Utterly Beyond Us. Dost Thou Think We Have Gained Intelligence, Improved, And Progressed So That We Might Imitate Thy Stupidities? Contradiction, Contradiction!" Both breached slightly. An enormous volume of water cascaded over the *Caribe,* drenching its occupants.

"We Could Not Do Such A Thing," the younger male said. "We Do Not Hate Humans. We Ignore Thee. Were We To Engage In Any Form Of . . . Of . . ." He hesitated, searching for a word to use. ". . . Of Organized Destruction Of Human Lives, That Would Mean Paying Attention, Devoting Time, To Thee. We Would Pay Thee As Little Attention As Possible." Another gigantic double splash, and the two disappeared.

Cora wiped salt water from her face, tried to wring out her hair. Many more such physical adjectives, and she would have to don her gelsuit.

Lumpjaw pivoted on his tail, a balletic mountain. The other eye examined them now.

"If not you, what about other catodons?" Merced inquired.

"What Holds True For Us Holds True For All," the whale declared with certitude. "We Are Not Subject To The Kinds Of Individual Madness That Afflict Humans. We Think As One. Only In That Manner Can We Hope To Aspire To Our Great End."

"What *is* your 'great end'?" Rachael asked curiously, mechanically entering a variation or two into her neurophon's memory.

"If We Knew That," Lumpjaw told her portentously, "We Would No Longer Be Aspiring."

"What about the other cetaceans?" Merced persisted. "The baleen whales, for example?"

Cora's earphones were filled with an eerie high-pitched whistling the headset could only make audible. It might have been laughter, as had been that of the porpoise herd. It might have been amazement. It might have been a combination of things, but it came from many members of the pod. When Lumpjaw did not elaborate, a puzzled Merced turned to Sam for explanation.

"The catodons and the orcas are by far the smartest of the cetaceans. I'm sure you know that"—to this Merced nodded—"but because of the lack of information, you may not know how great the gaps are.

"There are many degrees of intelligence, and among the cetaceans the gaps seem to be widening, not closing. For reasons which our limited studies have not been able to establish, the baleens are the mental primitives of the Cetacea. They're big, but comparatively stupid. The pod," and Sam gestured out over the dark water, "is reacting in surprise at the possibility anyone could seriously consider such an idea."

"I have to consider every possibility." Merced sounded miffed.

"Our Toothless Relatives Are Incapable Of Conceiving, Far Less Carrying Out, Such An Adventure, Even Were They So Inclined, Which They Are Not. They Have Not The Mental Ability To Do Such A Thing. They Can Join Together To Defend Against An Attack, But The Kind Of Effort Thou Suggestest Is As Far Beyond Their Capability As Is The Thought Of Our Doing So. Thou!" His eye focused on Cora. The head came closer, touched the railing once more. The eye stared at her, spitting distance away, and she did not have time to consider the remarkable feat of balance.

"Touch!" It was a command.

She hesitated, glanced at Sam. He said nothing. Incongruously, the worst thing about the confrontation was not the proximity of enough weight to smash her flat, or the nearness of those huge teeth, but the breath that emanated from a distant gullet.

She reached out, ran a hand along one tooth a quarter of a meter long. Her fingers trailed down the tooth, touched the thick lower jaw. The whale pulled away and she instinctively jerked her hand clear. All bravery has its limits.

"Those Teeth Never Have Nor Ever Will Damage Anything But Food," Lumpjaw told her somberly. "To Do Otherwise Would Be To Surrender Everything The Cetacea Have Accomplished On This World, To Snuff Out In An Instant The Progress Of A Thousand Years."

"If you're not responsible, if the other whales aren't responsible, we're left with two possibilities," Merced declared. "Some variety of local life"—he hesitated, but Lumpjaw did not volunteer any suggestions—"or humans, for reasons we can imagine but cannot yet confirm."

"The Latter I Can Well Believe!"

"If that's the case, could you help us locate those who have caused the destruction?"

"Certain It Is That We Could," the whale said, "But We Will Not."

"Why not?" Merced asked.

"The Great Question," Lumpjaw said, not being particularly profound. " 'Why' Indeed? Why Should We? Why Waste Our Time On Such Triviality? We Live And Die. Thou Livest And Diest. Better To Spend Time Exploring Life Rather Than Death.

"All Humans, All Whales, Die All Too Soon, Before The Great Mysteries Can Be Explained, The

Great Questions Answered. Those Who Perished On Thy Floating Towns Would Have Perished Soon Enough. Why Waste Time Trying To Learn The Cause Of Their Passing? We Work For The Ends Of Thought. No Time To Waste."

"Do youu nott underrrstandd?"

Cora looked down and to the left of the balancing sperm whale. A black and white head peered up the cliff of Lumpjaw's side, unimpressed by the vast mass hovering near it.

"Whhen willl you slowww swwwimmers underrstandd?" Latehoht asked. "Underrstandd as do the orrca and the porrpoisse, underrstandd as wwe havve comme to, thhat all liffe and all the questions of liffe, hummman as welll as cetacean, arre interrelated. Thhat all quesstions that so concerrn catodon allso concerrn mann. Thhat we arre tied togethher on this worrld byy ourr alienness to it."

Lumpjaw slid down into the water, keeping his eyes above the surface. "Ah, Small Cousin, Is It Indeed, Then The Porpoise Who Is The Greater Because He Has Sense Enough Only To Play With Man And Not To Deal With Him? What, Then, Would The Orca Choose To Do? Have Hands And Feet And Walk About On Land?"

There was a splash in front of the great catodon's gnarled forehead as another shape slid whippet-fast past it.

"Ayye, arre you grreaterr in weight and lengthh. Thhat does nott mean you knnoww the wayyy forr yourrselves anyy morre than you do for alll. Do nott attempt to speakk forr us, to coddle orr tease us," Wenkoseemansa warned, "forr you did nott act so superriorr lo those manyy centurries ago on Earrthh, and you arre no morre superriorr noww. We choosse onlly to rrelate to mankindd. Nott to becomme as menn."

Cora moved to stand close to Sam. "I thought

you just said that cetaceans don't fight among themselves."

"Only verbally," he explained. "Some bad feelings
between catodon and orca have always existed,
though they're among the most closely related of all
the whales. I guess it goes back to the ancient times on
Terra, when the orca packs would eat any great whale
they could kill. Just because the orca no longer eats
the catodon doesn't mean they've grown to love one
another. Respect, yes. They won't fight physically, but
they're not the best of friends. Don't forget that they're
cetaceans together, though."

"Enough Of This!" the irritated old whale roared.
"Enough Time Wasted! We Shall Not Help Thee," he
told Cora. "Not Because We Wish To Hinder Thee.
Understand That." He let out a long, modulated whistle. In a wonderful demonstration of the unity of
thought the old male had talked about, three hundred
massive backs arched as one. Enormous flukes came
up, filled the surface with a temporary forest of gray-
brown flowers, and dipped into the ocean with
hardly a ripple as the herd vanished beneath the
waves.

In seconds it was as if they had never been more
than a dream.

VIII

No violence marred their passing. They were simply gone.

"Simultaneous sounding," Cora murmured.

"Yes." Sam studied the surface. "They'll come up to breathe somewhere far from here, where we won't be around to disturb them. We could track them, of course, but they wouldn't take kindly to that." He smiled. "What the old one—Lumpjaw—said about not fighting with man is very true. In fatal incidents between the great whales and men on Cachalot, the fault has always rested with the persistent stupidities of the people involved. We won't make those kind of mistakes."

"What about letting Wenkoseemansa and Latehoht follow them?" Merced ran a hand idly along the rail.

"To what end?" Sam asked. "You heard their leader. They know nothing about what caused the destruction of the towns."

"Or they're not saying."

"That's possible," he conceded. "But you're still not taking into account their massive indifference toward mankind. That's genuine. They really don't care one whit what we do or what happens to us as long as we leave them alone."

Merced persisted. "Holding back information wouldn't contradict their policy of ignoring us. At the same time it would passively encourage whatever still unknown force is conveniently ridding their ocean of humanity."

The big man considered that, then leaned over the side. "She-Who-Rises-Above-The-World!" A head appeared, dim in the starlight near the bow. It floated back to linger below them.

"Tell me, Beautiful Swimmer, what did you think of the old catodon's comments?"

"Forr all that wwe arre rrelated, theyy arre a conceitted rrace," she announced readily. "Likke wwe nott theirr companyy orr theirr philosophyyy."

"Wwe like nott theirr thoughts," Wenkoseemansa added from nearby. "Theirr grreaterr intelligencce has brred in themm a grreat contemptuoussness. Yea, forr all thhat theyy mayy bee the smarrtest of the Cetacea."

"Ayye, though theyy mayy bee the smarrtest of us allll," his mate agreed. "Butt thhat does nott makke themm wise."

"No," Sam agreed, "that does not make them wise. Annoying, yes. But I want you to be more specific about what they said."

"Theyy arre sharrpp and yyet vague, talkativve yet coyyy. Annd neverr as prroperrly poetic as wwe," Latehoht said.

"Maybe they don't fight, but they snipe," Merced whispered to Rachael. "Certain vices seem to go with expanded intelligence."

"Shush," Cora admonished him, trying to concentrate on the orca's words.

"Wwe believve," Latehoht went on, after consulting with her mate, "thhat the Olld Onne was telling the trruth. Wwe listened carreful and close, to worrd and inflection. Wwe slid inn and ammong themm, ammong even the garrulous young, beforre wwe camme to rejoin you. Beforre we lefft the podddd."

"Thhey murrmurred of manny things," Wenkosee-mansa added. "Of grreat shoals of voula fishh, of battles withh the great mallost inn the depths. Of calvvings and matings and arrguments ammong the philosophher bulls. Butt nevverr did we hearr talk-ings of mann orr his worrkks. Not of the towwns destroyyed, not of the people killed and missing. Not of thhose still activve, fishhing orr gatherring orr mminning. Theirr callous indifference is as hhonest as it iss monumentally foolishhh."

"Thhat iss all we werre able to learrnnnn," Late-hoht finished. "Whhat noww, frriend Sammmmm?"

"To the Rorqual Station, and the reefs by which it kept company. But slowly. Our ship will follow your path, but we must have some sleep."

"Ahhhwww, poorr humanssss!" Latehoht commis-erated sadly. "Sso little alivve timme, so muchh of it spent in the brreathing deathh. We'll go and eat, we twwo, and watchh forr youuu." She and Wenkosee-mansa turned as one, vanished supplely beneath the starlit surface.

Rorqual Station Towne, the last attacked, was the nearest to Mou'anui. Its proximity was both conven-ient and ominous, for that hinted to Mataroreva, Hwoshien, and the others responsible for keeping Cachalot's citizens quiet and secure a growing bold-ness on the part of whatever was behind the assault.

As the town most recently destroyed, it was also the most likely to yield any clues to research. And if any trouble arose, skimmers from Mou'anui could reach the *Caribe* more rapidly than if it were to anchor at the town site of, say, Te iti Turtle, which lay a thou-sand kilometers farther out in the ocean.

Thinking of destruction as she slipped into her bunk made Cora think of Silvio. And of her breakdown. Rachael had been five at the time of her father's death and her mother's collapse. She knew of both only vaguely. Someday Cora would have to explain both, explain what had truly happened.

Mataroreva was at work on the bridge.

"What are you doing?" Cora asked as she approached him.

"Oh, good morning, Beautiful." He glanced up momentarily from the console and smiled hugely.

"Just plain Cora will do."

"Okay. Good morning, just plain Cora." He touched a contact switch. "I'm setting the stabilizers. Wouldn't be much fun if we spent a few hours diving and surfaced to find that the ship had drifted out of sight."

"Stabil—we're here, then?" She looked around in surprise. The ocean looked no different from what they had crossed in days of traveling out from Mou'anui.

"More or less. I'm picking a spot. Have a look over the side."

She did so, moving to the upper railing to peer at the water. She almost blinded herself in the process.

Several hexalate formations grew almost to the surface, and their reflected glare made her blink. The intensity was not as bad as that from the sands of a motu, however. By not looking directly at the uppermost growths and by squinting hard, she could gaze into the water without protective goggles. She could not see any end to the reef. The *Caribe* hovered above it, adrift in a sea of emerald and yellow. "This is where the town was located?"

He nodded. "The position was fixed by the first vessels that returned here after the destruction—the survivors of the town, those who'd been out working." He pointed, and she noticed several widely spaced, floating blobs of red: polymer marked buoys, each containing its own directional transmitter.

"What was the town doing here?"

"This is a fairly good-sized, well-known fishing reef.

The Rorqualians had it staked out for organic mining purposes. The survivors indicated that the town had taken its limit and was preparing to depart only a couple of days after it was hit. But they were primarily the fishermen. They weren't sure precisely what was being stocked in the town's holds."

"And, just like the others, they didn't find any bodies?"

He shook his head. "Not so much as a finger. You would think at least one or two would sink, or be trapped under falling debris and pinned to the bottom. But nothing."

She stared at the water. "It's hard to believe anyone ever lived around here."

"Oh, the town was here." He started for the ladder. "Get into your suit. I haven't explored the area myself, but records say there's still plenty of evidence around."

He finished setting the stabilizers and the automatic warning network. The latter was engaged as a matter of procedure more than anything else, since the two patrolling orcas provided a far more efficient advance detection system than anything composed of circuitry and transceivers.

Cora was first in, followed closely by Rachael, Mataroreva, and Merced. Pristine beauty she had anticipated. The reef did not disappoint her. Great hexalate heads like crystal trees rose from the sandy bottom, while diamond tunnels pierced labyrinths of frozen cloud.

She did not expect the nudge from behind. It compounded her shock when she spun and encountered massive jaws lined with even white teeth. A dense whistling filled the air around her, and a moment passed before she remembered to switch on her suit-mask translator.

"Sorrry iss this one to havve starrtled you-she," Latehoht said. "It was not meanntttt."

"That's . . ." Cora caught her breath, relaxed. "That's all right." She kicked easily, enjoying the familiar freedom that came with being underwater. Latehoht barely flicked her flukes as she spiraled over and around the tiny swimmer, keeping her right eye always on her smaller human companion. The gelsuit had already turned comfortably warm. Cora grew lazy within her transparent armor.

"To thhis placce has comme a sadness," the killer whale moaned. "Inn the waterr lingers still the effluvia of deathhh."

"Don't believe a word she says."

Cora looked around, saw the graceful bulk of Mataroreva moving up to join them. "Latehoht revels in the rhythms of languid depression."

"I doo notttt!" the orca whistled indignantly. "Thhe smmell iss herre. It does *too* linnger." She left Cora, twisted to charge Sam. At the last second he ducked below her rush. She swatted at him with her tail, but he anticipated the swing and clutched tight to one fluke. He hung on for several seconds until she flipped free, came up and around to bump him in the belly. Cora heard him grunt. Kicking around, he snatched at her dorsal fin.

There followed several minutes of violent choreography as she half tried to buck him off, but he was not as easy to shake from her back as he had been from her tail.

"Pllay theyy well together, well annd frreeee."

"Yes, they do." Cora managed not to jump this time, although Wenkoseemansa's approach had been stealthy.

"Havve I enjoyed to thhink, in momments of quiet contemmplation, in timmes of idle speculation, thhat the humman Sammm would havve made a passable cetacean."

"Certainly," she admitted, unsure of how to interpret the orca's observation, "he's built more like you than like most of us."

"Iss he? You mmust underrstandd, and carreful I amm not to sayy thhis with derrogatórry intent, thhat you hummans arre so smmall thhat to us any phhysical differrences of sizze orr shhape arre so superrficial as to makke us strrain to notice them."

"Yet for all our smaller size, we have a greater variety of features."

Wenkoseemansa considered. "Thhat only adds to ourr confusionnnn."

She looked back through the clear water, trying hard to ignore the wondrous diversity of alien piscatorial life swarming about her in order to concentrate on the problem at hand.

Where were Rachael and Merced? Had they sneaked off somewhere? "Rachael!"

"Over here, Mother!"

She turned a circle. "Where?"

"I esppy thhemmmm." Wenkoseemansa swung his seemingly weightless mass around, presented a black and white wall to her gaze. It occurred to her that he was offering her a ride.

"Theyy are a modest distance, byy your standards. I will convey you to yourr offspring."

She hesitated only a second before locking her gloved palms over the front of the towering dorsal fin. Then the water was rushing past her so fast it put pressure on her suit. In an instant (or so it seemed) she had traveled several hundred meters through the clear water.

Rachael was swimming alone beside a crystal castle. It looked like an interlocked series of colored, spiraled shells that rose to within two meters of the surface. Several smaller constructs, miniature versions of the larger, grew from the reef base farther down.

"Isn't it grand, Mother?"

"Isn't what grand? Yes, it's beautiful, but—"

"I'm sorry. How could you know? Listen!" Rachael held a small metal sampling tool. She used it to tap one side of the growth. A distinct, mellifluous tone ran through the water. "It must be partially hollow."

Yellow and blue stripes ran around the shell spirals, a collection of unicorn horns. The shells were pale green to transparent. In the center of each shell pulsed crimson organs, sending colorless fluid throughout the individual organisms.

"Okay, it's grand." Cora glanced around, relieved to find that Merced was nowhere in sight. She still couldn't keep herself from asking, "Where's Pucara?"

"Off somewhere, investigating on his own. Think he follows me everywhere?"

"Doesn't he?" Cora quickly added, "I'm sorry, that's none of my business."

"That's right, Mother," Rachael agreed with disarming cheerfulness. "It's none of your business." She swam up a meter or so and tapped the spiral central cone where it tapered considerably. Again Cora heard the ringing, only an octave higher this time. "I'll bet several people working in unison could play these."

So that was it. For just a moment, Cora had believed her daughter's scientific interests had been stimulated by the cone creatures. "Must you always be thinking of music?"

"I don't see any harm in combining my work with my music." Then, more seriously, "There's something else here you probably ought to have a look at." She arched her back, kicked downward. Cora followed.

Strewn between the crystal pinnacle and its lesser companions were several huge fragments of metal. The battered pieces of coated stelamic still retained their sheen and even markings. The inscriptions showed that they had been components of some large structure; a warehouse, possibly. Several of them were a third the size of the *Caribe.*

Cora drifted over one, studying the torn edges. "It

doesn't look as if this has been severed—by an energy beam, for example."

Rachael was inspecting another fragment nearby. "Here's one that's badly dented, but it's still intact."

Cora joined her daughter, saw that she was right. Torn supports were still fastened to an unbreached container. The tank itself was bent almost in half, flattened in the center by some tremendous force.

"A whale's tail could do that," Rachael murmured. She looked behind her. "What do you think, Wenkoseemansa?"

The orca swam over, turned his head, and examined the ruined tank with his right eye. "Howw frragile arre the arrtificial constrructions of hummankind. A whale's tail?" He sniffed, sending bubbles skyward. "Could doo thhis little thhing a whale's *brreathhhh.*"

"We've no evidence yet to support that hypothesis, Rachael. A weapon could do the same."

"What kind of weapon?"

"I don't know, dammit," her mother snapped. "I'm a marine biologist, not a munitions specialist. Pucara might know, and Sam surely will have some ideas. Wonder where they've got to?"

"Sooon will thhey rejoin you." Wenkoseemansa let loose a sharply rising whistle that the translator could not refine into human terms, then vanished in a rush of displaced water.

He wasn't gone long before he returned with Pucara Merced clinging to his dorsal fin. Latehoht and Sam rejoined the others seconds later.

The four humans drifted, exchanging thoughts and theories while the two orcas waited interestedly nearby.

"What about the possibility of a rogue whale?" Merced suggested. "A deranged one."

"*One* whale?" Mataroreva was properly skeptical. "Well, what kind of weapons, then?"

"Any number of possibilities there." The peaceforcer eyed the twisted tank, which they had tentatively identified as a type used to store liquid protein. "Let's not forget that the force of another, nearby explosion could have caused this. Also, there are compressed gas weapons which could directly do such damage. Or a storm wave could have caused it. I'm afraid this isn't much in the way of evidence."

"And no hint that energy weapons were used," Cora added. "That's obvious even to me."

"Could someone," Merced continued, "be trying to make it look as if the whales are causing the destruction, to cover their own activities? By using those compressed gas weapons, for example?"

"Could be," Mataroreva agreed. "It would add up with what the old catodon told us about the impossibility of any whales actually being responsible."

"There's more over this way." Merced had drifted off to their right, down a glass canyon. "Smaller stuff. We might find something more specific."

"I doubt it." Cora moved to join him. "The local experts have undoubtedly sifted everything already. Though you never know. What do you hope to find, Pucara?"

He shrugged. "Who knows? Maybe someone had a personal tridee recorder going at the moment of attack, though, as you say, it's likely the initial search teams would already have checked for such items. But it would be good for us to make our own search of the reef."

Mataroreva started to protest, intending to cite the size of the reef and the thoroughness of the previous inspectors, but decided not to. Cora and the other two were not as familiar with Cachalot growths and formations as were the residents. Therefore they might search where a local scientist would disdain to.

"Anything that looks helpful, we take aboard for detailed analysis," Merced continued, looking at Mataroreva.

"Sounds like a reasonable suggestion. I know that you're all experienced in underwater work, so I'll say this only one last time and never mention it again. Watch yourselves. As soon as we think we've identified every danger, some innocent-looking new creature appears with a unique form of protection. We've already catalogued twelve entirely new indigenous types of toxin. I don't want any of you discovering the thirteenth.

"Everyone should report in to the *Caribe*'s receiver" —he checked his chronometer—"at least on the hour. Give your approximate position in relation to the sun and the ship." He studied them each in turn, said finally, "That's all I have to say."

"Everyone pick a compass point," Cora said, anxious to begin, "and let's start hunting."

They learned nothing from the many fragments of town cleaned that day from the reef and sand. Subsequent days of searching added more material but no revelations.

Among the material recovered were many personal effects: bits of clothing, water-sealed foodstuffs, shreds of expensive pylon netting, electronic instrumentation, and whole gelsuits. One morning Rachael excitedly directed them to a half-buried case that contained two dozen tridee tapes. They were perfectly preserved in a watertight inner container and of no value whatsoever. All were entertainment tapes.

It was very frustrating to Cora. The frustration built as night ran into morning. It was pleasant enough work, swimming through the exquisite reef, idly examining the exotic and occasionally bizarre native life of Cachalot. Only an isolated tropical rainstorm arrived from time to time to break the routine.

But they were finding nothing. The growing mountain of debris still held its secrets. They could not even tell whether the assault had been made by an animal or a human agency.

Merced believed that this very lack of clear evidence pointed to the work of belligerent humans. The absence of clues suggested to him a careful, methodical attempt to destroy or eliminate any such evidence. He could not attribute this type of attempt to blind animal rage.

Cora still kept an open mind. Barring the recovery of some deus ex machina such as the hypothesized tridee tape of the town's moment of destruction, she would settle for a hint that Merced was right or, conversely, that some local life was responsible. She rather hoped the little scientist was correct. The thought that some unknown and immensely powerful whatsis might be lurking out in the depths bothered her more than the prospect of piratical humans.

While they found something every day, no plethora of debris lay strewn across the reef. For one thing, the town had been anchored off the edge of the reef instead of directly above it. Much of the town had sunk to depths beyond their diving capabilities. They could have requisitioned a deep-diving submersible to search the three-thousand-meter level, where the sea floor evened off, but she and Merced agreed they were as likely to find something near the surface as in the abyss. More so, in fact, since in the depths most everything would have been distorted by pressure.

But as the days passed in continued ignorance, she began to wonder if they ever would find anything. What made it worse was the certain knowledge that whatever had destroyed the four towns remained at large out *there,* cloaked in ocean and mystery, watching, waiting.

IX

Cora was sitting on the rear deck of the *Caribe*, trying to decide if a shred of fabric had been torn by a weapon or by teeth. It looked like part of a pareu.

A ripple ran down her back. Her hair tingled. Looking around, she lifted her eyes to the roof of the main cabin. Rachael sat on the edge, her legs crossed. Her right hand manipulated the double set of strings of the neurophon while her left fingered the contact controls of the axonic projector.

A warm feeling of well-being crept over Cora, the result of the perfect combination of lilting synthesized song and proper stimulation of her nerves by Rachael's playing. She felt as if she were being caressed by a pair of giant velvet gloves.

Abruptly the melodic massage changed from soothing to plaintive, then sank into melancholic. Despite the warm air, she found herself shivering. The reaction was stimulated as much by the melody as by the accompanying neuronics.

"Can't you play something happier?"

Rachael leaned over to look down at her mother. "I play as the mood takes me. I know that's not very scientific." Her mouth twisted. "But it's aesthetic."

"I don't want to argue about it, Rachael." Cora turned back to her study of the burnt bit of material.

"Then why did you bring it up?" Rachael continued to play and Cora continued to shiver, saying nothing.

Merced was sitting beneath Rachael, just under the overhang of the upper deck. He was laboriously examining a huge pile of water-damaged tape fragments. Cora wondered what he hoped to find in that massive, messy mound of communications numbers, personal histories, pay charts, and medical records. He confessed quite frankly that he wasn't sure, but at least the information was varied, and more relaxing than going cross-eyed picking through chunks of torn metal and plastic. She could sympathize. He was obviously frustrated, too.

Mataroreva came up from below. Since he wasn't directly involved in the research, he should have been more bored than any of them, what with nothing to do beyond seeing to the maintenance of the *Caribe*. But he was relaxed, even appeared to be enjoying himself. While they studied, he dove and recovered additional artifacts, concentrating on the edge of the reef where he had forbidden them to travel. There were large pelagic predators out there, where reef gave way to open sea, and he preferred not to have his charges tempt them. And he only hunted there himself when accompanied by the two orcas.

Now he looked over Cora's shoulder, noting her discomfort. "I've got to admit her current choice of dendritones doesn't lighten my day, either. How about a dive? Not for work this time, for a change. Just to relax."

"I can't," she told him. "Just because we're having a hard time doesn't mean we aren't making any progress."

"Really? You're making progress, then?"

"Well . . . take this piece of burnt fabric here."

Mataroreva looked at it. "So?"

"Don't you see that?" She paused, eyed it herself, then looked over at the knee-high ridge of similar fragments. She saw no answers there, only additional frustration.

Then she picked up the bit of water-soiled material, wadded it into a ball, and threw it angrily over the side of the ship. "You can take it and do what you want with it! To hell with it—let's go!"

"That's the spirit!" He moved to don his gelsuit.

No, it isn't, she thought exhaustedly. She didn't have much spirit left.

The strains of the sobbing Trans-Carlson tune followed her over the side, and the neuronic projections tickled her for several meters more. Then they were out of the instrument's preset range. Once more she was cruising among the delicate hexalate formations.

Sam continued to point out unusual examples of Cachalot life as they encountered them. There hadn't been much time for such sightseeing in days past. He spotted one advanced variety of pseudoworm, far more spectacular than any of the Terran nudibranchs that were its closest visual relative, fluttering in and out among the reef formations. It was about half a meter in length and swam with an incredible suppleness. Hundreds of long, thin streamers trailed from its flanks. The feathery filaments were a rich azure blue, spotted with yellow and pink.

"Gorgeous," Cora muttered, overwhelmed as she had so often been already by the endless beauty of this world.

"That's not all. Watch." Sam kicked on ahead, ran a finger down the creature's slowly rippling ventral side. A thin, cloudy pink fluid filled the water around it.

She winced instinctively. "Protective mechanism?"

"No." He was grinning. "Slip off your mask and smell just a little. Inhale as much water as you can without choking."

"You're crazy." She was giggling.

"Just once," he begged. "Quick, before it dissipates."

"Well . . ." She raised the mask, breathed in a tiny amount of water. It set her coughing as she hurriedly replaced the mask and cleared it.

But she hardly noticed the cough. Her head was swimming. She drifted dazedly, feeling as if someone had just increased her olfactory sensitivity a thousandfold. She was no longer swimming in salt water but in perfume. Her body was smothering under the concentrated scent of a million wildflowers.

Unperturbed, the pseudoworm fluttered gracefully away, disappearing into a crevice in a turret of emeralds.

"Lord!" she gasped when she could finally breathe easily again. "That's the most incredible fragrance I've ever smelled in my life."

"That's a Ninamu Pheromonite. They aren't common, but they never have any trouble locating each other." He started downward. "Incidentally, that could have been the reason for the town's anchoring here." She followed him, still stunned by the overpowering aroma.

"As I said, there aren't too many of them, but even one like the individual we just encountered would release enough essence to make it worthwhile for an entire town to spend a few weeks hunting for him. I believe that a centiliter of the essence costs about half a million credits on the open market. You just got dosed by five times that."

"Surely," she murmured, her thoughts dreamy, "it's not sold that way. No one could enjoy it."

"I wouldn't know," Sam said. "I expect it's diluted. But aromatics aren't my business."

They had descended some thirty meters. Sam leveled off, swam down a narrow natural canyon. The light at this depth was barely evident. The normal spectrum-spanning colors of the hexalates were homogenized to a uniform dark blue.

"I guess there are some rich enough to afford to use it straight," Sam was saying. "Though they don't swim in half liters like we just did. No one smells that bad." He chuckled. "A very tiny amount would be sufficent."

"You couldn't measure it small enough to use it straight," she argued. "It *has* to be diluted. There can be such a thing as being too overpowering."

She looked below them. A bottom fish was crawling across the crystal sands. It walked on its lower fins and sported a trunk like a tiny elephant, which it used to probe at the sand for the small creatures dwelling therein.

"What's that one called, Sam?" There was no reply. She looked around. "Sam?"

He had vanished. Seconds ago he had been swimming parallel to her and just behind. She turned, kicked hard. Perhaps he had made a turn behind some hexalate protrusion. But the canyon was steep and relatively smooth-sided.

She stood treading water, hands on hips in a most unhydrodynamic pose. "You're not being funny, Sam." She was still drowsy from the effects of the perfume. "I'm going back to the ship."

Something hard and unyielding wrapped around her ankle. She felt it keenly through the gelsuit, gave a little scream, and tried to pull free. She couldn't, but when she looked down, it was to see Sam grinning at her behind his face mask. He was leaning out of a modest hole in the reef wall.

"Don't go back just yet," he said easily, ignoring her furious expression. "I've something to show you. Why did you think I brought you down here?"

More curious than angry now, she followed him as he disappeared. She could touch both sides of the tunnel by extending her arms. Her suit light showed that the roof and the floor were equally close. Of course, if Sam could fit through . . .

They swam for several minutes. Then the tunnel angled upward slightly. It was completely unexpected when she broke the surface.

"What on earth? . . ." A soft hissing sound came from nearby.

"Air cylinder from our chemical stores," Sam said. "Switch off your light."

She did so, blinked as her eyes adjusted, and then sucked in her breath in surprise.

Lining the curving ceiling of the cave were a thousand creatures that resembled starfish, only they boasted nine dancing tentacles and a single greenish eye in the center of their bodies. At the tip of each tentacle was a glowing jewel, and the arms and central body sparkled with lambent dust.

Each animal was a different color from its neighbor: green, crimson, argent and gold, white and purple. Doubtlessly the larger lights on the end of each weaving tentacle were used to attract prey when the cave was filled with water, as it would normally be. She had the feeling they were outside on a clear night. Only now she could actually reach up and touch the stars. The ghostly firmament, constantly shifting to some instinctive choreography, hummed down to her as the massed creatures chatted at one another.

"Never . . . I've never seen anything so beautiful." First the perfume, now this, she thought. The stars were moving, crawling across each other as the animals hunted for better places on the ceiling.

"I don't understand . . . the air . . ." Hesitantly she lifted her mask. Not only was the air breathable, but it was fresh and sweet.

"There's enough pressure from the cylinder to hold the water back for roughly half an hour," he whispered to her. "The chromacules can survive much longer than that without it."

He was behind her now, treading water easily, his enormous arms enveloping her around her shoulders, hands locked in front of her. The fresh oxygen, the crawling, semaphoring stars on the ceiling, and the lingering aroma of the Pheromonite combined to overwhelm her. The tenseness that had been with her in varying amounts since she had first landed on Cachalot left her completely. What was more, some of that other, permanent tenseness faded away.

"You know," he was whispering in her ear, "the water's not *that* cold."

"That cold? How cold is 'that' cold?" Her gaze was fixed on the stars that weren't.

"That all depends, doesn't it?" he murmured. He nodded toward the large cylinder. It lay on a flat area several meters wide that was just above the waterline. A smooth glass beach.

Cora had never before made love under the stars. The fact that the stars were alive and that she and Sam were thirty meters beneath the surface of an alien sea did not matter. Nor did the fact that they were watched by a thousand dispassionate green eyes.

"Find anything?" Rachael extended a hand, helped her mother back onto the deck.

"Not really." The bright sunlight burned Cora's face.

Mataroreva was right behind her, slid up his mask. "We did a lot of looking. Found many beautiful things, but nothing that would help the investigation, I'm afraid."

"You looked long enough." Rachael studied Cora's back for a moment more, then added, "Pucara thinks he's found something significant."

"That's more than any of the rest of us have been able to do. Where is he?" Cora was grateful, no matter what the little researcher might have discovered.

"He's still down below, using the ship's duplicator to make a copy of what he's found. Just in case."

"It must be significant." They all moved below.

Merced was working in the one large, below-decks room, surrounded by familiar apparatus. He glanced up briefly as they entered. "Any luck?"

"Not a thing." Cora shook her head. "You've had some?"

"Maybe. I think it could be." He moved aside, switched on the duplicator's viewer. They crowded around the tiny screen. Cora felt Sam pressing close behind her, shifted her stance ever so slightly. Apparently he understood, because he moved back a step.

"Figures," Mataroreva muttered as he examined the screen. "Another list. So what?"

"The figures line up economically with some manifests I found. Here." Merced adjusted the instrument. Words and quantities were superimposed alongside the lists of numbers. "I found out what the town was working, here on this reef." He looked up at their guide. "Do you know something called Teallin?"

"Sure," Mataroreva said. "It's a mollusk, looks like a perverted abalone. That's what the town was harvesting?" He nodded thoughtfully. "It would explain why we've come across so few of them in our search. The mature ones were all harvested, then?"

"That's what the records indicate."

"What's the significance?"

"I've been through the lists of what the first search teams found when they arrived here to hunt for evidence. There are fragments of everything you can imagine, but no Teallin. Yet the town was just getting ready to move, according to its fisher survivors. After three months of anchoring here."

"It's a luxury item," Mataroreva said interestedly. "Like most of the foodstuffs that are exported from Cachalot. You can extract about a kilo of meat from one mollusk. That may not sound like much, but the stuff has a strong, smoky flavor. It's combined with other foods, mixed to give them spice. And they'd been gathering it for three months?"

Merced tapped the viewer screen. "Two shiploads packed for transfer at Mou'anui. Several thousand kilos. Just a footnote in the regular records, mixed in with all their other work and their own food imports, medicines, power packs, and other general inventory. Just another statistic."

"So that's it," Mataroreva muttered.

"So what's it?" Rachael wondered. "Somebody put it together for me, please." She looked apologetic. I'm afraid I wasn't listening too closely." She tried to hide her neurophon behind her.

"Teallin is perishable. It's packed in polymultiene containers, vacuum-sealed until it can be transported to its eventual processing destination."

"Oh—*oh!* Vacuum-packed?"

"Not only that," Mataroreva continued, "but polymultiene is a chemical relative of the polymeric material that the towns themselves were built upon. When the search skimmers out from Mou'anui arrived here, they found thousands of fragments of the stuff, from finger-sized all the way up to square meters of town-raft. And a lot of other related, unsinkable material."

"I see," Rachael said.

"I've got to check this." He turned, hurried upward. Moments later they could hear him mumbling into the ship's communicator. The signal would go out instantly via satellite relay to the Administration Center on Mou'anui.

"If this proves out," Cora said, "is it sufficient basis for us to declare that a human agency was responsible for all the destruction? Any local life thorough enough to devour every human inhabitant would only naturally consume all the available food it could get its teeth into."

"But we found packaged foodstuffs ourselves," Rachael countered. "Some were exposed to the water and decomposing."

"I know. And the Teallin was vacuum-sealed, too. I don't see any attacking creature or creatures being able to detect the food inside such containers. Yet it's all gone. You'd expect that the previous searchers would have found some of it."

"We're forgetting one thing," Rachael reminded her. "All the attacks took place during a storm. Even a mild storm could have dispersed any floating debris quite rapidly."

"Yes, but every single container?"

Mataroreva rejoined them, glanced at each in turn.

"They didn't find anything?" Cora asked.

"On the contrary, they did. Polymultiene vacuum containers, each about a meter square."

Merced looked disgusted. "That kills it. We're back at square one again."

"Not necessarily," Mataroreva told him. "They found *some*. Twelve, to be exact. They didn't show on your list of recovered materials," and he indicated the still glowing screen of the viewer that Merced had been studying, "because all the edibles, for example, were grouped together. What's more," and his eyes gleamed, "all twelve were damaged. Now, friends, what does that suggest to you?"

"Twelve!" Amazing how everything is falling into place, Cora thought. "All broken. If animals had been responsible, they would have emptied the twelve and left the others. Instead, it seems we've exactly the opposite situation." She looked at Merced. "How many containers did the town manifest list as ready for shipment?"

"Eight hundred."

"Seven hundred and eighty-eight unaccounted for, hmmm? Allowing for dispersal by wind and wave," and she nodded to Rachael, "I'd say that left rather a large number which have unaccountably disappeared."

"Even allowing for extreme weather," Merced agreed. "It would normally be expected that somewhat more than twelve should have been recovered. If animals were involved, they would not break into sealed cases and leave a dozen that were already open." He glanced at their guide. "What about container fragments?"

Matareva shook his head. "Uh-uh. Only the twelve. No pieces."

"Couldn't they have been listed with other containers of approximately the same size and composition?"

"No," he said positively. "Each polymultiene crate is stamped with the name of its town, the day it's sealed with whatever it's holding, who provided the contents, and most importantly, the contents themselves. The searchers found other containers, but none holding Teallin."

"Well." Cora slapped both hands on her knees, stood up. "That's that, then. No more mystery. Somehow a group of belligerents—local, human, or offworld—are raiding the floating towns and destroying any evidence that could implicate them."

"Pirates," Rachael said.

"Oh, Rachael, I'm not sure such an archaic term—"

"Why not?" Matareva asked. "As many millions of credits, as many deaths, as we have? I can't think of a more appropriate term."

They split, Merced to recheck his lists, Rachael to strum her neurophon. She kept the range down, and Cora left the stimulating projections behind as she walked up on deck and moved to the stern of the ship. Matareva went with her.

"But why?" she muttered, staring down into the clear water. Purple and yellow fish drifted beneath her, vanished under the stern. "Whole towns, entire populations? . . ."

"If you kill ten people or a thousand, the penalties

are the same," Sam told her softly. "Once the first step, the first multiple murder, is committed to cover one's tracks, subsequent actions become routine. You'll be wiped and personality reimprinted for the first as much as for the second and third. Why risk witnesses?"

"I suppose you're right." She tried to consider the situation coldly, as a question of statistics and not of individual lives. "At least we know what we're looking for now, if not who."

"I imagine they're from off-planet," he speculated. "I can't believe even part-time residents of Cachalot committed mass murder for profit. For *any* reason. But you're wrong about one thing. We're not going to be looking for these people. At least, you're not. I'll communicate our information and our theory to Administration and they'll turn it over to my people. This is peaceforcer work, not biology."

"I'd like to keep working," she argued. "Maybe we have a good idea who to look for, but not how to locate them. They've covered their work thoroughly. How can your people find them?"

He considered. "If this was a more technologically developed world, I'd set up a scan for any shuttle-craft leaving or arriving and have it searched for contraband materials. But Cachalot's satellite system is nowhere near sophisticated enough to watch the whole planet. Though they have to be getting the stolen merchandise off-planet via shuttle.

"As to finding the local end of the business, that's going to be tougher still. We can't search every town and independent gathering vessel. Not only isn't it practical—illegal goods could easily be dumped or destroyed—but the Cachalotians wouldn't stand for it." He grinned slightly. "Our citizens are very independent, as you may have guessed."

"What does that leave you with?"

"Trying to catch them just before they act." He sounded grim. "I don't like the implications there."

"Were the other lost towns also getting ready to make full shipments?"

"Sorry. I had the same thought. That was one list *I* checked. Not only did they have varying stocks on hand, but I'a, the second town attacked, had just finishing sending off its quarterly production only a few days before it was wiped out."

"It could have been mistiming on the part of the attackers."

"It could have been." He shrugged. "It doesn't matter."

"Why not?"

"Because I think we'll find, when we check the records, that all produce, regardless of quantity, disappeared," and he went below.

He was gone quite a while. Cora did not move, continued to watch the subsurface denizens, to envy them their freedom from thought. Much better to be able to rely only on instinct, she mused.

"Well?"

"Everything crated for shipment," he told her. "No sign of it. And that's not all. Merced and I made a detailed study of the recovered-articles lists. Absent from them is just enough in the way of water-resistant valuables—power packs, generator units, converters, and personal effects like jewelry—to give credibility to our theory.

"Many personal items were recovered—sunk to the bottom or found inside pieces of town. But enough is missing to fit with our analysis. Our pirates were careful to limit their greed. The absence of all such items would have pointed to human agents long ago. But just a few—now, they wouldn't be missed." One massive fist punched gently into its opposite palm. "I'd like to meet these folks." His expression now was anything but boyish. "Yes, I'd like to meet them."

"Sam, how can you predict where the next attack will take place since they don't rely on information regarding which town is ready to ship?"

"Time for some inspired guesswork, I suppose. We do know that every attack has taken place under cover of bad weather. All towns have been alerted to that fact. I've requested meteorological reports for this quadrant of sea for the next week. All four towns were within two thousand kilometers of each other. Now we have something else to alert the towns to."

"Two thousand . . . that doesn't exactly pin them down."

"There are only a dozen or so towns within that region now, and another dozen bordering it. Of the two dozen, the ones that will have to be extra careful are those that will be subject to bad weather. That reduces potential trouble spots somewhat," he insisted.

"We still have no idea what kind of weaponry they're using."

He looked helpless. "No, we don't." There was a yell from below. He and Merced exchanged words.

The report he had requested had been provided. For the next five days only three towns were likely to be subject to storm conditions.

"What were the time intervals between the previous attacks?" she asked.

"That's just it. There weren't any. Two of the towns were destroyed within days of one another, and then it was weeks before the third attack. There doesn't seem to be any predictability to it."

"So all we know," she murmured, "is that three towns might possibly be attacked within the next week."

"I'm afraid so. We'll travel to one of them. Vai'oire is closer to us than Mou'anui, and I want to talk to the town council in person about what we've learned. Certainly Wenkoseemansa and Latehoht ought to be available at one town for sentry duty."

"Why Vai'oire, other than its proximity?"

"No reason. It's as likely a target as Hydros or Wasser. But there is another reason for our going to a town, and it's because of you, not me."

"What's that?"

"After weeks on this boat I suspect you'd all enjoy sleeping on something that doesn't rock quite so much."

"Amen!" Rachael was coming up from below, with Merced behind.

"Speaking for myself, I could certainly do with a change," Merced admitted.

But Cora added nothing, instead turned silently to gaze back down at the crystal reef. The rocking motion never troubled her. She was as at home in the arms of Mother Ocean as ever she was on any stable land.

X

Vai'oire was not land, of course, but it certainly was stable. Cora could not see any motion when the *Caribe* slid into one of the several docks that extended into the ocean.

It was a quiet morning. Only a freshening breeze hinted at any possibility of the predicted storm. A few sooty clouds scudded past overhead, uncertain as yet whether to retain their independence or to join together to bleed life.

As the craft entered the dock it passed above the outskirts of the reef Vai'oire was exploiting. Sonarizers kept the suprafoil well apprised of any dangerously high hexalate formations.

"A coincidence," Sam assured her as they prepared to link to the dock. "True, Rorqual was anchored off a reef when it was hit. So was Warmouth. But the other two were over open ocean, moving or following schools. Sure, if they'd all been attacked when sitting off a reef, we could predict exactly which town would be struck next. Unfortunately, that's another common denominator that doesn't exist, except as wishful thinking."

The *Caribe* gently touched the starboard dock. A click sounded from bow and then stern as the suprafoil locked into the dock. Then the boarding ramp slipped into place. They descended, standing rubber-legged on a surface that did not sway beneath them.

They were met by four locals. Three men and a woman, all middle-aged or older. One of the men, a short, portly Polynesian type, stepped forward to shake hands with each of them in turn. He was bald on top, had a fringe of white hair that ran around his head like a three-quarter halo. All his features were round and soft, like those of a cartoon figure.

"Ja-wen Pua'ahorofenua," he announced. Cora decided that "Ja" would do. "I'm the current mayor of Vai'oire. We received a General Alert report from Mou'anui yesterday. Said that you folks had determined that human *pirates*—I had to look the term up —or other Commonwealth intelligences were responsible for the crisis we've been living with these past few months. That's hard for us to accept."

"Hard but not impossible, Ja-wen," the woman behind him said. Cora had noticed her first. She was so enormous that beside her Sam looked skinny. Yet as with Sam, the immense volume of flesh looked firm, and the rolls were minimal. "But then all of these attacks are hard to accept."

"I know that, H'ua," the mayor said. "I just can't imagine how any kind of human assault could get through screens and prewarn systems, not without leaving at least a hint of how it had happened."

"Four towns lost and nobody knows anything," one of the other men grumbled sourly. He wore an object around his neck which looked like a single tooth. It was at least sixteen centimeters across at the base, and the point hung halfway to the man's navel. Cora wondered what creature it might have been wrenched from and thought of what might still lie unobserved in Cachalot's deeps.

Beads and shells formed the rest of the necklace, alternating with light-emitting units. She wondered if it was some kind of personal ornament or perhaps a local badge of office.

"At this point," the last speaker concluded, "I'd believe anything."

"That's the truth," the fourth member of the greeting party said. "My five-year enlistment is up in a couple of months. We're thinking of taking our savings, Suzette and I, packing up the kids, and maybe moving to New Riviera or even someplace like Horseye, where the dangers are known."

The mayor turned incredulously to his companion. "You, Yermenov? You're lived on Cachalot all your life."

"I know, and I want to live the rest of it. I'd rather risk thirty years somewhere else than end up a missing statistic here."

"Well, I wouldn't worry about Vai'oire." Ja-wen turned confidently back to his visitors. "You can understand our concern. We're all worried, but now that we have some idea what to look out for, I'm sure we can handle it. Vai'oire's a big, well-financed town. Our defensive equipment is the latest available to private buyers. If you people are certain of your—"

"We're as certain as we can be at this point," Cora told him, "that people are responsible and that there's not some unknown entity lurking about that's swallowing towns whole."

"We knew that from the start, Ja-wen." The huge woman spoke in a voice that bordered on the girlish. "Too many pieces left floating about."

"Yes." Ja-wen leaned close to Cora, spoke conspiratorially. "I'm sure you've heard that part of our trouble is preventing this information from starting rumors we can't control. If something isn't done soon, some shuttle pilot's going to hear about our problem and word will get off-planet. Then it'll get on a liner going out-system, and before you know it, well—look at Yermenov. A lifelong resident. If people like him start leaving, before long this world will be less than a colony. We've already noticed unusual trouble in hiring new specialists." He looked away, upset and embarrassed.

"What do you think the reaction of our young people is going to be? Especially our brightest, away at University? There's no institute of higher learning here. You think they'll want to come back to face obliteration?" He shook his head.

"This has to be stopped, and soon." How like Hwoshien he sounds, Cora thought. "Too many of our friends have died already." And business is off, she thought coolly. Then he said something which made her regret her harsh appraisal.

"I understand you've come from the last docking site of Rorqual Towne." She nodded. "The assistant mayor there was my cousin. We've all lost friends or relatives. For all its size, Mou'anui is a tightly knit community, even if our knitting is via satellite. We feel the loss of any of our fellow citizens personally. But entire towns!"

"Whoever's responsible," Merced said confidently, "is a candidate for mindwipe."

"Mindwipe," the mayor echoed, nodding slowly. "If any of us lays hands on the perpetrators of these outrages first . . ." He left the sentence unfinished, but elaboration was unnecessary. If the inhabitants got to the pirates first, there would not be enough of the outlaws left to reimprint with new personalities.

"Well, they won't find us unprepared!" he said loudly. "We've nearly eleven hundred permanent residents here, and they all know what their day-status is. We don't rely just on our automatics. Since the trouble started, we've had people watching the monitors twenty-five hours a day. We go on about our business, but with an eye on each other's backsides." Cora wondered if the brave speechmaking was for their benefit or for the mayor's.

"What's Matamoreva doing?" The portly executive was looking past them, toward the far end of the dock. "I haven't seen him since last Harvest Holiday."

Cora turned with the others. Their guide was bent over, conversing with the water. "We've a pair of orcas with us. He's probably chatting with them." She noticed he was wearing his translator.

"Drifters or associates?" one of the other men inquired.

"I don't know the precise meaning of those terms," Merced said, "but if you mean do they work with Sam and humans on any kind of regular basis, I'm fairly certain that they do, judging from what we've observed thus far."

"Very nice," the enormous lady, H'ua, chirped. "They're the best early-warning system you can have. I've always been sorry we've never been able to induce one or two to associate with Vai'oire."

Matamoreva rejoined them, confirmed that he had been talking with their black and white companions. "I was setting them a patrol," he explained. "They'll circle the town about a kilometer out. How shallow is the reef you're working?"

"Breaks the surface in some places," Yermenov said. "I'm fisheries supervisor for the town, by the way. We're backed up to one end of the reef. It spreads out in a fan shape, more or less, from where we're sitting now. It's hundreds of meters across on the other side of town, expanding to kilometers at its greatest diameter."

"What are you thinking of?" Cora asked the pensive Polynesian.

"Submersibles. They would be the most effective means of attack. If they're emission-silent or screened, or both, no satellite would detect them. And if they're small enough and fast enough . . ." He shrugged. "They could be the explanation. The reef here will screen about a quarter of the ocean approach from any such underwater assault. I'm building an imaginary defensive ring around the town."

"It doesn't matter," Mayor Pua'ahorofenua said testily. "We'll keep our systems operative three hundred and sixty degrees. Just in case."

"That's just what I'd do if I were in your position."

To Cora, the simple fishing and gathering village was fascinating. On several of the ocean worlds on which she had worked, floating resorts had been constructed on polymer rafts. Occasionally she had encountered an isolated floating research facility. Never anything of this complexity, she mused. Not a complete community, with homes and places of work and recreation, of local commerce and schooling. Right now the illusion was that people actually worked and walked on solid land. It was at its most effective near the center of town, away from the sea. The walkway under her feet did not sway at all, yet she knew only meters of extruded polymer separated her from the depths. The compensators held the walkway and the buildings surrounding it as steady and secure as a padre's thoughts. If anything, it was more than naturally stable. The surface she trod was smooth and seamless, not shifting like the glass sands of Mou'anui Atoll.

Some of the buildings rose three stories from their raft foundations. Most roofs sported a fringe of small dish antennae, like split bivalves, to receive and broadcast via satellite.

"Looks like weather coming in," Mataroreva observed as they turned toward a long structure which the large woman had identified as her home.

H'ua glanced up at the darkening sky. "We're due for a day or two of rain. Nothing serious, according to the forecast. Mild winds and light chop. Besides, the rain is good for us."

Merced frowned. "Why? I thought the floating

towns produced all the fresh water they required through desalinization."

"*E mau roa*—that's very true," H'ua replied. "For drinking and cooking and most other functions, the desalinated sea is quite sufficient." She winked at Cora and fluffed the mane of long black hair that framed her moon face. "But some of us traditionalists believe that for washing one's hair, rainwater is a necessity. Rain is also good for the soul."

They passed the house, turned up another street, and eventually reached a two-story, molded rooming complex. They entered a small reception area.

"You are our guests. It's not often Vai'oire has a chance to display its hospitality to off-world visitors." H'ua looked at Rachael, nodded toward the object the girl held under one arm. "I understand you can actually play that witch's lyre?"

Rachael looked surprised. "How could you know? Many people carry them and can only practice with them."

Mataroreva smiled hugely. "That was one of the less serious pieces of information I broadcast prior to our arrival."

"You would honor us with a concert," H'ua added.

Rachael looked embarrassed. "Now, wait, I'm not a professional, only an enthusiastic amateur and—"

"Anyone who can make a neurophon do more than simply wail is more than a mere amateur." A huge hand patted Rachael on the back. "Anyway, you are a new and exotic quantity. Wear something skimpy. If the music and projections are weak, the men won't notice." She eyed the girl approvingly. "They may not notice anyhow."

With a long, infectious, little-girl giggle, she turned to lumber from the reception station. "You all have a good time while you're here. Each room has its own autochef, communicator, and tridee. There are broadcasts from Mou'anui every day. If there's anything else you want, buzz me through your room com on the local network. I'm one-forty-six. My husband's name is Taarii Maltzan, by the way. You won't get him. He's out working the reef with the rest of the gathering teams."

"Thank you," Cora barely remembered to say as the woman left them.

The door to her assigned room was locked. That was to be expected. In an area as restricted and isolated as a floating town, privacy would be highly prized. The door opened at the sound of her voice and the application of her thumb to the recess in its frame.

What was inside was totally unexpected, however, and she nearly let out a yell. Her surprise was due to the apparent absence of floor. Then she saw the reflections in the corners. Gingerly she stepped out onto the transparency.

Her uncertainty rapidly gave way to delight. The floor of the surprisingly spacious room was completely transparent. Six meters below she could see wonderfully bizarre, multihued creatures swimming back and forth, lit by lights someone had thoughtfully turned on for her prior to her arrival. Meters farther lay a sandy bottom spotted with hexalate formations.

On the clear floor sat a lounge and bed woven from some dried blue sea plant, an exquisite chunk of polish hexalate containing the tridee unit, and scattered mats of spiral design and exquisite workmanship.

Cora knelt and ran her hands over the smooth floor. The glassalloy was perhaps half a meter thick. The room-wide shaft that continued deeper on all sides was part of the polymer raft on which Vai'oire rested. It was the lack of motion which had deceived her into thinking she was stepping out into nothingness.

Further investigation revealed a hatch in the far corner. It was part of the same transparent material.

Steps cut into the white wall of the raft structure led down to a bench resting just above the water. There a guest could sit beneath the floor of her room and bathe in complete privacy in the warm sea.

The guest building was located on the edge of the town, so the water beneath would be relatively warm. Rising, Cora found the one-way window which looked out over the ocean and the small docks holding pleasure craft. Outside, people walked past clad in the familiar pareus, occasionally in a diving gelsuit. Small children often went naked.

Such casual imagination expended on behalf of the rare guest hinted at an industry only marginally exploited on Cachalot: tourism. She envisioned floating hotels anchored above or near the seamount reefs and atolls—and chided herself. Tourism and science rarely mixed. No doubt the resident cetaceans would vigorously oppose any such form of permanent floating development. She should be devoting all her thoughts to the serious mission at hand.

Though perhaps not too serious any more. Her thoughts were not on enigmatic sources of death and destruction, but on a cave filled with living stars. She glanced around the empty room again and for the first time in a long while felt the key word in the description to be "empty." Maybe Sam would enjoy sharing a dive. There was a new reef to explore.

She checked the other rooms assigned their party. Merced was luxuriating in the shaft of his. Rachael, he told her, should be on her way back to the boat, in whose lower cabin she would practice frantically for the demanded concert. As to the whereabouts of Mataroreva, he had no idea.

She thanked Merced, cut off, and left her room. Vai'oire was not so enormous that she wouldn't be able to locate him. In the air of a muggy afternoon she asked questions of the townsfolk.

For a while the answers were identical. "No,

haven't seen him; yes, know who you mean, but I've been out fishing all day; no, sorry . . ."

As she wandered around the town she came to feel progressively more isolated. The differences hadn't been so obvious back on Mou'anui. Many technicians from off-planet worked at the Administration Center and its processing facilities. Here on Vai'oire the majority of the population was of traceable Polynesian ancestry. Their massive bodies and café au lait color, encased only in pareus or skimpy diving gear, made her feel like an awkward splinter of jet set among twenty-karat topazes. She felt smothered by sweaty, heaving flesh, pressing in on all sides.

Eventually she ran into someone who had seen Sam. "The peaceforcer captain?"

She nodded energetically.

"He *was* headed over that way." The young man pointed, added good-naturedly, "Two buildings down, you turn to the left. Town Communications. I'll bet he was going there."

Communications—yes, that made sense. She thanked the youth, followed his directions carefully. She needn't have been so intense. One could not become very lost on Vai'oire, since all steps led eventually to the sea.

The structure was clearly marked, with curved corners. Its walls, like all on Vai'oire, were formed of a light but extremely durable honeycomb plastic that was impervious to salt corrosion and placed little burden on the supporting polymer base. Several small domes protruded from its upper sides and roof, along with a broad dish antenna. An impressive array of electronic webwork connected antennaes and domes and other projections, spun of titanium and magensoy and glass instead of silk.

Inside she found not a single worker. She was not surprised. Automation and robotic sensors could handle the prosaic, monotonous chores of aligning anten-

nae and distributing long-distance bulletins. The bulk
of radiowave information went directly into the inhabitants' homes, ready for display on individual
tridee units.

She finally found a man using one of several public
viewers. His home unit had blown a module and had
not yet been repaired.

"Mataroreva? Big fellow, real easygoing?" She
nodded. He jerked a thumb to his right, his attention
still wholly on the viewscreen. "Went into the library,
I think."

Two rooms farther on she found the town storage
bank. Thousands of tape chips with information on
everything from how to dissect local forms of poisonous fish to entertainment shows imported all the way
from Terra filled the slots in the bank. The room was
very small. No one except the librarian needed to use
the room, since the chipped information could be
called up on any screen in town.

Maybe Sam was hunting a restricted chip, or providing information to be stored and shipped hard copy
to Mou'anui, to back up his broadcasts. She tried the
transparent door. It wasn't locked. Yes, he was probably encoding a chip. For all his seeming frivolity, she
knew he was a diligent and conscientious worker.

She could surprise him as effectively as he had surprised her. She opened the door quietly and slipped
inside. There was no sign of him . . . no, there, toward
the back of the room, some noise. A local technician
was probably helping him, she realized. That would
spoil some of her surprise.

As it developed, her surprise was as total as she
could have wished, but she drew no joy from its effect.
A technician was also present, as she had suspected.
The trouble came from the fact that Sam and the
woman weren't engaged in research or programming.

Cora simply stood and stared, her expression completely blank, like a mindwiped idiot awaiting imprinting.

Oddly enough, her attention was focused mostly on the technician, the stranger, who was taller, fuller, at least ten years younger, than Cora. Sam moved slightly away from the woman, shattered the incredibly awkward tableau by doing the worst possible thing. He smiled apologetically.

"Pardon me," Cora finally managed to say, with the incredible calm that so often occurs in times of emotional paralysis. "It wasn't anything important."

"Cora?" She had already left the room. He did not follow.

Still icily composed, she exited the building. She managed to get halfway back to the visitors' apartments before she broke into a run. A few locals eyed her curiously. There was no need to run on Vai'oire. Everything was close to everything else.

Cora entered the reception area. The fates had chosen to bestow a small favor: Rachael was not to be seen. Stumbling into her room, Cora sealed the door behind her. Then she collapsed on the woven bed and lay there interminably, trying to cry. She discovered that she could not. She laughed wildly, her throat burning. Out of practice. Old habits die hard. No tears fell from her eyes. Not for Sam, not for herself.

Exhausted, she eventually rolled over. Her head hung toward the floor. Rainbows danced and swirled beneath the distant water.

Why so upset? she asked herself silently, angrily. What do you have to be so upset about? He promised you nothing, he forced you into nothing. It was the mildest possible seduction.

Yes? What about the cavern, then? Beauty that he knew would overcome you. And you were overcome, but he and the beauty were separate, and you willingly drank of both. So you wanted to make love to him.

Integrate critical query: do you want more than that? Don't know, don't know god I don't know. You went into this with your eyes open. Yes, eyes open and brain shut. Serves you right. You deserve what you get in this life.

Then stop acting like a sixteen-year-old! You're always harping at Rachael for acting immature, and you're acting worse than she ever has. When you see him again, you go right on as if nothing has happened. Yes . . . he's still in charge of the security end of this expedition. You treat him that way. Polite, friendly—and distant. If he so much as touches you . . .

Again the fury rose like lava in the throat of a volcano, subsided as quickly. How interesting to speculate, she told herself, on man's continuing familial relationship with the ape. Don't blame Sam for a species-wide lack of progression.

She rolled onto her back, studied the ceiling. Always the male must prove himself. You cannot be mad at the leader of the baboon pack for acting like himself.

She could cope with that reality. She had done so for years. No reason to regress now. Sam had made his point. She did not bother to debate the thoughts behind his ludicrous little grin, back there on the floor. How jejune!

Running back to her room, memory and confusion and hurt all mashed together in her mind, she had thought he had been taunting her, deliberately flaunting the woman at her. The male peacock flares his feathers, she mused.

But that was asking too much of him. He had never laid claim to eloquence or cunning, and now he had demonstrated his lack of both. You were the one, Cora reminded herself with satisfaction, who took the situation in hand and spoke, made the decision to move. That smile was nothing more than a truthful mirror of his inner vapidness. She had made a mistake. Sam Mataroreva was not merely boyish in appearance and manner, he was a boy in all things. She should simply treat him as such. Her expectations had been too, too high. How she had permitted herself to regard him as an admirable *man* she now could not imagine.

Enough. She would relax with some tapes the remainder of the afternoon, dine with the others as pleasantly as possible, and have a good night's rest. There was still much of the town to be seen, for who knew wherein might lie the critical clue? Perhaps she might even seek out that girl and ask her to show them about Vai'oire. Yes, that was it, show *her* how a mature woman can act. Let the other be the nervous one, awaiting the explosion that would never come.

For now a nap would be a good idea. She would have no trouble falling asleep. The autochef could dispense things other than food. At the last moment she changed her mind. Naturally induced tranquility was better than drugged.

She lay back down on the bed, rolled over, and darkened the window and floor. The anger had subsided, the anxiety vanished. But though the room was now as dark as night, she could not shut out the afterimage burned into her retinas of two bodies entwined on a floor.

Dinner proceeded with a forced amiability that fooled no one. Rachael knew something was wrong with her mother, but for once had the sense not to open her mouth. Mataroreva ate with an unusual single-mindedness, letting Rachael and Merced carry the conversation.

After dessert he brightened, however, at a thought. "Listen, there's going to be a spectacle on the reef tonight. The townsfolk are used to it already, so we ought to have the entire reef to ourselves."

"What kind of spectacle?" Cora displayed more interest than she felt.

"Well," Mataroreva hurried on, believing that he had genuinely aroused her interest, "it involves a native cephalopod. It doesn't look like a squid or sexathorp. More like a ball with tentacles."

He withdrew a sketch film from his pareu pockets, then a stylus. The instrument was wielded with surprising delicacy by his thick digits. The creature he outlined was actually more ellipsoidal than spherical. Four squat fins protruded from one end while a ring of six or seven tiny eyes orbited the other. Each eye had a long tentacle set just above it. A single round mouth rested in the center of the ocular ring.

"They range in color from a vitreous green to a light lavender," Sam told them animatedly. Rachael and Merced were listening with interest. "They school in the thousands over this reef."

"How big?" Merced asked.

"About the size of my fist." He made one by way of example. "Plus the tentacle length."

"The town hunts for them?" Cora was intrigued despite herself.

"No, not for them. There's a small fish, about the size of my little finger . . ."

"You have expressive hands," she cut in. "Two examples already."

He eyed her uncertainly for an instant, hunting for hidden meanings before continuing. "The fish live in millions of crevices in the reef. When they school, the cephalopods arrive to hunt them—and to mate. When they're mating they pulse like fireflies: the males, different shades of blue; the females, of red. They're powerful bioluminescents. And they dance, a kind of figure-eight weave. Thousands and thousands weaving together, and pulsing every shade of red and blue."

"Sounds like a subject for a new composition," Rachael admitted, thinking of the neurophon languishing back in her room. As she did so, her expression drooped. "But I promised to do that concert."

"You didn't promise a particular night," Merced reminded her. "You can put off our hosts for a couple of days."

"All right, tomorrow would be as good as tonight, I suppose." She rose from the table. "Sure. I'll go tell them, and get into my suit." She suddenly glanced over at Cora, asked concernedly, "You coming along, Mother?"

What an odd tone to her voice, Cora thought. Surely I'm acting perfectly normal. "Of course I'm coming along. It sounds very exciting."

"Good." Mataroreva put away his sketch film, from which the drawing of the cephalopod was already fading. "At the northeast end of town you'll find a long, isolated pier. It's tangent to the nearest portion of the reef shallows." He checked his chronometer. "Sundown's in about an hour. We should meet at two in the morning."

"That long?" Rachael was looking out a window. "It's dark already."

"Clouds," he replied, following her gaze. "It's not the darkness—the cephalopods have a particular time of night. We'll all simply have to remain awake for a while. The rain won't affect them, if it comes."

Excitement overcoming her sleepiness, Cora made her way through the dimly lit streets of the town. So late at night (early in the morning, she corrected herself), the majority of the townsfolk were long since sound asleep.

She reached the edge of town, heard the water lapping at the polymer raft. Ahead lay the pier. At its far end she could make out several shadowy figures.

"We're all here," Rachael offered as Cora joined

them. She was already poured into her gelsuit. Merced was adjusting his mask. In fact, they were more than all there. Now five figures were standing at the end of the pier.

"This is our guide." Sam pointed to another shape making final tunings of its own equipment. "There are enough ins and outs to nightdiving a strange reef to make it tricky. It would be hard to lose anyone, but this is safer."

"I know that. You think I'm a complete idiot?" Rachael looked sharply at her mother, and Cora could see the puzzlement on her daughter's face through faceplate and darkness.

"I'm sorry—I know you don't," she apologized. "Naturally it would be sensible for us to have a guide."

"I'll do my best, Ms. Xamantina," a voice said. The fifth figure turned toward her. Cora stared. She trembled just a little, and the quivering passed quickly. It was the girl Sam had been with.

She extended a hand. Even in the dim light Cora could discern the tenseness in the youthful face across from her. "My name's Dawn. I'm the town librarian." Cora resisted the urge to say something like, "That's not all you are, lynx." Besides, Cora was not going to lapse into adolescence now. She reached out with her own hand, tried to will the nerves to numbness as they shook.

"It's an honor to meet you." The girl spoke with apparent sincerity. "We all know that you've been brought in by the government and the administration all the way from Terra to help us with our misfortunes. If anyone can solve them, I'm sure you can."

Come on, dear, Cora thought to herself. You're overdoing it. Nonetheless, staring at the unlined young face, she sensed that, given half a chance, this was a woman she could come to like. At the moment she was unsure whether she still hated her or merely felt sorry for her. This was an oceanographic expedition, no matter its aesthetic coloration. Not a sequence from a tired old tridee fiction chip. "Let's get going," she said briskly. "It's late. Very late." That was true enough. The sun would rise in another few hours.

Clouds blotted out the stars. A few drops, harbingers of nocturnal precipitation to come, dampened their now masked faces. Mataroreva produced a set of diving lights, tiny high-intensity beam throwers that could be held easily in one hand.

"What about predators?" Merced was speaking through his headphone system now. "I'd expect there would be many, unless Cachalot's carnivores are all day feeders."

"They're not," Dawn informed him, "but the large pelagics never swim in the reef shallows. Those that do are too small to trouble more than one swimmer, and there are five of us."

How obvious, Cora mused. Was Merced trying to make the girl feel comfortable with them by providing her with a chance to display some knowledge? It had to be that. She had seen and heard enough of the little scientist to suspect him of several things, but naiveté wasn't one of them.

Naturally there wouldn't be a swarm of dangerous predators about, or the cephalopods would not have chosen this place and time for mating.

One by one, they turned on their hand beams, the projectors clipped protectively to individual wrist latches, and slipped quietly into the water.

The beam throwers were necessary to illumine their surroundings. It was not necessary to search out a companion with the lights because the gelsuits, in addition to being thermosensitive, were also thermoluminescent. While the gel controlled body heat, that same heat was enough to excite the atoms of the suit ma-

terial to fluorescence. So each swimming figure glowed
a soft yellow.

As they moved farther into the reef they encountered a myriad of phosphorescent hexalates and other
creatures, but nothing particularly unique. Cora had
observed similar phenomena on other worlds.

Then the reef seemed to drop abruptly away on all
sides and they were swimming in a vast open hollow, a
natural underwater amphitheater. Within that watery
bowl was one of the most magnificent sights anyone
could imagine. For a time Cora forgot her worries
about their assignment, forgot any memories of the
painful confrontation with Sam and Dawn back in the
town library. Forgot everything. Before her was glory
that eclipsed all anxiety.

If anything, Sam had underestimated the number of
cephalopods they could expect to encounter. Tens of
thousands wiggled and fluttered before them, around
them. Some danced in threes and fours. Others were
naturally partnered, while thousands more sought
partners amid the iridescent orgy of liquid copulation.
Myriad searchlights flared and pulsed around her.
Soon something neither Sam nor Dawn had mentioned
commenced about them.

The gelsuits shone yellow. Not red or blue. That
mattered not. Driven by curiosity, passion, or forces
unimaginable to mankind, the cephalopods began to
scurry around each bipedal figure. Cora discovered
herself enveloped in a multiple waltz of other-worldly
beauty and grace. She let herself drift, suspended in
luminescence, as blue and red spheres jigged and
courted about her hands and head and legs.

Peering through the tentacled brilliance, she saw the
yellow figure of Rachael surrounded by an attentive
court of dazzling luminaries, a flavescent nucleus orbited by blue and crimson electrons.

She raised one of her hands. Immediately two of

the blue cephalopods began a stately pirouette about her fingertips, twisting and somersaulting with gravity-defying grace. Another bumped against her faceplate, making her jerk instinctively. But it was a soft, powder-puff collision. She stared into septuple alien eyes, cat-slitted and rich purple, trying to bridge a chasm of intelligence and evolution. Blankly, the disappointed creature drifted away with a hypnotic wave of its tentacles.

Treading water easily, she remained above the bottom, below the surface. There was no sky above, no ground below. She was adrift in a sea of stars. She had to force herself to think of the proximity of sharp hexalate blades which could rip gelsuit or airflow headpiece. In such light, devoid of reference points, one could easily become disoriented and swim into the reef wall.

Despite such dangers, she found herself wishing she could slip free of the suit skin to swim naked and clean in the dark water, convoyed by gently bobbing blue and red lights.

She held up both hands now, watched as a dozen males teased and courted her fingers. She moved her hands up and down and the ellipsoidal forms matched her movements exactly, never pausing in their generative ballet. I'm a conductor, a conductor of life, she thought in wonder. She crossed her arms, and the hopeless suitors again changed their dance to mimic her motion. Bodies tumbled and spun, stubby fins producing astonishing agility in the water. Two opposing tentacles were always held stiffly out to the creature's sides, acting as stabilizers.

Wondering how they would react, she brought her two hands together, forming a single, larger yellow mass. Would they fight, or freeze in confusion at the unexpected merger?

The did neither. Instead, the obsessed dozen vanished with appalling speed. She blinked, wondering if her vision was at fault. Not only were her suitors gone, they all were gone, as if they had never been there. Thirty thousand azure and vermilion globes had disappeared as if cut off by the turning of a single biological switch.

XI

For several long, horrifying moments she was utterly alone, suspended in black limbo save for the penetrating beam of her hand light.

Then she made out other swimming, yellow forms and their individual hand beams.

"What was that?" she inquired of everyone in general and no one in particular via her mask broadcast unit. "What happened?"

"Where did they go?" Rachael asked, sounding concerned.

"Did we frighten them?" Merced appeared on her right. The five figures came together.

"Dawn, I thought you said that there are no large predators in here." Predators did seem a likely explanation for the cephalopods' reaction. They would douse their lights and scatter for shelter.

"I don't think there are, Cora." The girl sounded curious, not defensive, which was why Cora was inclined to believe her.

They were interrupted by a flash of dull light from overhead. Cora wasn't the only one who experienced an instant of panic before the explanation reached them in the form of a low rumble of thunder, muted by the water.

"Lightning," she muttered. "Could that scare them?"

"It's possible," Dawn agreed. "I'm not enough of a specialist to be able to say."

"Possible perhaps." Cora recognized Merced's thoughtful tone. "But why should other light startle them that way, when they generate such an immense display themselves? Maybe that particular wavelength? . . ."

As she listened, Cora was distracted by a peculiar tickling inside her head. It was almost familiar. She had the strangest sensation—Then she felt herself being moved forcefully to one side.

But no hand had touched her, not even Sam's massive ones. As enormous volume of water had been displaced somewhere nearby. Yet Dawn continued to insist on the absence of large predators. Maybe the girl was no specialist, but Cora granted her the benefit of local experience, which she knew was often worth much more than theoretical studies.

But there was *something*. She sensed it, felt it through her suit. It had moved a mountain of ocean and frightened the milling cephalopods into instant oblivion.

Another flash from above momentarily lit the translucent water, a second dim rumble echoing forever behind. She briefly saw her companions outlined in light blue. Still no sign of anything else. Only gleaming hexalates and nothing more. Whatever had terrified the cephalopods had done the same to all other local motile life.

In the center of Vai'oire was a tall, thin building within which was a dense assemblage of the most complex machinery in the town.

Two men monitored the instruments. They were conscientious and attentive to their tasks. One was presently visiting with a member of the opposite sex in a corridor just off the main chamber. His companion remained behind, until he decided that it was vital he attend momentarily to certain critical bodily demands.

No one saw the dial on one panel swing from one end to the other. No one saw a fluorescent grid suddenly swarm with electronic pollen. The aural alarms went off seconds later. Alert functions were beyond the immediate reach of the busily occupied man in the corridor. Ignoring pants and awkwardness, his partner in the bathroom rushed for the general alarm. He was also seconds too late, as the general alarm system, the men, the building, and the community of Vai'oire began to disintegrate.

Cora rested in the water, puzzled by the inexplicable sudden swell. Hasty questions and theories were exchanged by the five swimmers. Before any conclusion could be agreed upon, the water around them fragmented into a dozen arguing whirlpools, accompanied by a continuous, modulated rumble.

Cora was thrown about like an ant in a storm. She kicked frantically to recover her equilibrium before the turbulence threw her against an outcropping of sharp reef. In the darkness and chaos something locked onto her right arm. Water pulled the opposite way. She felt as if her arm would be torn from its socket and screamed inside the face mask.

But the grip held her tight. Looking around, she saw the contorted, straining face of Sam Mataroreva behind his faceplate. His other arm was locked around the protruding spine of a hexalate bemmy. Another figure also clung tightly to the formation: Rachael.

Then Sam had drawn her back to the sheltered side of the growth. The water there was still angry and confused, but the violence that had tossed Cora was greatly diminished.

As the rumbling continued, rising and falling to no recognizable pattern, Cora thought of a seaquake. She suggested it to Sam.

"Can't be," he replied, sounding tired and frus-

trated. "Not that these old seamounts aren't subject
to seismic disturbances—they are. But this one's too
localized. We would be feeling the effects more where
we are right now, more toward the center of the
mount and the reef. Instead, the disturbance is off-
shore, toward the deeps."

Other figures fought their way toward the three
refugees. First Merced, then Dawn, drifted past. Like
a hesitant fisherman, Sam swam out to aid first one,
then the other. Soon all the swimmers were huddled
fearfully behind the protective mass of the bemmy.

"It's definitely coming from the area of the town,"
Mataroreva murmured. "I'm going up. Maybe I can
see something."

"Me, too."

He looked at Cora's glowing, tiny form, said nothing. Then he was swimming surfaceward, keeping
safely behind the bulk of the formation. Cora followed.

As they neared the surface the turbulence increased
considerably. Cora had to climb upward, keeping a
constant grip on the hexalate protrusions lest the surge
knock her from its protective mass. The disturbance
did not suggest a storm.

They broke the surface. This time Cora almost lost
her grasp as a huge swell smashed into her. It knocked
her face mask askew and she had to fight to clear and
reposition it. A fresh flash of lightning lit the roiling
waters and unmuted thunder assailed her exposed
head. It was raining steadily, but the wind was mod-
erate. The violence of the waves allowed them barely
half a minute above the water, which was sufficient
to imprint forever on her memory the fantastic im-
ages before them.

Bits and pieces of the town of Vai'oire were floating past and around them. Violent smashing sounds
mixed with a few faint, distant screams and the action

of wind and wave. All of the town lights had gone out, including those independently powered.

Four colossal, monolithic forms rose from the water like a piece of the planet's crust. Breaching in unison, the quartet of blue whales fell simultaneously onto what remained of the now exposed central portion of the town. Huge sections of plastic wall and roof exploded in all directions. Something irregular and heavy made a *whooshing* noise as it flew past Cora's head, to land in the water far behind her. Something smaller *wanged* metallically off the front of the bemmy. Then Sam was practically dragging her below.

The rumbles continued to assail the swimmers, reaching their hiding place in the depths. The noise was growing fainter as Cora numbly informed the others, "We thought it was people, but it's been the whales all along. I was so sure a human agency was responsible."

"Then the catodon lied to us." Rachael treaded water slowly.

"Lumpjaw insisted he knew nothing. Maybe they don't."

"Probably not." Mataroreva's face was ashen behind the mask. "What the old one said to us about the baleen whales being incapable of mounting such a co-ordinated enterprise is damn true. Yet you and I just saw four of them operating in perfect unison. They knew exactly what they were doing, and they were going about it as methodically as any intelligent military group could. I'm pretty sure I had a glimpse of a couple of humpbacks working off to the west. Humpbacks! They're usually as gentle as children. If we'd been able to look around, I suspect we would have found fins and seis and minkes and all the other baleens out there, too.

"But I didn't see any toothed whales, and I was looking for catodons. Until we have proof they were involved, I'm not going to condemn them with their less intelligent cousins."

Dawn's voice was agonized. "How can you hold the baleens responsible? I'll bet the catodons are controlling them, directing them! It's all! . . ."

Mataroreva shook her. "I know this doesn't make any sense. Crazy—it's all crazy. Let's not fantasize, though. Let's stick with what we know."

"What about our defenses?" she mumbled. "Someone . . . we should have detected the approach in plenty of time to give the alarm."

Mataroreva considered. "The whole business was planned perfectly from beginning to end. They knew exactly what they were doing. Probably they hit the defense center first. What went wrong there is something we'll never learn."

"How could a bunch of dumb baleens know all that?" Dawn moaned.

"Someone must be telling them. Someone has to, unless . . ." He hesitated, then went on. "Unless the baleens and the catodons, all of them, have been hiding abilities and desires we know nothing about."

"That's a pretty far-fetched hypothesis," Cora commented.

"I'm willing to accept a better one."

"Could a human agency somehow be controlling the baleens?"

"I don't see how." But she could see he was seriously considering the idea. "No group of humans could so completely dominate and direct a pod of intelligent whales. Not by any known technique." His hand gestured, a glowing pointer in the water.

"There must be a couple of hundred cetaceans functioning in chorus out there to generate such total destruction in so short a time. No wonder the other towns never even had time to send out a warning."

"I think we'd all do well to be silent for a while."

Merced was looking away from them, around the hexalate tower.

"Why?" Cora asked.

He pointed toward the town, to where the reef sloped off into deeper water. "I think I just saw something move."

They went quiet, huddling together tight against the finger of silicate. The rumbles had vanished, and the water, though still disturbed, was silent.

Cora couldn't be certain, but she thought she saw a great silver-gray wall sliding past in the blackness. It was only a dim outline on the far boundaries of perception. She cursed their gelsuits' irrepressible luminescence. The sight reminded her of nothing so much as a shark on patrol, and she shuddered, cold now despite the warming efficiency of the suit.

The outline faded into the blackness from which it had emerged, but they continued to stay bunched together and silent. With their suits automatically assisting in respiration, they might have slept in shifts, those awake monitoring the regulators of their somnolent companions. They tried to do so, but no one could fall asleep. The gelsuits could modulate air and warmth but could do nothing where fear was concerned.

Gradually, an eternity later, the water around them began to lighten. The storm had long since moved on. Sunlight was once more turning the water to glass, sparkling off the brilliant reef growths. The day swimmers appeared, poking at crevices in the hexalates for food and amusement. Long, multihued fronds hesitantly unfolded from their hiding places, began to strain the water for microscopic sustenance.

All was normal save for the presence of thousands of inorganic objects drifting on the surface. Some sank slowly past the five tired swimmers, who made their way carefully to the light. Around them drifted the remnants of the town of Vai'oire, shattered and torn.

Sections of housing, packages, clothes, and personal effects bobbed eerily on the gentle current. Meter-square hunks of polymer raft dominated the flotsam like miniature icebergs. The superstrong polymer had a breaking point of several tons per square meter, a point which the rampaging cetaceans had handily exceeded.

Incongruously human in the sea of technological corpses, a doll drifted past. It was half sunk, badly waterlogged already. Its head was bent and hung beneath the surface. Cora shied away from it as if it could poison her through the water.

They remained next to the crest of the bemmy, hanging onto it as they studied in stunned silence the section of sea where the town had been anchored.

Considering that all her friends and associates, perhaps relatives as well, had been killed, Dawn was holding together surprisingly well.

"I'm going to hunt for survivors," Mataroreva announced.

"What about remaining cetaceans?"

He started swimming around the bemmy, looked back at Cora. "I don't think so. I don't see any plumes or backs. Not a fin in sight. They finished their work last night."

Fin . . . fin . . . the way he said it made Cora think of something else. Then she had it. There was no sign of either Latehoht or Wenkoseemansa. Yet she had been told the cetaceans did not fight among themselves. The cooperative action of the different whales the previous night proved as much. But the effort itself, the hostile premeditated attack by the herd of cetaceans, was so unprecedented that she wouldn't be surprised to learn that the baleens had killed the two orcas because they had been working alongside mankind.

Come to think of it, the orcas had been on patrol last night but had sounded no warning. Were they dead, or in league with the baleens? The plankton-eaters had no teeth, nothing to bite or chew with. But a tail weighing many tons could smash the skull of a much smaller orca as easily as it could a section of polymer raft.

Which survivors was Sam really worried about?

He searched for some thirty minutes before rejoining them. The current was already dispersing the broken skeleton of the town. In the bright sunlight of morning the remaining fragments took on a surreal aspect. It was as if the town had never been, and something had poured tons of garbage into the waters surrounding this reef.

"No sign of them," he announced and then, seeing Cora's questioning look, confirmed her thoughts. "Either of them. I called and called. No one responded." He forced himself on. "I didn't spot a single body. What the hell *do* they do with the bodies?"

"I can't imagine," Cora said carefully. "The throat of even a blue is too small to pass a whole man, and they've nothing to chew a person up with." Rachael looked ill. "Anyway, why would they suddenly switch, after millions of years, from a diet of krill to much bulkier food?"

"Then what do they do with the bodies?" Sam muttered again.

No one had any ideas. At that point, everything caught up with Dawn. They took turns comforting her, calming her. Only Cora stayed aside. She was nauseated by her own thoughts: the wish that Dawn had perished along with the rest of the town. Her reaction was only human, but sometimes the thoughts that cross a human mind can be appalling. How thin is the veneer of civilization.

Rachael and Merced did a better job of soothing the distraught girl anyway. Cora forced personal matters from her mind by concentrating relentlessly on the problem at hand.

"We have enough nutrients in our suits to keep us going four or five days." She pulled herself up onto the smooth top of the bemmy, slid aside her mask. "We can rest here without having to swim and can conserve our strength." She looked at Sam. "I'm sure we can find something in the way of local life to supplement our suit diet." She gestured at the surrounding debris. "There should be some useful material among all this, food included. We'd better start looking for it before the current carries it beyond our reach." And, she mused silently, it will give us something to do besides think.

Even Dawn participated in the search, hiding her sobbing behind her mask. They found a considerable amount of packaged food floating on the surface. Much of it was inedible. Either the vacuum seals had cracked, or it was designed only for use in automatic cooking units. But some was both intact and directly edible.

A great deal of torn, lighter-than-water cable drifted about like yellow seaweed. These lengths served to tie the packages of food to the tops of several bemmies. The pattern thus formed would also serve to attract high-flying skimmers.

Merced suggested they employ one or more of the emergency transmitters located in the instrument belt of every gelsuit. The idea was vetoed by Mataroreva. They still could not discount completely the possibility that a human agency was somehow involved in the attacks. Setting up an emergency beacon might draw visitors to the reef other than those desired. Besides, the lack of communication from the town would draw investigators soon enough.

Quite unexpectedly, they did come across three closely grouped watertight containers from their own sunken suprafoil. Two contained delicate research equipment for the study of underwater life. That was a laugh, Cora thought. They would be doing nothing but studying undersea life for the next several days, perhaps for weeks, until someone thought to send out a skimmer or a ship to see why the town of Vai'oire was not responding to signals.

She couldn't decide whether to be pleased or disappointed at the contents of the third container. It was filled with personal effects that were of no use to anyone in the water, and included Rachael's neurophon. Her daughter, of course, was overjoyed. To Cora's relief, however, she wouldn't chance playing the sensitive instrument, much as it would have relaxed her.

Not that the sealed, solid-state electronics would be damaged by a little water, but Rachael was unwilling to risk dropping the device from the uncertain perch of a bemmy top. It would not float. So she left it sealed in, together with the other two containers, and tied to the top of a silicate projection.

They spent the next few days examining the rest of the debris as it was dispersed by wind and wave. Mataroreva made longer and longer swims out to sea, disdaining the comparative shelter of the reef. He claimed to be searching for weapons as well as for additional food supplies.

Cora knew otherwise. She stayed tuned to his broadcast frequency, listening to his plaintive calls. He was still seeking the pair of missing orcas. As the days passed without any reply from the empty sea, he grew more and more morose. Less time was paid to his companions, to eating, to anything other than his muscle-wearying swims. Cora began to feel that his attraction for the two whales was obsessive.

Or was it simply that in spending so much time seeking them, he was ignoring her?

At least his obsession was inclusive. He ignored Dawn as well. And despite herself, Cora felt increasingly sympathetic toward the girl. She was too young to take so much death in stride.

They continued hunting for a body or two. A

drowned human would eventually rise to the surface through the production of gas via decomposition. But they found not an arm or a leg or anything to indicate that hundreds of human beings had once occupied this section of sea. To Cora, their absence posed as great a mystery as the still inexplicable assault of the baleens.

The food from the packages was a welcome change from the bland liquid nutrients supplied by their suits. Cora finished her lunch, slid back into the water. They were entering their fourth day in the sea.

Such an existence compelled her to consider the catodon's way of thinking. Four days of eating, sleeping, and living in near open ocean is enough to affect anyone's outlook on life. Once she had spent fourteen consecutive hours in the water, but that was nothing compared to four days.

A gentle current rocked you to sleep. You would awaken beneath the surface of the sea, to find a glass-faced human hovering above you and mumbling concerns. Once or twice a day it was time to bathe outside your gelsuit. It began to seem foolish to get dressed to get back *into* the water.

The reef became home as well as refuge. Certain hexalate growths grew as familiar as any furniture. Several territorial teleosts greeted the swimming humans as associates, if not friends. Cora found herself worried one morning when a favorite blue and pink fish failed to appear on schedule, and was relieved when it finally did.

At night they glowed alongside their protective bemmy, one remaining on watch while the others slept. Thousands of nocturnal reef dwellers commenced to fill their half of the daily cycle of life. She nearly forgot what it was like to be a land-dwelling creature. Her legs were accustomed to functioning in smooth, alternating kicks now. How much easier, more graceful, it was than walking!

Given gills instead of the confining gelsuit, she believed she could adapt readily to an oceanic existence. She found that she didn't miss solid land at all. In fact, if assured of an ample supply of food and fresh drinking water, she felt she could live this way for months on end.

Her enthusiasm was not shared by her companions. Of the four, only Mataroreva seemed at home in the water. There his great bulk was neutralized and he became as graceful as a seal. But his moroseness turned to bitterness as the days passed. When he talked to Cora or the others, it was with an increasing and unnatural brusqueness that was quite unlike him.

By now the last floating fragments of the town of Vai'oire had been carried off by the current. Anything potentially useful to the five refugees had been secured. Rather than drift and think, Cora tried to do some serious work.

It was while she was studying a particularly interesting anemonelike creature that Dawn swam down to join her. Bubbles rose like clear jelly from the back of her breathing unit.

"You mustn't blame Sam, you know."

"What? What makes you think I blame Sam for anything?"

"I've seen the way you watch him, react to his presence," the girl said. "It's there in the way your body moves, and in your eyes behind your mask."

Cora turned away from the purple fan she had been examining, looked around. She and Dawn were alone. Whatever expression the girl wore was distorted by the mask. Only her eyes could be seen.

"Sam—Sam's problem is that he genuinely loves everybody," Dawn explained. "You mustn't think of me as a rival."

Cora looked away nervously. That was precisely how she had come to regard her.

"It wasn't only me, you know," the lithe young

woman continued. "I think Sam must know half the women on Cachalot. They all like him. Why shouldn't we? He's a wonderful, charming man. But a permanent mate?" She shook her head, the motion given an unintentional portentousness by the resistance of the water.

Cora checked to make certain her broadcast unit was operating with only enough power for this intimate person-to-person conversation. "What makes you think I was considering Sam as anything more than a . . ."

"Oh, come on," Dawn scoffed gently. "You're as transparent as the water here. Don't you see that I'm trying to help you?"

"Don't do me any favors," Cora replied coolly.

"Sam—he . . ." The girl looked thoughtful. "He isn't designed to love just one woman. Some men and women aren't. He truly loves everyone, and feels—though he might not be able to articulate this feeling—that he should spread that great love around."

"I think you and I define love in different ways."

"Maybe we do, Ms. Xamantina. Maybe we do."

"Call me Cora."

"Thank you." Dawn smiled gratefully. "I'd like that. I'm only giving you a piece of advice, believe me. It's absurd for you to think of me as a rival for Sam's permanent affection. You can't compete for something that isn't available."

"That remains to be seen. You seem awfully certain of yourself and your appraisal of Sam."

"It isn't just Sam," the girl said, oddly reflective. "It's Cachalot. Sam was born here. So was I. If you had been born here, you'd understand his attitude better than you seem to. The competition is more than you imagine, and yet isn't really competition at all."

"If you're trying to puzzle me, I don't pay much attention to riddles."

"No, I'm not trying to confuse you." Dawn sighed, partly out of resignation, partly from exasperation.

"Then tell me straight what you're talking about."

The young woman hesitated. "I think it may be better for you if you find out for yourself. I'm not sure you'd believe me anyway."

"You're still doing a poor job of putting me off through confusion and mystery."

"Never mind." Dawn turned to swim away. "Forget it."

"Just a minute." Cora put out a restraining hand. "Whatever happens, you should know that I'm terribly sorry for the destruction to your life here. I know that most everyone you liked or loved probably perished with that town. But I've been through too much in my own life to give up a chance at a man like Sam. I've tried to hate him for being with you, but I can't." She shrugged. "There's no such thing as a scientific approach to love."

"I'm not asking you to give up anything," the girl insisted. Then she smiled shyly and unexpectedly. "In fact, though you probably won't believe this, either, I wish you the best of luck."

"Thanks. I wish you the same."

Dawn shook her head again, slowly. "You still don't understand. Someday I hope you will."

XII

"**I**'m beginning to get itchy, and it's not from living in this gelsuit," Merced said as he and Cora sat atop the familiar bemmy. They had their masks pushed back and were breathing real air. It seemed unnatural to Cora. The gaseous world was cold and harsh compared with the gentle homogenized environment below the surface. She was anxious to return there.

"There should have been an inquiry by now," Merced continued. "A skimmer ought to have arrived to check up."

"Not necessarily," Cora argued. "It may not arrive for another two, three days. Even if they tried to contact the town immediately after the disaster, it would still take time to decide that the quiet was due to some catastrophe rather than, say, to a power failure, and then more time to get a ship out here. Remember how long it took us."

"Why a ship? A skimmer would be faster."

"I know, but a skimmer doesn't have the carrying capacity of a—" She stopped in midsentence, staring.

Merced tried to see what had caught her attention. He located it as she identified it. "A skimmer would be faster, but not if there's a ship in the area."

Two dark blotches marred the southwestern horizon. Merced had a bad moment when he thought they might be whales coming back to make certain no one

172

had escaped. Then the slight spray from their flanks became visible. "Suprafoils!" He slipped his mask back over his head. "Thank goodness. I was getting sick of field work. Let's inform the others."

Together they dropped into the water, where their transmissions could be picked up by their companions.

Rachael was the first to rejoin them, towing the crate containing her neurophon. "I can play again! It's been too long."

"Withdrawal symptoms?" Cora commented sardoically.

"Yes." Rachael was too excited to respond to the sarcasm.

Dawn arrived next, followed closely by Mataroreva. "You sure they're foils?" He spoke to Merced.

"Unmistakable. Two of them."

"That's funny." He sounded puzzled. "I would've thought a skimmer from Mou'anui would have arrived first. It's too soon for a foil from Administration Dispatch."

"Probably these were fishing in the area," Dawn suggested hopefully, "When Mou'anui got the word." Her voice dropped. "Or rather, didn't get the word. They would come here if a general broadcast was made, as it should have been."

"Makes sense," Mataroreva conceded. "We'll know in a few minutes what they're doing here."

Cora frowned at him. "What are you talking about, Sam? You still subscribing to the theory that humans are somehow directing the baleens?"

"I'm not subscribing to anything except caution," he shot back. "We've nothing to lose by spending a little while longer in the water. We can wait a bit more. And watch."

They did so, clustered tightly behind the bemmy, their heads just above water. The pair of foils slowed, settled into the nearby section of sea where the town of Vai'oire had floated in peace not long ago.

Distant splashings reached the hidden watchers. Divers in gelsuits were dropping from both foils. Frantic activity marred the smooth lines of the two ships.

Cora pushed back her mask, spoke directly to Mataroreva, as he had insisted they all do. Suit-unit transmissions, he had declared, were too easily detected.

"See? They're looking for survivors." She moved as if to start around the mound of hexalate.

He put out a hand, grabbed her. "Maybe." He stared thoughtfully across the thin ridge that broke the surface. "But if they're searching for survivors, why haven't they broadcast their location?"

"Maybe they're just investigating, after receiving orders from Mou'anui to do so," Rachael suggested. "Maybe they know from previous experience that there are no survivors."

"Investigating for what?" Mataroreva went silent.

They had their answer soon enough. Divers began returning to their ships. Blocks and winches, magnetic and straight, were dropped over the sides of each vessel. Soon the men were hoisting individual crates and bits of selected debris on deck. The flotsam was then neatly stacked and tied down. It had the air of a well-practiced operation.

"Instrumentation." Mataroreva squinted across the sunlit surface. "Ah, and there's a couple of freshly sealed containers. What do they look like to you, Dawn?"

"Those are vacuum cylinders." Her voice was low, almost trembling. "They would hold fragrance extracts and spices: town cargo."

Mataroreva glanced over at Cora. "Do you think they're salvaging that stuff to put the proceeds of sale into an account benefiting surviving relatives of Vai-'oire's dead? Or maybe to raise a memorial to them? Look how fast they're working! They're pushing themselves to finish before the first official observers arrive.

"It makes sense now. Our first guess was right. We suspected either whales or men, but not both functioning in tandem. Somehow these people *are* controlling the cetaceans. I can't believe the whales are working for them of their own free will. They have nothing to gain.

"First the whales, their activities somehow coordinated by these vultures, destroy a town. Then their human Svengalis rush in and rake up anything of value. If anyone happened to stumble in when a town was under attack and get safely away, the cetaceans would get the blame."

"I can't imagine," Cora muttered, "how anyone could control and direct a large group of cetaceans like that."

"Neither do I. But I *will* find out."

"What do *we* do now?" Rachael asked.

Mataroreva continued to study the busy operation. "There appear to be about twenty crew per ship. Many of them are diving. Maybe we can take one of the ships. Even if we can't get away, possibly one of us might make it to the ship's transmitter. We could at least explain what's been happening. That would doubly alert all the other towns. Might even frighten these people off. We have one advantage anyway."

"I'd trade all our advantages for a beamer," Merced murmured, his right hand tightening around an invisible one.

"We know the reef," their guide continued. "We've been swimming over and through it for days. We'll head for the nearest foil at dusk. In the dark, we'll glow just like those pirates. They'll still be diving after the sun goes down, as anxious as they must be to finish up and clear out of here. If we can just get on deck before someone raises the alarm, we should at least have a good chance at their transmitter."

"I'm for the transmitter." Dawn looked eagerly at the nearest bobbing vessel. "I know communications.

I bet I can get off a signal faster than any of you. In the dark, if need be."

"Sounds good. We'll take the boarding ladder the last diver uses. I'm up first."

"No. Let me go."

Mataroreva stared in surprise at the soft-voiced Merced.

The little scientist continued with gentle relentlessness. "They may not have any oversized specimens in their crews," he explained. "Your suit glow will be the same, but your mass will not. I'm more normally built and less likely to be noticed than any of you. Also less intimidating."

Mataroreva considered, then nodded slowly. "You make good sense. Now, what about weapons? We can't chance jumping one of their divers. They'll probably work in pairs or trios, and one would be sure to sound a warning."

"There are some blue echinoderms on the bottom," Cora suggested. "They have three to five large poisonous spines. We can break them off at the base. The spines are pretty tough. Even if their toxicity fades after separation, they'll make serviceable knives."

Mataroreva smiled thinly at her. "I didn't think you'd notice such bloodthirsty details."

"Part of my job. And I'm not bloodthirsty. I'm mad."

An orange sun hung just above the water, fire balancing on a sheet of silvered clay, when they started toward the nearest foil. Mataroreva and Merced led the underwater procession. All eyes turned anxiously, seeking the telltale glow of another approaching diver. None came near.

They could not know how many of the crew remained aboard, but the craft offered little room in which to hide. Each was built for speed, with only a single modest forward cabin. Most of the area was open rear deck and cargo hold.

Two boarding ladders dipped like straws into the water on either side of the ship, one forward and one astern. The swimmers intended to mount the forward ladder, nearest the central cabin and the transmitter. That would also keep them away from the region of greatest activity near the stern, where salvage was being loaded.

Each of them carried a twenty-centimeter-long blue spine, four-sided, taken from an unlucky bottom-dweller. The spines would not stand repeated use. Mataroreva felt that if each spine found a throat, it would more than have served its purpose.

He articulated that desire at every opportunity, running his hand along the sides of his own weapon and making repeated stabbing gestures as they swam. Cora couldn't share his lust for killing, despite the ghastly crime that had been committed here. But she was quite prepared to wound.

They reached the hull of the suprafoil without a challenge, hovered beneath its bow. Gestures served in place of words. Merced moved upward and grabbed the bottom rung of the fore port ladder. Still there was no challenge.

As soon as he was clear of the water he removed his suit fins, but did not drop them. If he appeared on deck without them, he would attract immediate attention, whereas if he acted and looked like a normal diver, he might escape curiosity for a precious second or two longer. It was possible the divers on one boat knew those on the other only casually. And it was dark.

A minute passed while those remaining in the water waited nervously. Then Merced reappeared, leaning over the side and gesturing frantically. Mataroreva started up the ladder. Cora was right behind him, followed by Dawn and Rachael.

Then they were all standing on deck alongside the

only cabin. Lights glowed from within. They were not
interrupted by moving shapes.

The only sign of habitation was a limp figure on
the deck at their feet. Its head was twisted around at
an unnatural angle and blood trickled lazily from the
gaping mouth. Merced's spine-knife was unstained.
Mataroreva glanced curiously from the corpse to
Merced.

"I broke his neck. The opportunity presented itself," the smaller man whispered. Then he turned
and moved on, crouching like a spider.

Cora passed the body and wondered at the unexpectedly lethal talents of the wiry oceanographer. His
athletic ability had been amply demonstrated. Mataroreva, who knew more about such things, had
reached the conclusion that Merced was somewhat
more than merely athletic. But there was no time to
discuss such mysteries now. The real problem at hand
was far more prosaic in nature.

From the side of the cabin they had an excellent
view of the rear deck. Two men were studying a dark
gap into which an automatic crane was lowering a
basket filled with cylinders of varying size. There was
nothing resembling crew quarters. A couple of luminescent panels completely lit the interior of the cabin.
That was good. It made it difficult for anyone inside
to see into the blackness beyond.

Mataroreva bent around a corner and peered briefly
into the chamber. He turned and held up a single finger. Gestures and whispers followed. They would first
attempt to silence the single inhabitant of the cabin.
Then they would rush the pair monitoring the loading.
If the one inside the cabin managed to cry out, Merced would lead an immediate attack on the two load-
ers. It was hoped that the other ship was anchored too
far away to notice any screams.

They did not have as much success as Merced in
sneaking up on their quarry. One of the men operat-

ing the crane glanced back and stared straight at them. For a long moment he simply stood there, a puzzled expression on his face. His companion might have proved more voluble if given time. Instead, he had only seconds in which to gaze at them in shock.

They were indeed not used to the presence of survivors. It was good they were surprised as well as outnumbered. After so many days of moving horizontally through the water, the boarders had a difficult time running across a solid surface.

The second loader reacted. He wore nothing in the way of a weapon, so he hefted a slim, salt-stained cylinder full of supercooled argon and swung it in the general direction of the onrushing Merced.

The scientist's leg came around in an unexpected arc to connect solidly with the loader's forearm. The cylinder fell to the deck. Without pausing, Merced continued to spin, flying through the air. His back foot landed on the other man's chin. The man collapsed like a waterlogged steak.

Meanwhile, Mataroreva had returned from forward and was able to help Cora and Rachael subdue their antagonist. Neither woman had any military training, but each was sufficiently enthusiastic to keep the first loader occupied until Mataroreva could arrive to finish the job.

Breathing in long, painful gasps, Cora walked over to join Merced. "Odd sort of talent for a biologist to have. Do you find you have to knock out many fish?"

Merced grinned uncomfortably at her. "You know that sort of thing won't work underwater. Too much resistance. It's only a hobby. It's a good way to keep yourself in shape when you spend a lot of your time on your butt studying tape chips."

"Uh-huh." Cora did not sound at all satisfied, though the explanation was perfectly sensible. She watched as Rachael finished hauling a container they had brought with them onto the deck. It contained the best of the food concentrates—no crew quarters likely meant no autochef—and, of course, her damnable instrument.

"In any case," Merced began, looking down speculatively at the man with the shattered jaw, "I don't think that . . ."

"What's the matter? Pucara?" The biologist was gaping past her. He made a funny sort of gargling noise. Then his eyes rolled up and he toppled over onto his victim.

Spinning, Cora confronted two gelsuited figures standing on the foredeck. One flipped back her mask. She had short blonde hair, an unfriendly grimace, and a tight grip on the handle of the weapon she cradled. It was stubby of body, with an incongruously long barrel, all stinger and no bee. Cora recognized it readily enough. The gun was intended for underwater defense and used compressed gas to fire small darts. Each dart contained a powerful soporific. The intensity of the drug varied according to what one expected to have to defend oneself against.

As the woman had just demonstrated, the weapon worked very efficiently out of the water. It was tubed to her gelsuit airsystem, powered by the carbon dioxide from her own lungs.

Her slightly taller male companion stood alongside her. A similar device was held loosely in his left hand. The other was peeling gelsuit.

"Where did you people spring from?" The woman's query was a mixture of resentment and surprise. "You, fat boy—hold it right there or it's sleepy time for you, too." Mataroreva, who had started edging toward the railing, was forced to halt.

Rachael was kneeling alongside Merced, showing somewhat more than ordinary concern. "How strong was the dosage, damn you?"

"Not very. He'll sleep for a while and be good as new." The woman's tone turned threatening as she studied the two bodies by the hold opening. "That's more than you can say for Solly and Chan-li."

"We're from—" Cora started to explain.

Dawn cut her off quickly. "We're the last survivors of Vai'oire. Don't talk to us about sympathy."

"That may be." The woman leaned against the inner wall of the cabin. Her companion, Cora saw to her dismay, was already yammering into the ship's transmitter. "It's no concern of mine. We'll let Hazaribagh decide whether it's necessary to know where you come from." She smiled meaningfully. "There's no doubt in my mind where you're going. Though I may be wrong."

"You've killed several thousand people," Cora said angrily. "Why pretend you're going to treat the five of us any differently?"

That caused the woman to frown. "We haven't killed anybody. At least, I don't think so."

"What are you talking about?"

"I said, we haven't killed anybody!" The woman, to Cora's great surprise, appeared honestly upset. "I think that's about enough talking." The muzzle of her weapon swung several degrees to starboard. "And if you take one more step, fat boy, I'm going to put one of these into you. At this range I couldn't miss."

Mataroreva, who had used the conversation to gain another couple of meters toward the cabin, said quietly, "You keep calling me fat boy, and I'll make that toy pistol into a necklace for you."

"Okay." She took a couple of nervous steps backward. "Standoff, then. You keep your feet still and I'll do the same with my mouth."

For all her initial bravado, the woman did not strike Cora as a coldblooded member of a band of ruthless killers. What was going on here?

Undoubtedly they would soon find out. Other divers appeared, to desuit on deck while muttering with seeming confusion about the presence of the five

strangers. The subjects of their attention had been
herded together just in front of the open hold.

Mataroreva and a groggy Merced gave some
thought to their making a concerted charge for the
railing, figuring that if they all went in different directions, the woman couldn't hit more than two of them
before the others were well on their way to the secret
places of the reef.

It was Merced who finally vetoed the idea. Even if
three of them made it successfully over the side, these
people doubtless possessed at least the standard varieties of detection equipment. They were obviously
adept at ferreting out sunken valuables. It would not
be difficult for them to find a few divers.

A better idea might be to rush the woman, since no
one else had yet thought to bring up additional weapons. Unfortunately, this idea lost its appeal when five
more divers appeared, all of them armed with identical gas-dart weapons save for one. The latter carried
a squat device that projected explosive shells for dealing with particularly stubborn forms of sea life.

So the captives waited and pondered the possible
profile of the person the woman had called Hazaribagh, who would decide their fate. At least they
weren't to be murdered out of hand. And why should
they be? Hadn't the woman insisted she and her co-
horts had killed no one?

It seemed to Cora that the more they learned about
the destroyed towns of Cachalot, the less they knew.
It was like breaking an egg. Instead of finding a yolk
inside, they found two more eggs. And four inside the
two. And so on and so on, on to utter frustration.

A guard kept watch on them all night. In the morning they were given a surprisingly pleasant meal. Rachael asked for permission to take possession of her
neurophon.

The woman withdrew it from the watertight container but paused before handing it over. As Rachael

watched anxiously, the woman and another of their guards removed a back panel. The two of them consulted before the first dislodged a pair of tiny solid-state modules. Then the instrument was handed to its owner.

"Now you can play all the music you want," the stocky blonde told Rachael pleasantly, "but without neuronics. In the proper hands, that otherwise delightful device could be very disconcerting if someone knew how to maltune the projections."

"I wasn't thinking of that," Rachael protested indignantly.

"Maybe not. But I am."

The midday meal passed with the divers continuing their salvage operation. Soon after, another vessel appeared on the horizon. It was much larger than either of the suprafoils. It was also of old-fashioned but proven design. There were no foils. Beneath the double hull of the massive catamaran, a foil could fit neatly alongside hull doors and portals. There it could unload even in rough weather, shielded by the bulk of the mother ship.

The sleek mass anchored nearby and their foil pulled in underneath. Cora noted the blotches on the twin hulls and on the huge deck shading them. The craft was well used.

An elevator descended to the deck of the foil. They boarded and were carried up to the larger vessel's main deck. A walkway took them to a second deck near the stern. In addition to communications equipment and a recorder, they found chairs, tables, a portable autochef, and several very large men holding large guns.

There was also a small, dusky character clad in a khaki-colored shirt and vest. Several necklaces framed his thin brown chest and the white and black hair sprouting there. White teeth alternated with faceted red and yellow gems in the necklace. Straight black hair was combed directly back and tied in a knot with red and yellow cord. Extremely bushy white sideburns flanked the narrow, tiny face.

A thin black and white mustache curled upward toward ink-black eyes, was dampened slightly when the man took a drink from the tall metal glass on the table in front of him. He looked for all the world like an elderly bureaucrat on vacation. But his face, as he turned to inspect them, was troubled.

"Hazaribagh. Dewas Hazaribagh," Mataroreva murmured.

"Yes. Mataroreva, isn't it?" The man's voice was high, and as sharp as a paper cut.

Cora's gaze traveled from stranger to companion.

"Yeah, I know him now," Mataroreva said. "He manages this factory ship. Independent operator. The two foils are gathering and scouting craft for the big one, in case you haven't figured that out already. A modest operation, if I recall the lists right. Not the largest working on Cachalot, nor by any means the smallest."

"A correct appraisal," Hazaribagh agreed easily. "Honest folk trying to make an honest living by fighting whole floating towns financed by huge interstellar companies and big new ships bankrolled by wealthy merchant families. That kind of competition makes mere fiscal survival a matter of thin margin."

" 'Honest living,' " Dawn sneered. "I could laugh, if you hadn't just murdered every friend I ever had!"

"You're a former inhabitant of Vai'oire?" Hazaribagh looked shocked. "I was told, but I didn't . . ." His voice changed as he abruptly took a different tack. "Are you all former townsfolk? Which of you are and which of you aren't?"

No one said anything.

"Come, come, it really doesn't matter where you're from. I'm just curious." He pointed at Mataroreva. "Him I know from the planetary gendarmerie. The young lady who just spoke," and he indicated Dawn, "has confessed that she resided here. What of the rest of you?"

Cora, Rachael, and Merced remained silent.

"Well, you disappoint me. But as I said, it doesn't really matter. Keep your little secrets, if you must."

He looked back at Dawn, his fingers flicking away the condensation from the chilled flanks of the glass in his hands. It exuded a sweet aroma.

"I'm being perfectly honest with you. I said 'honest living.' Well, perhaps 'semihonest' would be more accurate now. But we're no mass murderers, no matter what you think."

"How do you do it?" Cora blurted, unable to keep her curiosity in check any longer.

"Do what?"

"Control the cetaceans. Order them to destroy—" She stopped. Hazaribagh was laughing. In the face of such callous indifference to death, Cora could say nothing. He did not laugh so much as chirp.

"Really, lady, you ascribe to me qualities and genius I truly wish I possessed. Sadly, it is not so. I am not the mad scientist of so many tridee thrillers. I'm not even a scientist. Only a businessman casually employing oceanographic technology. Certainly I don't have the knowledge to carry out mass murder, even if I wished to do so. Control the Cetacea? No one can do that."

"Then," Rachael hesitated, "then how? . . ."

Hazaribagh put up a hand for silence. Walking over to the upper deck railing, he stared in the direction of the reef and the former anchorage of Vai'oire Town.

"We happened on I'a immediately after it was destroyed. It was pure accident. There was no signal from them, no indication of trouble. We just happened to be in the area. We were utterly stunned by what had taken place, and the first thing we did was look for survivors." Dawn made a noise. He turned, glared hard at her, his voice rising.

"Yes, we searched for survivors! We suspected it was the whales. Maybe they hadn't perfected their method of assault yet—I'a was the first town to be hit. We saw a couple of big backs floating around. When the baleens noticed us, they vanished. Our sonarizer patterned them before they all got out of range. We noted fifty, and more had probably fled before we arrived. If they hadn't run as soon as we appeared, we'd have been the ones doing the running, I tell you.

"That was the first and last time we saw any whales near the towns. We found no survivors." Dawn said nothing this time. "Nor any bodies. It puzzled us greatly. Our first thought was to beam in notification of the disaster, but"—he spread his hands—"to what end? As I said, there were no survivors. And there was a great deal of very valuable material floating around our ship, preparing to sink or drift off into the sunset. What could we do but recover what was available? The ancient laws of salvage apply.

"After that, we tried to plot the location of towns which seemed near unusually large concentrations of baleen whales. We also learned that the attacks always took place under cover of storms."

"Just baleens?" Cora asked.

"We never saw any toothed whales," Hazaribagh informed her. "Most curious, I tell you. You would suspect them the most likely of all the Cetacea to plan and carry out such an attack.

"I want you to know also that we always searched for survivors, but never did we find any. At Warmouth, other vessels arrived before us. Vai'oire makes four out of five for us, however. A good percentage of prediction. Salvage is far more lucrative than gathering fish or molluskan products. We have several off-world buyers who are pleased to purchase our offerings, whether they be cargo the towns were storing preparatory to shipment or valuable electronics, or even personal effects. We are not discriminating, I tell you."

"If you're not controlling the cetaceans, then who is?" she wondered aloud.

"Why must anyone be controlling them?" Hazaribagh asked. Perhaps no scientist this one, but an astute observer of life. "Why can't they be controlling themselves?"

"Baleens are incapable of such concerted action," Mataroreva insisted.

The factory manager turned on him. "How do we know that? How much do we really know about the Cetacea beyond what they choose to tell us? Abilities may mature in a thousand years. Simply because a man does not talk is no indication he is an idiot. He may simply be a noncommunicative genius."

"Only one thing prevents you from receiving absolution," Cora stated. "You knew! You knew from the start that whales were responsible. If that information had been communicated to Administration on Mou'anui, then Vai'oire, Warmouth, and the others might have survived, knowing precisely what to expect. But you couldn't do that."

"Of course we couldn't," Hazaribagh admitted. "I don't see how you can hold us accountable for the nondistribution of knowledge. We've harmed no one. There's nothing criminal in opportunism, I tell you. If we had found survivors, now that would have presented us with a problem. But we never encountered any . . . until now."

He tapped the sharp edge of his chin with the rim of the cold glass. Ice clinked within. "Now there are five of you. A situation I hoped I would never have to deal with." He paced in front of them, gesturing with hand and glass. "You see, this has become an extraordinarily profitable operation for us. One I am loath to relinquish."

It took considerable courage for Cora to say, "By withholding this information, you become guilty of murder by oversight."

The accusation did not upset Hazaribagh. "Oh, I doubt that a Church court would convict us on that. If I were to let you go freely, however, it could complicate things for us by leading, as you say, to the prevention of such unfortunate incidents in the future. I am not sure we can go back to the ill-rewarding occupation of fishing. While I would not go about destroying towns with a casual wave of my hand, even if I could control the baleens, I think I could see my way to order the elimination of five embarrassments . . . I tell you."

Cora stiffened. So they were to be killed after all, though not for the reasons she had first suspected. It was small consolation to see Hazaribagh wrestling with the decision.

"You must try to understand my position. My people and I have made more profit in the time since I'a was destroyed than in our previous thirty years of licensing on Cachalot. We're not ready to give it up. And while we would not murder the town people, we of the boats bear no love for them, I tell you.

"As to why the baleens have suddenly become subject to organized mass insanity, I have certainly given it some thought." He shook his head. "I have no better idea than any of you. Unlike you, I do not much care, as long as they continue their actions. We have passed many whales, many baleen. None have bothered us.

"If we should eventually be discovered salvaging the ruins of some town, then and only then will we have to curtail our activities. But such an operation would make us guilty of nothing beyond illegal confiscation of private goods. The court would fine us and warn us, but that would be all.

"Three more months," he told them firmly, "at the current rate of destruction will enable my people and me to make enough credit to quit Cachalot forever and retire en masse to one of the pleasure worlds like New Riviera. Perhaps at that time," he added thoughtfully, "we will reveal what we know about the baleens' responsibility. Thus we will retire as heroes as well as newly wealthy."

In a perverse fashion Cora discovered she was disappointed. She had expected some extraordinary genuis to be behind all this. Instead, the only humans so far known to be involved had turned out to be nothing more than petty crooks.

"If you intend to quit in three months," Rachael pleaded, "why not just hold us for that time and then let us go?"

"I'm sorry," Hazaribagh said genuinely. "I don't think that would be good business. You now know all about our activities. Despite any promises you might give, I'm not sure I could trust you to be silent in this matter. I think it would be safer to dispose of you, much as I regret the necessity. As to the manner of your death, I think that it will be ascribed to the general destruction of Vai'oire."

Two guards shoved and pushed them toward the railing, then down to the lower deck. Hazaribagh followed. A section of rail was lowered, leaving them backed against the sea below.

"You could keep us for three months and then decide!" Rachael argued desperately. "We'd still be your prisoners. You could kill us any time after. Why spoil your claimed record of not having murdered anyone and maybe have some jealous crewmember expose you for it later in the future?"

"We don't have any jealous crewmembers," Hazaribagh informed her. "We suffered together. Now we're growing rich together. And we'll all be equally guilty." He stood back while the guards, who had grown to six, checked their weapons.

"We have reasonably efficient facilities on this ship

for processing large quantities of meat." He finished his drink, tossed the foil glass over the side. "We wouldn't want to spoil the whales' record of not leaving any bodies to be found. We'll process you as quickly as we can.

"As for holding you for three months and then deciding, why should I give such obviously resourceful folk as yourselves ninety days to escape or sow dissension or put out a call for help? If I kill you now, then I won't be troubled by such possibilities, and this unfortunate business will be off my mind, I tell you."

One of the guards stepped forward slightly and raised a weapon. Cora noted it was one of those that fired explosive shells, and tensed. Hazaribagh apparently meant to finish them off as quickly as possible. The guard sighted down the narrow barrel at Mataroreva.

Something huge and fast flew through the air like an ancient express train, blotting out the sun.

XIII

There were faint thumps. Half the gunman went one way. His lower torso and legs stood tottering on the deck while blood fountained everywhere. The immense shape landed on the planking, nearly breaking through the tough metal into the hold below. A second guard was crushed beneath it. The others fled in understandable panic.

Hazaribagh was stumbling backward for the nearest walkway leading to the upper level as four and a half tons of killer whale thrashed about and made a shambles of the stern deck, instrumentation, and any human being foolhardy or blind enough to come within range of flukes or teeth.

"Now!" Merced shouted, flipping his mask into place. "Over the side!" He turned and leaped for the water. Mataroreva, Dawn, and Cora followed. Once in the water they surfaced. Cora looked around for Rachael, finally spotted her still on the deck above. In a moment she joined them, preceded by a sealed container. Cora did not have to ask what it held.

"Have to replace those modules," her daughter was complaining.

Water geysered around them as three more massive black and white shapes exploded from the sea to join the first. The stern of the catamaran began to buckle under their combined weight.

Cora tried to right herself in the confused water, saw a huge shape rushing at her. There was an instant of unavoidable, primeval panic before she recognized it. The shape dipped beneath her and she slid back until she could clutch the slick dorsal fin. Merced was right behind her. The moment they were securely seated, the whale turned and accelerated. She thought to switch on her translator.

"Sorrry as the windds arre wwe to havve taken so long, sorrry arre wwe thhat wwe had to abandonn youuuu."

"Hello, Latehoht," she said weakly. "Never mind your timing. For some reason I just can't find it in my heart to criticize you."

The five of them were deposited alongside the abandoned catcherfoil still anchored off the reef. Cora slipped off the wide, slick back as another huge blunt head surfaced near them. Thick ivory teeth gleamed in the sun.

"Healthffullll?"

"Healthful we are, Wenkoseemansa, and thank you."

The whale disappeared, was soon replaced by his mate. Cora watched the Dantean scene taking place around the catamaran. "What about the? . . ."

"Badd mmen on shhip arre in flight rrather thhan fight," Latehoht sang lustily. "Sit somme within the rreeff whherre wwe cannot go. Thhey arre fearrful and hidden. Thhey will trouble you not, thhey will not bothher you. Onn thhe shhip stand fewerr and fewerr. Only in its depths hidde somme like their afrraidful brrethrren inn the rreef. Thhey mayy yet comme out. Wwe will kill thhen only thhose necessarrry. Did wwe wellll?"

"Most well." Cora saw Sam offer Rachael a hand up the foil's boarding ladder. The girl disdained the offer, instead carefully handed up the crate containing her precious instrument.

"Got to go nowww," Latehoht whistled. She nodded at her human friends, slapped the water once with her jaw, and dashed off to rejoin the fading battle.

They stood by the stern of the badly damaged ship and stared incredulously as a few of Hazaribagh's team attempted to regain control. The orcas were so fast that the hapless crewmembers barely had time to take aim with their weapons. One or two of the whales were hit by the hypodermic darts and had to be kept afloat by their fellows, but for the most part the resistance was as ineffectual as it was sporadic. It is difficult to aim at something hidden beneath the surface of the sea, more so when that something emerges like a rocket straight toward you.

Only one orca was badly wounded, by an explosive shell. The watchers near the reef could hear its cries for help via their headphone units. The fight shifted as the crew of the factory ship soon discovered that several tons of killer whale jumping at one's face inevitably had serious effects on one's aim. Those still resisting retreated to the second deck, where the prodigious leaps of the orcas couldn't reach them.

Hopes of driving off the attackers faded quickly for those on board. The moment the gunmen moved out of range, the orcas concentrated their assault on the interior of the twin hulls. Their attack had already sunk the second suprafoil. Now they pounded at the fibermetal hulls, working in relays. Eventually the constant pressure of many tons would breach one hull or the other and the factory ship, too, would sink.

The transmitter behind the watchers buzzed for attention. Mataroreva moved to the battered cabin, acknowledged the signal.

"Call them off!" a voice from the speaker pleaded. Cora recognized the anxious voice of Dewas Hazaribagh.

"Call whom off?" Mataroreva replied, thoroughly enjoying their former captor's discomfort. " 'Why

should I give such obviously resourceful folk as yourselves a chance to escape?' " he added, mimicking the
manager's former evaluation of their own status.

"Call them off, I tell you! We'll do whatever you
wish!"

"Of course you will. You can't bring weapons to
bear between the hulls unless you open the service
bays—which would promptly fill up with large, unwel-
come visitors. You're stuck, Hazaribagh. You'll last
less than most once you're all in the water."

"I will not beg for myself, but as for my people—"

"Uh-huh." He turned to the railing. "Cora, you tell
them."

She leaned over the side, adjusted her mask to
make certain she was speaking into her translator
pickup. Several strange orcas waited in the water
below. They looked up alertly when she spoke.

"Tell your companions they've done well enough.
Stop the attack." She looked back toward Sam.

He addressed the transmitter. "Throw all your
weapons over the side, Hazaribagh. You can worry
about salvaging them later." He pronounced the word
"salvage" in a particularly unpleasant manner.

Splashes began immediately, dotting the surface
around the assailed factory ship.

"Fine," Mataroreva told his distant listeners. "Now
all of you sit tight. I don't want to see anyone on deck.
You can drink yourselves into a stupor, commiserate
in groups, make love, do anything you want. But
don't try to start your engines or I'll have you sunk.
And once you're down in the water, I don't think I
could keep control of my friends."

"As you wish."

Minutes later a cetacean call sounded near the
bow. "Samm! Samm!" All whale voices sounded much
alike, but this one's pitch and phrasing Cora had
learned to recognize. The voice was that of a happy
Latehoht.

Mataroreva jogged out of the battered cabin, shouted a hasty "Take over!" and jumped over the side.

Latehoht swam delighted circles around him and he around her. He kicked water in her face and she spit it playfully back at him. Wenkoseemansa floated lazily nearby.

"Frriends comme behind ussss," he offered, noticing an intent Cora staring over the railing at the male-whale waterplay.

"I guessed as much," she murmured. "I didn't think you'd return with only cetacean help. Sam worried that you might not have escaped." She watched as the subject of her thoughts let out a whoop. Latehoht had slipped her tail beneath him, and the gentle flip that resulted sent him soaring through the warm afternoon air.

"What the hell happened?"

"Doing werre wwe whhat Samm hadd asked us to, had requested of ourr timme and abilities. We watched the waters frromm farr out in the Deeep, frromm distant lookking-places.

"Thhe Mad Ones whho kill swwam in silence. In grreaterr silence than thhat of any podd everr havve I known, everr has any whale known. Knew thhey exactly whhat they werre about, she-frriend Corra. Knnew thhey beforehand whhat thhey would do. It wwas . . ." and he sounded terribly confused, as well he had a right to be, ". . . it wwas not a thhing to bee beelived. I would not beelieve so, hadd not I witnessed it myselffff.

"Nothing thhey said, but camme thhey silent frrom all directions at onceee."

"A coordinated attack. But coordinated by whom?" Merced muttered from nearby.

"Neverr did wwe hearr thhem," Wenkoseemansa continued, "but instead felt at lasst the prressurre of thhem in the waterr, of manny comming frrom all dirrections. Could it thhus mean only one thing, could it therreby signify only one evvent forrthcoming. Chose wwe the seconds rremmaining to us to flee beforre wwe could bee encirrcled, forr in madness such as thhis even the Covenant could havve been brroken, and wwe would then do neitherr ourrselves norr you any gooodddd."

"I didn't think orcas were afraid of anything that lived in the sea," she replied.

"Fearr wwe nothing wwe can underrstand, but thhis was a thhing not to be underrstood. It is not wrrong orr cowarrdly to fearr and flee insanityyy.

"Fast as wwe did rrace, ourr passage was not unnoticed. Severral Mad Ones turrned frromm theirr courrse to chase us! Thhey werre Rights and thhink wwe one Humpback. And thhey chased *us!*" Astonishment filled his voice.

"Twwo to one, and wwe would havve turrned and fought, sizze notwithstanding. But therre werre sixx, and thhey did not act at all as thhe baleeen should. Faced werre wwe with suchh a horrrrible perrverrsion of naturral law, with events beyond ourr comprrehension, and with hundrreds of otherr Mad Ones nearrby, we determrined it best to find help for any thhat might surrvive. So gladdddened arre wwe to find you well! Knewww wwe thhat if any would livve, thhey would bee underr Samm's guidance.

"Chhased us forr many leagues did the baleen, forr a grreat distance and timme thrrough the waterr. Neverr havve I seeen such perrsistence of purrpose in a baleeen, let alone in severral acting togetherr. Outrran wwe thhem eventually. I believe had wwe turrned to the depths thhey would have followed and died behind uss. Had therre beeen among thhem Fins, wwe might havve beeen caught, forr is therre in the sea little that can outrrun a Fin whale. But therre werre none nearr us and had wwe a good starrttttt." He paused and Cora could almost hear him thinking.

"Sommething thhis is forr all the Cetacea to discuss, sommething thhis is thhat must be sent arround the worrld-ocean. Forr havve I no doubt thhat had those Rights caught uss, thherre would havve beeen a death-fight. A death-fight among Cetacea!" Mutters of disbelief swelled in Cora's earphones from the assembled orcas gathered around the suprafoil.

"Has upset sommething all of cetacean society. Has perrverrted ourr peaceful meditations sommething of grreat evil. Sommething thrreatens the peace wwe havve had forr morre than eight centurriessss."

Cora recalled a theory first propounded by her colleague Merced. "Could the catodons be controlling the baleens, directing these attacks for reasons of their own?" She expected a quick denial, but hardly the thunderous outcry that arose.

"No—neverr—it is not a thhing to be considerred!"

When the outrage had quieted, Cora spoke patiently to Wenkoseemansa. "You've just admitted yourself that the attack was not a thing to be considered. Yet *it* happened."

"Thhis is so-o-o," the orca confessed. "Yet sooonerr would I believe myself brreathing waterr than would I hold the catodons rresponsible forr such madnesses. Thhey arre closerr rrelativves to us thhan to the baleeen. Obstinate and stubborrn thhey arre, but not lacking in courrageeee."

"I understand what you mean." Merced crowded closer to Cora. "You're saying that if the catodons wanted the towns destroyed, they'd be doing it themselves."

"Thhat is so-o-o," Wenkoseemansa insisted. "Farr morre efficient and deadly would thhey bee thhan any baleeens could possibly bee. Would bee a lesser madness then thhan the otherr you say, forr no cetacean can control anotherrrr."

"Catodons don't think like us, or even like other

whales," Dawn said from nearby. "I'd believe anything of them."

"We've already learned a little about their indifference to mankind," Cora replied. "Destruction of a town would constitute interference of a sort they profess not to want. Destruction means notice, and they insisted they chose not to notice us."

"Still," Vai'oire's sole survivor wondered aloud, "as your friend in the water just admitted, something has upset the balance of cetacean existence. Something has to be directing the baleens. I don't for a moment believe they're doing this of their own choice." She chewed her lower lip thoughtfully.

"Could you tell," Cora asked, leaning over the side once more, "if anything was controlling the attackers?"

"If so, it was not noticeable to uss," Wenkoseemansa confessed. "But swwift wwe fled the region of Insanity, flying fastest through the waterr. Ourr thoughts werre on brringing back assistance and on surrviving until wwe could do so. Might well wwe havve missed such evidence as would provve the contention."

"If the catodons aren't involved," Cora mumbled, "and Hazaribagh's been telling the truth about simply following up on the destruction, then we're just about back to where we started: looking for some unknown, probably human, outside agency. Or some other off-world intelligence."

"At least we know it begins with the baleens," Merced commented. "There's another possibility we have to dispose of first." He addressed Wenkoseemansa. "You called the attackers the 'Mad Ones.' Have there been many instances of mass cetacean insanity?" Cora wondered how that might translate into orca, but apparently Wenkoseemansa understood, because he answered readily enough.

"Havve happened such thhings. In the passt parrticular, in ancient timmes, whole podds would commit

suicide, as did theirr ancestorrs in fearr of the geno-
cidal harrpooon. The harrpooon was long passt, but
the fearrs still lingerred. In ancient timmes men
thhought such mass strrandings of whales due to dis-
ease or weatherr, not realizing the cause was despairr.
Even so, in madness lies not the resourrces forr plan-
ning and carrying out such a vast, orrganizzed at-
tackkkk."

"I agree," Merced said. "Insanity could account for
the attacks, but if the baleens are insane, then they
can't organize well enough to mount those same attacks. Contradiction. Damn!"

While Cora still felt no particular fondness for the
little scientist, that didn't prevent her from sympathiz-
ing with him on the professional level. She fully shared
his frustration. "At least we have a beginning now."

A violent splash sounded beneath them. Wenkoseemansa was battering the water with his tail to get their
attention.

"Distant brrotherrs and sisterrs relay thhis newws:
the neww hummans commeeee."

"Distant?"

"Fearred wwe much the rreturn of the Mad Ones,"
he explained. "Brrotherrs and sisterrs patrrol much
distance away in watch forr thhem. But it is good
newws thhey givve nowww."

Cora was angry that she hadn't thought to suggest
such a lookout, consoled herself with the knowledge
that her thoughts never took a military bent. Somewhere behind all this, she thought furiously, lay minds
as cold as they were efficient. It was harder to believe
them cetacean than human.

Another vessel soon hove into sight: a long, sleek
suprafoil. It was considerably larger than the ruined
craft they waited on or the long-since sunken one that
had carried them out from Mou'anui a short eternity
ago.

They made preparations to meet it, moving the injured catchership alongside the catamaran. None of Hazaribagh's crew appeared to challenge them. They remained huddled below, mindful of Mataroreva's threat to unleash the orca pack against them a last time.

The four anxious researchers and single survivor waited on the empty deck of the factory ship to greet their rescuers.

Moving quickly up the ladder and the first man on deck from the larger foil was Yu Hwoshien, not the least embarrassed at revealing most of his elderly form in a pair of swim briefs. His eyes swept the deck, noting the absence of any but the five survivors.

Somehow the absence of clothing on an individual Cora had come to think of as the epitome of dignity was more shocking than expected. Divested of his black uniform of office, he was at once more and less human than he had seemed back on Mou'anui.

A host of armed, grim men and women followed him onto the deck. Cora recognized none of them, but they greeted Sam with a mixture of relief and deference. He directed them across the ship. The number of peaceforcers was sizable. No doubt additional assistance had been brought in for this rescue from other sections of Cachalot.

While Sam was directing the counting and recording of the factory ship's sullen, disgruntled crew, Hwoshien joined the other survivors. His attention went first to the one person among them he had not yet met.

"What of the town?" he asked Dawn simply.

She shook her head.

"You are the *only* survivor?"

"And that only because I wasn't in the town at the time it was attacked." She gestured limply to Cora and the others. "I was on the reef, guiding these people."

"We know the first cause now," Cora said. Hwoshien turned to her. "It's been baleen whales all along, at every town. They attack in military formations, as if they've been drilling for such assaults all their lives, and after each attack they disperse and disappear."

"But we still have no idea why they're doing this," Merced picked up for her, "or if they're doing so on their own or under the direction of someone else."

Hwoshien put both hands behind his back, wandered to the railing that had not been flattened by whale weight. "Another town," he finally rumbled. "Another population lost, more financial disruption and distress." He looked back at them. "The baleens are responsible, you say? That's bad. Very bad. We had already been told as much, but I wanted to be certain. Transmissions can be garbled and—" He stopped, breathed deeply. "Not that I doubted the source of the information, but I wanted to hear it directly from you."

"How could you have been? . . ." Rachael looked surprised at her mother's forgetfulness. "Oh, of course. Latehoht and Wenkoseemansa told you."

"The pair of orcas who operate with Sam, yes. Since whales were involved, and since in a thousand years no human has harmed one of the Cetacea, we thought that despite the severity of the situation it would be best to have one cetacean inflict an injury on another, if any had to be injured at all.

"There are always several pods of orcas hanging around Mou'anui, waiting for the chance to play with or inspect or work together with people. Latehoht and Wenkosee—whatever his name is—put out a call as soon as they told us what had happened. Locals put out the greater call to others of their kind."

"What do you think would have happened," Merced asked curiously, "if they had found the town intact but still under siege by the baleens?"

"I don't know," the old man admitted. "While humans and cetaceans no longer fight, the same is true ten times over for cetacean and cetacean. But even if they had elected, in such a case, not to interfere physically, they still could have talked to their cousins more effectively than we."

"It's all so frustrating," Cora burst out. "You make a dent in the problem and it makes a bulge on the other side of the same problem."

Hwoshien had turned to inspect the piles of unstored salvage on the factory ship's rear deck. "At least we know now what happened to so much of the valuable electronic equipment that disappeared from the area of the vanished towns. We suspected it had sunk into the abyss." He sniffed. "I would not expect such discrimination from people of this type, like this Hazaribagh."

"You know him, then?" Cora was surprised.

"Only by records and tapes. I recognized this ship readily enough. I know every ship and town on Cachalot. It's my business to know their business. But I would never have suspected such a modest operator and his crew to be tied into anything so extreme. He is not controlling or operating with the baleens, then?"

Merced nodded. "That's what he's said. We haven't had the opportunity to discover whether he's been telling the truth, but according to what we've seen and what you've just said, I would tend to believe him. So extraordinary an enterprise seems utterly beyond his capability. He's an opportunist, not a genius."

"We concur, then," Hwoshien said, "though, like you, I'm certainly not going to leave the matter at Hazaribagh's word."

"If he's lying," Cora said, suddenly concerned, "and he is after all controlling the baleens in some fashion, it's possible that . . ." Her gaze traveled nervously to the horizon.

"No, it's not." Mataroreva rejoined them, a beamer dangling from and almost lost in one huge hand.

"Latehoht and Wenkoseemansa's friends and relatives are patrolling far enough out to warn us in plenty of time if a single whale comes within ten kilometers."

Cora relaxed only slightly. The dozen peaceforcers looked very competent as they wrist-sealed the crew. But their suprafoil displayed only a single energy cannon at the bow. She doubted it would last very long under the assault of, say, twenty blue whales. The orcas were their best defense—assuming they would actually interfere with an assault by their larger cousins. If not, she reminded herself, the suprafoil below could outpace the fastest whale in the sea. So they were fairly safe.

Or were they? They had learned much. But Vai'oire had thought itself safe, too.

Only one thing kept Cora from asking then and there for transfer back to Mou'anui. While her fear was enormous, her curiosity was greater. That was ever the case with the scientist in the field, whose courage was born of brain and not of brawn.

"If this Hazaribagh person was controlling or directing the whales in any way, to any degree," Hwoshien was saying, "I should think we would have been attacked long before now."

"Yes, that makes sense," she agreed.

They followed the Commissioner of Cachalot as he walked over to confront Hazaribagh. The scavenger looked even smaller with his head bowed and his wrists sealed together. The chemical handcuff could not be removed except by a special solvent. The rest of his crew was similarly bound.

Hazaribagh looked up at Hwoshien, tried to assume an air of defiance.

"So," the older man began casually, "it seems you insist that you are not responsible for the deaths of several thousand innocent citizens."

"I've never killed a single person or had one killed." The ship leader sounded embittered by his sour luck. He threw a surreptitious glance at his former captives. "I confess that might have changed if your whales had not arrived when they did." He shrugged. "Who knows? Perhaps it's better this way. I had no wish to harm anyone."

"Or to save anyone," Cora snapped at him. "If you had no wish to do so? . . ."

"I told you why. For the chance to be wealthy. For the chance to sell this thin-seamed ship and get off this sweaty, salt-stink of a world!" He glared across at Hwoshien, the two men regarding each other like a couple of irritated banty roosters. "If I'm guilty of anything, it's withholding information. You can't even accuse us of not aiding survivors, because we never found any."

"We have only your word for that," Hwoshien replied ominously. "You were about to dispose of these good people to protect your activities. I wonder how many other inconvenient citizens you had to dispose of."

"None, dammit!"

"We'll find out when we question your crewfolk."

"Go ahead." Hazaribagh appeared unconcerned. "They have no reason to lie. And we still have the laws of salvage on our side."

"If you had adhered to them properly, you would," Hwoshien said. "But you did not report what you recovered for recording purposes. And salvage does not apply to, for example, personal effects, which are to be turned over to surviving relatives and which, I suspect, you have also heartlessly marketed."

"You can't prove any of that."

"We will. You just admitted that your people have no reason to lie."

Hazaribagh's defiance leaked away like sand through a sieve.

"You still insist you had nothing to do with the cetacean attacks?"

"Yes," he murmured. He looked toward Mataroreva, found no sympathy there. "I've already told him that. We're victims of circumstance."

"Victims of greed. You might have prevented the deaths of many people. What's done with you will be up to the courts, but they'll hear no cries of mitigating circumstances from me." Hwoshien turned to one of the nearby peaceforcers. "Put him on the other catcherfoil, together with any manifests or chip records you can find."

"What happens to my ship?"

"Nothing yet, though if you have so low an opinion of it, I wonder that you care. It will be sailed back to Mou'anui by your crew, under peaceforcer supervision. The courts will decide what to do with it as well as with its crew." Hazaribagh and the tall man guarding him started for the side.

"Just a minute." The downcast ship manager and his watchful attendant halted. "If you could give us some insight, if you have any idea what is causing the baleens to act in this inexplicably belligerent fashion, that might be a contribution in your favor the courts would recognize."

Hazaribagh's humorless laughter echoed across the deck. "If I knew that and admitted it, that would make me at least partly guilty of what you've first accused me of, wouldn't it? A neat trick." He coughed, said harshly, "I've not the slightest idea. My fishing experts have no idea. Mass insanity that comes and goes, manifests itself as rage against humanity? Who knows? Perhaps they are at last sick of mankind's presence in their ocean."

Cora felt disappointed. She hadn't expected any revelations from Hazaribagh, but she had had hopes. The ship manager was led down a boarding ladder to the suprafoil below. Hwoshien rejoined the others.

"Something else doesn't make sense," Cora told him.

"I seek clarification, not additional confusion," he muttered.

"In the attack we witnessed," she pressed on, "we saw two kinds of baleens—blues and humpbacks. Latehoht and Wenkoseemansa were chased by rights and worried about the presence of fins. Now, these are all plankton-eaters, but as far as I've read, they never school together. Joint schooling of, for example, humpbacks and seis is unknown. I realize that studies of Cachalot cetacean society are limited, but in all the preparation I did before we came here I didn't come across a single example of joint schooling."

"That's right," Dawn said excitedly. "Not only are they functioning as a group, the attacks involve mixed species."

"We've tried for weeks to find a purely scientific explanation," Merced said. They all turned to look at him. "Maybe we're going about this the wrong way."

"How do you mean?" Rachael asked respectfully, cuddling her neurophon. She had already been badgering the crew of the peaceforcer suprafoil for replacement modules for the instrument.

Merced appeared embarrassed, as he always did when everyone else's attention was focused on him. "We've been trying to find a biological explanation for the attacks. Now we intend to concentrate on the cetaceans. If we throw out the insanity explanation and assume there is some kind of intelligence at work behind all this, how would we go about determining the ultimate cause?"

"I'm not sure I follow you," Cora said.

"That's because you're still thinking in terms of cetaceans. We all are. Let's use the more obvious analogies rather than the less so. If a group of humans attacked a town but insisted they didn't know what they were doing, how would we begin to go about finding out the cause?"

"Capture one of them and question him or her."

Mataroreva looked at the little scientist approvingly. Merced nodded.

"That's impossible," Cora said immediately. "You can't restrain a blue whale without using something more than words. Even the use of a temporarily debilitating narcotic drug could be interpreted by the Cetacea as the use of violence. That would shatter the human–cetacean peace you're always telling us about. Anything milder than that, like a large net enclosure, would probably be torn apart."

"There must be some way," Dawn murmured.

Mataroreva looked at them thoughtfully. "There may be. You can't compel seventy tons or more of whale, but you may be able to convince it."

He went to the railing, slipping his translator unit back over his head. Loud squealing sounds rose from the water below, and Cora hurried, along with her companions, to adjust her own unit as they walked to the side of the factory ship.

Latehoht was already sounding. Moments later she returned, accompanied by a large, scarred male.

"Thhis is hhe whho is called Kinehahtoh," she informed them, "He-Who-Swims-Out-Front. Kinehahtoh of many battles, seniorr ammong the podd whho rescued you, as you requested, frriend Samm. Kinehahtoh the wise, who speaks forr the brrotherrs and sisterrs of the packkkk."

A surprise followed, for when she introduced the old male to the waiting humans, she used their cetacean as well as their human names. A touch ruefully, Cora learned that the name she had been given by Latehoht and her mate was Talsehnsoht—She-Who-Has-To-Know-Everything.

"Kinehahtoh," Sam began, "we must know why the baleens have been killing our people and destroying their homes."

"Surre you arre noww, surre beyond rreason or doubt, thhat thhey arre trruly rresponsible?" the patriarch inquired. Grandfather grampus, Cora thought, admiring him.

"I and my friends witnessed such an attack ourselves. A blue whale is not a cloud, to be mistaken for one. This is a truth-thing, Kinehahtoh."

"A trruth-thhat-is-not," the oldster agreed, shuddering. That quiver was ancient cetacean behavior, Cora knew. Not a reaction acquired from contact with mankind. "Though arre you knnown to us as one whho speaks the trruth, Samm Matarrorreva, this one and the brrotherrs and ssisterrs would not believe had not wwe hearrd it frrom two of ourr own. Would thhat I could will it not truth, yet what is, is, and cannot be wished awayyy."

"Then you understand our need to learn the cause behind this," Mataroreva said, "as we would yours if whole pods of the orca had been killed."

"Wwe underrstand, though it makes ourr hearrts fall to thhe ooze of the Deeep Places. Whhat would you havve us doooo?"

"We must ask the why of this terrible thing of one who was part of it." Kinehahtoh did not reply, lay waiting. "To do so, we must have the help of the orca so we do not risk the peace between man and Cetacea."

Still the old male did not speak. Finally he did so, choosing his words slowly and carefully. "One whho has beeen parrtnerr to so vicious a thhing may not wish to talk of it." Even in translation, the orca sounded distinctly troubled.

Matoreva took a long breath before responding. "That is why we must make this request of you. We cannot forcibly restrain a baleen to question it, as you well know. But if the pack assembled here were to gather tight around a single whale, as they have around this ship, there would be no fight."

"It could be interrpreted as a provvocation to suchh, a brreach of the peace, a challenge to the

Covenantt. Not forr a thousand yearrs has orrca tasted of baleeen. Wwe cannot rriskk the Covenantttt."

"I'm not asking you to," Matararoreva said quickly, before Kinehahtoh could set himself irrevocably against the idea. "There are fifty of the orca here. If so many were to surround a solitary bull, for example, what could be the result? The baleen thinks slowly. I suspect it would simply float in one place until the multiple obstruction was removed."

"I doo not knnow," the leader of the pack replied. "Not forr centurries has such a confrrontation taken plaaace."

"Just my point," Matararoreva pressed on. "The result wouldn't be anger. It would be confusion. The restraining need last only long enough for us to ask a few critical questions. By the time the baleen could make up its lumbering mind that it *might* possibly be threatened, maybe we'll have our answers and can leave it in peace. No one is being asked to fight anyone."

"A thousand yearrs of Covenant," Kinehahtoh murmured solemnly. "A thousand yearrs of peace ammong the Cetacea."

"The Cetacea as well as man are confronted with an unprecedented crisis," Matararoreva argued. "If men who do not understand the ways of Cachalot learn that the baleens are responsible, even indirectly, for the destruction, a greater threat to the Covenant will arise than any single confrontation could ever create." He did not add that since the cetaceans were fully protected, the trouble would more likely be between men.

"Will I askk the otherrsss," the old orca decided at last. His great head smashed into the water as he turned and vanished. Latehoht went with him.

Matararoreva clarified the discussion for Hwoshien, who had waited patiently nearby. Long minutes passed and still no sign of returning orcas. Cora wandered to stand next to Mataroreva and watch the sea. "What do you think they'll do, Sam?"

He didn't try to conceal his worry. "I don't know. As far as they're concerned, I've just made a dangerous request. It remains to be seen whether or not that will outweigh the threat posed by whatever is driving their larger relatives to madness."

"But they've already saved our lives once."

He smiled faintly. "Killing bad humans is a very different proposition from attacking or even threatening another whale."

"But we're not asking them to attack."

"I'm hoping they'll see that. If they don't, we may as well forget it and try something else. Not even Latehoht or Wenkoseemansa can change their minds once they've reached a decision."

Kinehahtoh returned. "The orrcas havve agrreed. Help you to finnd and encirrcle *one* of the baleeen wwe will. But iff it movves to escape," he warned, "orr calls otherrs to its aid, wwe will not trry to hold it. This abovve all must bee underrstood. Must not the Covenant bee thrreatened, or all will sufferrrr."

"Suppose," Merced asked disconcertingly, "the baleen we confront chooses not only to ignore our questions but to attack *us?*"

Kinehahtoh's instant reply left no room for misunderstandings. "Help and enjoy wwe worrking with hummans in many things. Butt wwe will not fight with cousins. Theirr actions arre theirr owwn. Wwe cannot interrferre. If one of the Grreat Whales turrns on you, you mustt cope with it as besst you arre abllle to."

"And you won't try to protect us?" Merced sounded more like a quaestor working a truthfinder during a trial than a biologist querying a killer whale.

"Must the Covenant bee kept," Kinehahtoh repeated firmly. "Follow noww, and wwe will huntttt." He turned away before Merced or anyone else could pose another question, to rejoin the waiting group of high dorsal fins stirring the water.

When informed of the orcas' limitations and the concurrent risk, Hwoshien did not hesitate. "Of course we have to go along. It is our best chance to find out what is driving the baleens to these deeds."

"And if a sixty-ton fin whale rushes our ship at forty kilometers per?" Mataroreva asked.

"You say the pack will not intercede for us. Then we'll have to take our chances. Dammit, people, it's *time* to take chances!" This was the first time Cora had heard Yu Hwoshien raise his voice.

"Could we outrun an attacking whale?" Rachael wondered, nervously running fingers over the strings and switches of her neurophon. The projectors were silent. Only aural music floated across the deck.

"Depends on its nearness at the moment of attack and on the type of whale," Mataroreva informed her. "A humpback, certainly. Probably a blue. A fin— that I can't say for certain. Over a short distance it would be a near thing. I agree with Hwoshien, though. It's a risk we have to take."

XIV

Peaceforcers and prisoners, catcherfoil and factory ship, all were soon cruising back toward Mou'anui and a distant justice. Hwoshien and the others boarded the peaceforcer suprafoil and followed in the wake of the searching pack.

Several days and nights of beautiful weather and dull sailing ensued. Working in tandem with the sophisticated tracking equipment on board, the orcas located first one solitary whale, then a second. The first turned out to be a humpback, the other a minke. Neither knew (or claimed to know) anything about the attacks on the floating towns. They were allowed to depart before they grew aware they had been restrained.

On the sixth day Wenkoseemansa split the water in his haste to report that half the pack had encircled another baleen and urged it to the surface. Their reluctant quarry was already confused and irritable. It would be best for all concerned if the humans were to hurry.

As Mataroreva and his companions checked out their translating equipment, the suprafoil swung around and sped toward the section of ocean specified by Wenkoseemansa.

Before very long the gentle rise of a small island broke the horizon. As they drew nearer, the island developed a modest geyser, whereupon it was clear to all on the slowing ship that the island was solid without being land.

Over thirty-five meters in length and weighing well over a hundred tons, the sulfur-bottom, or blue whale, lay at the surface and considered his unprecedented situation. He looked quite massive enough to Cora to fight off all fifty orcas, even if for some reason they elected to contest such a battle. A nervous twitch of that enormous tail would make a metal patty of the ship.

He was barely moving in the water. While Cora couldn't make out the tiny eye through distance and sea, she supposed it to be rapidly scanning its surroundings with considerable unease. The encirclement by the orca pack could only be interpreted by the creature as a potentially threatening gesture. It was up to Cora and her companions to obtain the answers to their questions before the solitary bull decided the threat was anything other than potential.

When the suprafoil coasted alongside, taking care to approach the living mountain from near the head and not the dangerous tail, he shifted with ponderous uncertainty. Initial conversation was opened by the orcas. The cetacean-to-cetacean conversation was strange to Cora's ears, even in translation. In comparison with the rapid speech of the orcas, the blue's was turgid and slow.

Wenkoseemansa asked most of the questions, swimming right up to the gigantic, striated jaw, which dwarfed his entire sleek body.

Meanwhile, Cora fiddled with her translator, struggling to bring sense out of cetacean chaos. Each species had its own whistles, its private clicks and colloquial howls. The translators converted the blue's chatter into a kind of stupefied pidgin that sounded unintentionally comical.

"You Great Brother know attacks on human-town,

on human-people?" Wenkoseemansa seemed to be asking. "All human-people their-kind killed and gone away. Great Brother savvy?"

There was no response. Hwoshien spoke around the pickup of his own translator. "Another blank. Is it possible all the whales who participated in the attack on Vai'oire have already fled this region?"

"Gone to another town, maybe?" Merced wondered worriedly. No one felt like commenting on that ominous possibility.

But the baleen finally answered. The reply was made with assurance, though with typically maddening slowness. "This One Great Brother savvy Little Cousin query. This One Great Brother aware muchly of attack on human-towns. This One Great Brother much sad at death of human-people, yes, muchly much."

"You One participate in attack?" Wenkoseemansa inquired carefully, his muscles tensed in expectation. "You One help kill?"

"This One participate," the blue said with appalling coldness, not to mention an obvious indifference to whatever the little knot of listening humans might choose to do. But while the whale's tone as conveyed by the translator contained no empathy, neither was it bellicose. Some of the crew shifted nervously at their stations. The helmsman's fingers tightened around Scanning screens on the suprafoil showed the tiny dots the controls.

Yet the blue did not move, remained peacefully if uncomfortably in the center of the hemisphere of orcas. He's so calm, Cora thought in admiration. Does he know we could kill or severely wound him? The energy cannon at the bow was purposely not aimed at the baleen, but it was manned. It could be adjusted to fire over and down in an instant.

Maybe he has even now sent out a distress call to the hundreds of others who participated in the attack on Vai'oire, Cora thought. That's absurd, she corrected herself. Any such call would have been intercepted and reported by the orcas, if not by the detection equipment on the ship.

"What for, Great Brother, you kill human-people?" Mataroreva asked, taking over the process of questioning from Wenkoseemansa. "Human-people Great One's friends. No attack, no threaten, Great One's self or children. What for Great One and Cousins do such terrible-bad thing?"

Slowly, with unexpected pain, the sulfur-bottom replied, "This Great One don't know. Subject hard to consider."

The orcas could not frown, but Cora received the same impression from the puzzled chatter that circulated among them.

"But you did participate?"

"This One did."

"Did kill?"

"Did kill," the blue agonized. "Don't know why. This One no know. No inner-savvy why This One attack. Hard think-back."

"Something-someone convince you attack?" Mataroreva pressed. "What say?"

"No savvy."

"Great One attack-kill human-people, what cause Great One do so? *Who* tell Great Ones do so? *Try* savvy." Mataroreva stared over the railing as if he could will the great whale to answer.

"Savvy . . . hard is. Hard think-back. Dark waters. No can straight savvy." He shook his head slightly. Sudden swells rocked the suprafoil, and those on board grabbed for support. "Hard think-back. Mind hurt bad. No sense makes." Again the head twitched and the entire body shuddered, throwing water over the low deck of the nearby ship. Clearly the immense creature was becoming frustrated and upset. *"No can remember!"*

The whale spun and the foil threatened to capsize
In the water the orcas fought hard to hold their posi-
tions against the powerful swell. Cora hung on tight to
the rail with one arm and wrestled to reduce the volume on her translator. The blue's voice was growing
deafening.

"Attack—kill—no like! No choice but. *Had* to do.
Ordered to do. Think-back hurts! *Leave now. This
One!*"

Up went the great flukes, like some huge gray bird.
Down went the head as the whale arched his back.
of the orcas sprinting out of the way as the multiton
bull plunged rapidly and unhesitatingly for the
silence of the depths.

Gradually the water calmed. The ship ceased rocking. Cora slipped her translator back on her head. "So
the whales are apparently not responsible. Someone is
directing them."

"Whoever it is can compel them to attack a town,"
Merced murmured thoughtfully, "but we can't compel
a single one to explain his actions."

"I still don't see how you can compel something
that weighs a hundred tons," Rachael insisted. "Let
alone dozens of them."

Cora snapped at her without meaning to. "Thoughts
don't weigh much. I think it's pretty clear we're up
against some kind of mind control. Something that can
force the cetaceans, but not people. Otherwise whoever's behind this could simply direct the inhabitants
of each town to blow themselves up. The Commonwealth watches anything having to do with central-
nervous-system or mental-modulation research very
tightly. But as isolated as the cetaceans have been in
their mental development here, by their own choice
—that would make them a perfect subject for anyone
wishing to try out such a control system."

"Not only doesn't it affect humans," Merced observed, "I would guess it doesn't affect the toothed

whales, either. Certainly not the orcas and the porpoises, probably not the catodons and their relatives."

"Not yet it doesn't," Cora said grimly. "Maybe it's not perfected yet. Maybe the catodons will be the next subjects, together with the orcas—and then us. We can't break this precious Covenant, can't even chance it, but I can think of some that ought to be ready to risk it, for their own sakes."

"We can't," Mataroreva protested immediately. "We tried it once and got nowhere."

"We know more now. I should think the catodons would be interested. They ought to be, if they know what's good for them."

"I keep telling you," he said tightly, "they don't think the way we do. No matter what we've learned, regardless of what we might say, they'll see it first and foremost as another attack on their privacy, on their thinking time. We might try another pod—"

Cora shook her head. "It has to be the same one we talked to before. We can't take the time to establish a relationship with a new pod, even assuming we could locate another one, and we can't take the time to go over old ground again. It has to be Lumpjaw's pod."

"They could consider a second attempt a provocation," he warned her. "They as much as told us so."

"Do you have a better idea?"

"No, I don't have a *better* one!" he shouted angrily at her. "But I don't have any as dangerous, either!"

Legally they were now subject to local administrative directives. So the question was formally put to Hwoshien.

"Let us try it," he finally told them. "It offers us the best chance of obtaining a solution fast."

"It also offers the best chance of eliminating our now experienced research team," Mataroreva argued. "If we get in among the herd and they then decide on a

unified attack, we won't have a prayer of getting out
alive."

"I am willing to trust the Covenant," Hwoshien replied. "I do not *think* they will break it this time
merely to protect their right to privacy. And our new
information may indeed, as Ms. Xamantina says, in-
trigue them."

"There's no telling," Mataroreva muttered. "You
know people, Yu. I know cetaceans. A group of people wouldn't react violently to the mild intrusion we
plan, but we're dealing with different moral standards,
with a different scale of values. I'm certain of nothing
except the catodon's unpredictability. Maybe it's the
smartest of the Cetacea, but it's also the most volatile."

"I have an obligation to protect the living,"
Hwoshien said firmly. "We not only require a solution
to this, we require one *now*. I cannot risk another town
in the name of caution." He adjusted his own translator and walked to the railing.

"Wenkoseemansa—Latehoht—pack leader." Two
familiar shapes instantly flanked the ship. They were
soon joined by a larger third: Kinehahtoh. Hwoshien
explained what they wished of the orca's. When he
had finished, Kinehahtoh spun distress in the water.

"Bad thhing is thhis, a woefful prroposal you
makke. Not at all goood. 'Tis bitter to thhe taste of the
packk.

"Like we not the catodons overrmuch, like they us
still less, and saltted is theirr irrritation with con-
temmpt. But theirr dislike of us is as swweet schools of
golden *madandrra* to the taste comparred with theirr
dislike of hummans. Dangerrous, woefful dangerrous
is this idea." He stopped spinning and splashing, gazed
up at the humans lining the low rail.

"Knoww you thhat if the catodons choose to vent
theirr discontent, wwe cannot prrotect you. Know you
thhis well! Even did wwe wish to, wwe could not. Arre

firrst among the Cetacea the catodons, whho alone in the sea arre strronger than the orrcas."

"We understand your position," Cora said, "but we have no choice. We've come to a dead end."

" 'Deadd end'?" a puzzled Kinehahtoh echoed.

"A place that cannot be swum through, like the bottom of the sea," Mataroreva explained helpfully.

"Awwwh. Underrstand wwe noww *yourr* positionnn."

"Can you find them, then?" Mataroreva asked expectantly. "The large pod we conversed with so many days ago?"

"Can find prrobably, cann overrtaaaake."

"Then do only that much for us," Hwoshien put in, "and the orcas are released at the moment of contact from any obligation to us." Mataroreva whirled on him, gaping.

"This Kinehahtoh has already restated their position, Sam. Close your mouth. There's no point in asking them to risk their precious interspecies Covenant. As he told us, the orcas couldn't protect us even if they wanted to. I don't want them holding any bad feelings against us if this doesn't work out." He turned back to the water.

"Take us to them. That will be sufficient. We will do our own talking."

"Fooolish thhing is thhis," Wenkoseemansa said, leaping clear of the surface and landing with a tremendous splash. "Fooolish. Arre therre not otherr ways, otherr means, to learrn the answwerrs you requirre?"

But no one could think of any, though all tried as best they could as the suprafoil sped northwestward, following the pack of coursing black and white shapes.

By spreading out, the orcas were able to search a tremendous volume of ocean, backed by the long-ranging sonarizer of the suprafoil. Even so, they located the pod sooner than even Hwoshien might have hoped. The catodons could be leisurely travelers, often following schools of food rather than any straight course. Also, they were hindered by the presence of many calves, which the hunting orca pack had left safely behind.

Cora, Hwoshien, Mataroreva, and Dawn moved to the bow of the ship as they neared the herd. Cora found herself wishing the other, younger woman had remained behind. She still had not accepted Dawn's insistent claim that she had no permanent designs on Sam, less so that Sam held no interest in her. Cora had too graphic a proof of the latter.

A call came to them from inside the cabin. "Twelve kilometers and closing."

"Thank you, Mr. Asamwe," Hwoshien replied crisply. His attention was also directed forward. "Yes, I can see the spouts." Cora strained, could make out nothing against the sea and sky. Whatever Hwoshien's age, there was nothing old about his eyes.

"I don't see them."

He pointed. "There . . ." and then he frowned slightly. "No, I don't see them any more, either. I thought they might do this."

Sure enough, the report soon confirmed the truth. "Reporting again, sir. The pod is sounding."

"All of them? Calves included?"

"It shows here," the crewman said. Hwoshien did not reply, continued to stare over the bow, his back as straight as an iron bar and his stare as cold.

"Well, they can't stay down for much more than twenty minutes," Cora murmured. "Not with calves." She turned and surreptitiously eyed Mataroreva. The big man was tense, obvious worry creasing his usually rotund, jovial face.

"They'll come up a damnsight sooner than that, once they've decided we're not going to leave them alone."

He's worried, she thought. Worried but not frightened. Never frightened. Morally innocent, but an admirable man nonetheless. One of the few. She might be just the one to cure him.

Wenkoseemansa was back paralleling the ship, leaping to confirm what the sonarizer had already reported.

"Why bother to sound?" Cora wondered. "Surely they know we're aware of their location. They can't lose us."

"Could be several reasons." Mataroreva studied the horizon. "They might be showing their displeasure and just incidentally giving us the chance to change our course—and our minds. Or they might not care one way or the other, since we haven't actually disturbed their activities with our presence yet. It might be a normal feeding dive." Now he smiled slightly. "It would be just like them to surface all around us and ignore our presence entirely, not to mention our questions."

Minutes later the helmsman reported, with admirable calm, "We're right over them, sir."

"Hold just aft of the pod, as near as you can."

"Yes, sir."

The suprafoil slowed. They cruised just behind their submerged quarry for another fifteen minutes before detection reported again. "They're coming up, sir."

"Good," Hwoshien said into the nearby com. "Keep us posted, please."

"Still rising." A pause, then, "Shouldn't we move a little farther aft of them, sir?"

"No. Hold your position and speed."

"Changing course, sir—they're going to come up all around us." Still no panic in the crewman's voice, though the words poured out a bit hastily, Cora thought. Impassive, Hwoshien said nothing, continued to stare interestedly over the bow.

"Twenty meters. Fifteen." The engine raced.

"Hold your position," Hwoshien ordered firmly. "Show them we're not concerned. They know they're

not surprising us. Don't show them otherwise. Besides,"
he told Cora, "it's too late to do anything anyway."

"Five . . . four . . ." the technician counted down.
"Three . . . two . . ."

Calm sea, tolerant sun, a few white clouds conversing in a sky as blue as a blade of azurite, made up
the momentary universe. Then it was filled with a
sight few humans had ever been privileged to witness.

With intelligence had come more than thought. It
brought with it an aesthetic sense, coupled with a
unique unity of purpose. The entire pod, some two or
three hundred adult, adolescent, and juvenile cetaceans, breached simultaneously. One moment the sea
was calm and the air deserted. The next, it was filled
with two hundred thousand tons and more of gray-
brown flesh.

The pod hung suspended in the air for a second no
onlooker would ever lose track of, before falling convulsively back into the sea. Wet thunder shook the
somnolent sky. The displacement of air was enough to
knock everyone off his feet. Only the fact that the pod
was now evenly distributed around the ship kept it from
being capsized. Still, all the silent efforts of automatic
stabilizers and gyroscopic compensators were required
to hold the suprafoil level on the surface.

Everyone knew that had the catodons so chosen,
several of them could have landed precisely on the
ship itself. The vessel would have vanished beneath
the sea, to rise in thousands of fragments minutes later.
Instead, it was the pod that rose, like several hundred
gigantic corks, to dot the surface with dozens of temporary islands. They did not remain, but cruised steadily on their unchanged course. The helmsman jockeyed
constantly, trying to avoid ramming the whale immediately ahead without being overrun by the ones just
behind.

A new sound filled the air, dozens of explosive
whooshes and pops as the pod flushed the built-up

carbon dioxide from its lungs. An organic fog momentarily obliterated the sky above the patch of disturbed ocean, until the gentle breeze dissipated it forever.

Hwoshien said into the com unit, without any change of tone, "Easy ahead, helmsman. You're doing fine. Don't screw up." He appeared completely unaffected by the titanic display of power and unity they had just been treated to.

Vast, sliding bulks hemmed the ship in. The majority of them were larger than the foil.

Mataroreva still looked worried. "What's the matter?" Cora asked.

"I know what you're thinking, but it's not the catodons now. I don't see Latehoht or Wenkoseemansa or any of the orcas."

"They said they wouldn't interfere. I expect Kinehahtoh and the rest of the pack accepted Hwoshien's offer to stay out of this."

"I know, but still, Latehoht and her mate . . ." His voice trailed away. A surprise, she mused. For all his railing about the cetaceans' different method of thinking, he still half hoped his two friends might have chosen to stay with him instead of with their kind.

Cora found her thoughts turning more to the minds of the catodons than to Sam's. What was their state of mind now? If she could see inside those massive brains, what peculiar, alien concepts would she share?

As yet they might not know that she and Sam and those who had intruded on them before were once more among them. Hwoshien's ship was larger than the little research vessel that had originally carried them out from Mou'anui. How irritable would they be? More importantly, how intractable when it came time to ask what had to be asked?

Mataroreva slipped down his translator unit. "Time to talk, before they make up their minds to do anything."

Cora adjusted her own, as did Hwoshien and Dawn.

Rachael and Merced rejoined them, already properly equipped for interspecies conversation.

It was decided that Matatoreva would speak first, as before. He leaned over the portside of the bow, chose a subject, and shouted hopefully, "How goes your journey, youngling?" The translator could interpret that query several ways. It might refer to the journey for food, the whale's personal odyssey, or the catodonian journey through life. She guessed that he left it purposely indistinct, perhaps to provoke a questioning response.

A very young whale, no more than four meters in length, responded by angling for the flank of the ship.

"Human ones, I have never seen that—" A vast mass suddenly appeared beneath the juvenile, nudged it aside.

"Will you talk, mother?" Matatoreva hurriedly inquired of the female who had interposed herself between ship and offspring. She and the infant slid away, and what she replied was not translated effectively.

Matatoreva managed a tight grin, however. "Scolding the child, I would guess. Trying to keep him from the evil influence of human beings."

Abruptly, a gigantic bulk emerged alongside the ship. A vast skull, larger than most of the creatures that had dwelled on the Earth or in its waters, reared above the surface. Cora immediately recognized the gnarls and whorls that slashed it, like markings on some ancient tree.

"Greetings, old one," Matatoreva offered in recognition.

"Human, I Know You," a vast, sighing voice said through Cora's headset. The eye set back and just above the wrinkled jaw flicked across the railing. "I Know Most Of Thee. We Did Talk To Little Purpose Not Long Ago." Lumpjaw paused, considering how to proceed.

"We Did All Our Talking Then. Why Dost Thou

Disturb Us Yet Again?" No one could mistake the urgent edge to that question, nor the implied threat behind it. Normal catadonian apathy was changing to anger.

"Thou Tryest The Patience Of The Pod. We Will No More Talk With Thee. Go—Now!" he finished emphatically. "Or We Will Not Be Responsible. We Know The Laws And Will Make Use Of Them! Nor Depend On Thy Small Servants To Help Thee. They Are Well Away From This Place And Would Not Help Thee If They Could, For They Also Know The Laws."

"What is there for them to help us *from?*" Matatoreva asked with an ease he did not feel. "If we are not friends, at least we are not enemies, for we have not harmed you."

"Thou Interruptest Thought, Thou Breakest Concentration, As Thou Didst With That Youngling, Thou Lengthenest The Great Journey!" the furious old cetacean stormed.

"We know and we're sorry," Matatoreva replied quickly. "We just want—"

A massive pair of flukes slammed dangerously near the ship, dousing everyone on board. "No More Talking! No More Wasted Time! Life Is Short!" Cora found herself wondering at their perception of time, since a healthy catodon could live well over a hundred years, as this patriarch probably already had.

"We Go This Side Of The Light-Giver. You Go The Opposite Way. Go *Now!*"

"That's enough," Hwoshien grumbled outside his headset. "We'll have to find another pod to question, or look elsewhere altogether." He yelled dispiritedly up at the helm. "Slow turn to starboard and quarter speed ahead."

"Yes, sir," the helmsman acknowledged; he needed no urging to comply.

"Wait," Cora pleaded with the Commissioner. "We

can't give up now. We need to ask only one or two questions."

"I'll take a reasonable risk," he replied carefully, "such as entering this pod's area. I won't risk a warning such as we've just received." The engines whined behind them.

She looked imploringly at Mataroreva, found no comfort there. "He's right, Cora." He turned away from her, spoke to his superior. "We might have a chance to locate an isolated . . ."

Cora looked wildly around. Anxious crewmembers were rushing preparations to depart. Mataroreva continued to converse in low tones with Hwoshien. Rachael fingered her neurophon and chatted with Merced. Only Dawn appeared unoccupied, and she was staring interestedly at the herd, not at Cora.

Frustration, loss, Silvio, Rachael, pride, and the eternal burning desire to slay ignorance that so often plagued her combined to push desire past reason in the mental race for attention that was screaming inside her head. Impulse overwhelmed rationality.

There was a zero-buoyancy rescue disc tied to the railing. She unlatched it, put her other hand on the rail, and vaulted over the side of the ship. The last words she heard were a startled scream from her daughter and a Polynesian oath from Sam.

XV

Her arms threatened to tear from her shoulders as the float disc sank only a few centimeters before bobbing insistently to the surface. She hung on, struggled to adjust her headset translator as she sucked air and climbed onto the stabilizing disc. Though the water was reasonably comfortable even out here in mid-ocean, she still felt cold without her gelsuit.

As she attempted to get into a lotus position on the disc, water cleared from her eyes and she discovered she was sitting not more than a few meters from a gray promontory. That towering cliff swung slightly toward her as it sensed her presence. Near the line where cliff-head met water, an eye the size of her head impaled her with an unwinking stare.

She froze on the disc. Too late now to reconsider, too late to apply reason. But commitment did not breed action. She could only sit motionless and stare back.

The cliff came close to her legs, the entire enormous mass balancing in the water with wonderful delicacy. Behind her, shouts of confusion and worry formed a meaningless babble on the ship. The sounds might as well not have been there, for all the attention she devoted to them. Only she and that curious eye existed.

Rows of white teeth a fifth of a meter long lay partly exposed in half-opened jaws. The slight movement of the whale in the water sent swells cascading over her legs and hips, but the disc's stabilizers held her level.

It required no effort to concentrate wholly on the creature before her. She wished she could see what was going through that huge mind, what emotions if any lay behind that speculative eye. Another impulse, perhaps less rational than the one which had forced her to jump overboard, induced her to reach out a tentative hand. The old catodon did not pull away from her touch. The feel of the skin surprised her. It was smooth and slick, not nearly as rough as it appeared.

"You Fell," a voice in her headset claimed, strangely noncommittal.

"No. I jumped." She wondered if the translator would convey her nervousness along with her words.

If it did, the whale gave no sign that it mattered, for all he came back to her with was, "Why?"

"You may not like us," she began, her mind functioning again. "You may not like *me*. But I am doing only what you or any member of your pod would do, defending the endangered and the calves."

"There Are No Weak, No Injured, No Calves On Board Your Float," the whale said.

"No, but there are calves on other floating towns as yet unharmed, healthy ones who stand to be injured, and all who are endangered. I have to help them now, before it's too late."

"So Thou Riskest Thyself To Learn. Preventive Sacrifice." Cora trembled a little, wondering what the whale meant by the use of the word "sacrifice."

"Noble. We Do Not Generally Think Of Humans As . . . Noble. Are These Questions Thou Wouldst Ask So Vital, Then, To Thee?"

"Not to me. To the endangered, to those who stand to die."

She waited tensely for the catodon to reply. He had

quieted behind her, as everyone on the foil waited breathlessly for the drama to resolve itself.

Eventually the old whale said, "What, Then, Be A Question In The Scheme of Things? I Waste Time With Thee. Yet The Pod Will Progress, The Pod Still Thinks. Ask What Thou Wilt, Female."

Cora tried to stop shaking. For a moment she marveled that the cetaceans would bother to distinguish sexual characteristics among humans. Then she hurried on.

"First I have to tell you," she said, feeling like an ant addressing a man, "that we know for a fact that the baleen whales are destroying our towns. We don't know if any of the toothed are involved. If you doubt this, ask your small cousins who travel with us." Silence. "Did you know this?" she added.

"We Did Not Know This," the whale replied. "Yea, Why Should We Believe Thee Or The Cousins Who Slave For Thee?"

"They don't slave for us and you know that," she snapped back, affecting an invulnerability she did not possess. "They would never lie to you, and you know *that*. Certainly not on human account."

"They Indeed Confirm What Thou Sayest. Normally The Doings Of The Baleen Are Of No More Interest To Us Than The Doings Of Mankind . . . But . . . This Is A Most Interesting And Disturbing Thing. Very Difficult It Is To Believe."

"I myself witnessed one of their attacks. So did my close companions." She gestured back toward the now crowded railing of the suprafoil, where Mataroreva and every other member of the crew stood watching in mute fascination. "They acted in unison," she continued, "according to some prearranged, thought-out plan. Blues, fins, humpbacks, rights, probably seis and greenlands and all other plankton-eaters. We saw none of your people among them, as I said."

"Naturally Not!" the old one roared confidently.

"No Catodon Would Participate In Anything So Foolish, To No Philosophical End. And Thou Sayest The Baleens Acted Together? This Is Not Possible. Our Great Cousins Have Not The Intelligence."

"Something has the intelligence," she insisted, "because it happened. Someone is directing them, instructing them in what to do. We found one who actually participated in at least one attack. It admitted this, yet could not explain why it did so. Whoever is controlling and directing the great whales in these attacks is doing so without their consent."

"That Is Possible." The old whale sounded a touch tired. "But As I Said, The Doings Of The Baleens Are Of No Real Consequence. It Is Interesting, But That Is All." He slid deeper in the water, preparatory to submerging.

"Wait! Think a moment, Lumpjaw. Anything that can control the baleens against their will might soon also manage to control your people."

"That Is Not Possible." He spoke with maddening self-assurance.

"Probably the baleens think the same thing." She slapped the water angrily, a pitiful gesture that nonetheless made her feel better. "You pride yourselves on your privacy, your chosen isolation and time to think and philosophize. You've elected for yourselves a special nomadic, noninstrumental existence and seek to develop your own kind of civilization. Don't you see that whatever's controlling the baleens is a threat to that, even if you're right and it can never control you? Mightn't it turn the baleens against you, as it has turned them against us?"

"I Have Said That We Will Not Concern Ourselves With The Activities Of The Baleens, Nor Do We Fear Any Actions Of Our Large But Harmless Cousins."

"Harmless?" She tried one last time. *"How do you*

know what they might be capable of under outside control?"

Silence for a long moment, and then a bellow that rang around inside her head.

"PEOPLE!" She forcibly reduced the volume in her headset as the shout reverberated inside her skull like a ball-bearing in a steel globe. "Thou Nearby Have Heard." Answering replies came from at least three dozen cetaceans. Cora had considered the conversation pirvate, but come to think of it, why shouldn't many others of the herd within range have listened in? Were not the catodons developing a cooperative society?

"What Think Thou," he finished, "Of This Unprecedented Anomaly?"

"Yes," she said loudly, "and what are you going to do about it?" She fervently hoped she was not overstepping her thinly stretched luck.

A great deal of rapid intercetacean communication generated a verbal blur in her ears, too rich and rapid for the translator to handle.

Finally the wrinkled brow turned to her once more. "We Shall Question The Baleens Ourselves About This Peculiar Matter."

"I told you we already tried that," Cora reminded him. "With a big sulfur-bottom bull. He admitted the attack, admitted being directed, but didn't know how or couldn't say how it was accomplished. Thinking about it gave him a whale-sized headache."

"All Thoughts Upset The Baleens. They Do Not Like To Think. They Only Like To Eat. Feeding Occupies Too Much Of Their Time. But We Will Question Them." He said it in such as way as to hint that Cora and her friends were guilty of either a wrong approach or collective stupidity. Well, that was fine with her. She had achieved as much as she had dared hope.

But the catodon added something completely unexpected, unhoped for. "Thou And Thy Companions May Come Along If Thou Wish To, Though I Cannot Say When We Might Encounter Any Of The Great Cousins."

"Thank you. We—" But the great head sank like a stone. Then Cora felt herself rising. She was preparing to jump clear when the ascent leveled off. She found herself moving toward the ship. Ahead, crewmembers ran in panic to left and right. The head beneath her dipped slightly. She slid a couple of meters to the deck, landed on her feet, and sat down awkwardly. The float disc clattered next to her.

Mataroreva was the first one to reach her, lifted her to her feet. A smile told him she was all right. She shook free, moved to the rail in time to see the massive skull slip back into the water. A vast, fathomless eye rolled at her. The old leader issued a high, squealing sound the translator could do nothing with. Then he vanished beneath the waves.

As if directed by a single source, the entire herd began moving northwestward. Their pace increased rapidly. Gigantic backs raced and rolled past the suprafoil, coming withing centimeters of its hull. None actually made contact.

Having also listened in on the conversation, Hwoshien had the presence of mind to order, "Slow ahead, helmsman. When they're completely past and a kilometer out, match speed and maintain that distance!" The suprafoil's engines hummed. Soon it was racing in the wake of the herd like a silver waterstrider.

Mataroreva stood near Cora, towering over her. Yet he no longer seemed so big. "That was a very stupid thing to do," he said quietly.

"Yes, I know." She ran the absorbent cloth across her legs, began drying her hair. "But we had no choice. We knew that the catodons were our best bet for finding out why the baleens were doing what they were. Our toothed friends didn't know, as it turns out, but maybe we're all going to find out together."

"Stupid," he reiterated, but it was muted by the admiration in his voice and in his face.

"Why? What would it have mattered to you if something had happened?"

"It would have mattered, *vahine*."

"Sure. It would have mattered no matter who had been in the water, right?" Not wanting an answer, she slipped past him before he could offer one she wouldn't like.

Dawn was waiting to confront her. She stared the older woman squarely in the eye, said, "That was the bravest thing I ever saw anyone do."

Cora hesitated, then smiled. "I didn't think of it as particularly brave. Sam was right. It was a stupid thing to do. I was lucky." Then it hit her, in detail, exactly what she *had* done. "In fact, I didn't think of it at all. I just did it."

Behind them both, Merced was nodding understandingly.

Cora was standing in the bow, watching the spouts and backs leading the ship. Mataroreva had rejoined her and they watched together.

"What do you think will happen when the catodons confront a baleen or two the way we confronted the blue, and demand an explanation?"

"I've no idea," he said slowly. "I don't think they'll risk the cetacean peace. But as you've already seen, they can be considerably more forceful than most of their relatives. And where the orcas couldn't do anything with that bull, a couple of catodons could."

"You think the baleens might fight rather than talk?"

"No way of telling. Normal relationships are being upset on this world." He nodded toward the distant, curving backs of the herd. "It's awkward, though.

They might risk a breach of the peace to sate their curiosity, but they won't do it to save a thousand human lives. It would be easy to learn to hate them for that."

"That wouldn't bother them, either," she reminded him. "They don't care at all how we look at them."

"Self-centered egotists," he muttered.

"Not necessarily. Maybe they're right."

"How so?"

"Maybe we're just not very interesting."

They went quiet, each absorbed in personal thoughts. A pair of familiar shapes raced the ship to port. Wenkoseemansa and Latehoht had rejoined them. The rest of the orca pack, they explained, had turned back for Mou'anui. They had come to rescue human from human. That task accomplished, they saw nothing to be gained by remaining with the suprafoil. And they found the company of their supercilious cousins wearying.

Somehow the sonarizer operator managed to keep a scan ahead of the cluster of blips that identified the leading pod.

"There's something out there," he reported over the communicators.

"Baleen?" Mataroreva asked quickly.

"Big enough to be. And there's more than one showing. I read five or six."

"Species?"

"Too far for resolution."

The catodons had sensed them, too. The herd turned with precision and the foil angled to remain with them.

As the distance closed, the sonarizer operator continued to report. "I make out seven now. Not humpbacks. Not rights. Fins or blues. Ten . . . no, close to twenty now. Fins, I think."

By now the lead catodons should be in verbal con-

tact with the baleen pod, Cora knew. "Fins could out-
swim them," she murmured.

"If they haven't by now, that means some of the
pod are on the other side of them, and probably diving to get beneath them," Mataroreva replied speculatively.

The fins did not try to swim away, though they
were the fastest of all the whales. But they did not
stop to answer questions, either. What they did was so
shocking that both humans and catodons were
equally stunned.

A sound echoed through the long-range pickup and
over everyone's communicator. A sound that Cora recognized as a whale in pain. Mataroreva was pointing
wordlessly over the bow as others ran to join and gape
alongside them.

Ahead, the water was churning as if disturbed by
the explosion of a series of heavy charges. Huge forms
breached clear of the sea and vast flukes battered the
innocent waters. The helmsman slowed the foil without waiting for formal orders. Commotion and chaos
made froth of the ocean around the ship, jolting it and
inhabitants unmercifully. If they had been traveling
among the pod instead of behind it, they would already have been swamped.

From the speaker emanated sounds diversified in
their anguish and all too familiar.

"What's going on?" Dawn wanted to know, arriving
out of breath.

"I don't believe it!" Mataroreva told her above the
cetacean screams and the noise of great bodies in collision. "I don't believe it!"

The fins were attacking the catodons.

If the humans on the foil were stunned, the pod of
catodons was more so. Surprise and shock rapidly gave
way to instincts equally basic, and they began to defend themselves.

Charging at great speed, a pair of fins would attempt to catch an unwary catodon between them. But they were badly outnumbered, and in any case, at a real disadvantage in having nothing to bite with. Nor were they constructed for butting, the only form of attack they could use against another whale. The more intelligent catodons soon overpowered their cousins.

All at once the fins ceased their assault.

The sonarizer was of little help now. Crowding the bow, the onlookers stared anxiously at the quiet surface as the craft moved slowly into the area of combat. It was left to the orcas to relay the critical information back to the ship.

"Noww havve thhey stopped theirr obscene activities. Now havve thhey ceased to do battllle," Latehoht told them.

"What are they doing now?" Cora asked.

"Lie thhey in the waterr devoid of movvement or response." She went quiet for a moment, then, "Wenkoseemansa says the catodons do quesstion thhemm. Says he thhat the Great Cousins appearr dazzed and lifeless, unawarre of whhat thhey havve just done. Unawarre to the point whherre thhey cannot feeel even outrrage at thheirr actions." Her voice was full of disbelief. "Woefful thhing is thhis. Sadness fills the waterrs. Not since thhis worrld was given overr to us has cetacean fought cetacean."

"I'd like to question them myself," Cora murmured.

"Out of the question." Mataroreva moved closer, perhaps to reassure her during a nervous moment, perhaps to be ready in the event of an unexpected leap at the railing. "Remember Vai'oire. Keep in mind that this bunch has just acted completely crazy and could do so again, and we're much closer now. We'll remain right where we are and let Lumpjaw and his brethren ask the first questions."

"The baleeen pod leaderr," Latehoht was saying, "knowws not whhy thhey attacked theirr cousins the catodons. Awww . . . theirr reaction if not theirr mo-

tivation is noww clearr. They arre ashamed beyond
measurre. They say they werre driven, forrced to attack, as if . . . as iff . . . thhey cannot descrribe it,"
she concluded.

"Never mind how," Merced said quickly. "Tell
Wenkoseemansa to see if he can learn *who* compelled
them to attack."

Latehoht passed the request on. Minutes went by.
Instead of answers, the water erupted in violence once
more. The helmsman was hard put to keep them from
being swamped by the behemoth shapes that filled the
sea around the ship.

"*Now* what?" Hwoshien wondered aloud, spitting
out salt water.

"Commpletely mad thhey havve gone!" a shout
sounded in their headsets. Latehoht maneuvered to
avoid ship and catodon alike. "They fight noww to
fleeee."

"They mustn't all escape!" Cora yelled frantically,
struggling to avoid being thrown overboard as the
suprafoil rocked and heeled against the best efforts of
the stabilizers. "We must hold *one* of them at least!"

But Latehoht was now too busy protecting herself
to relay requests or information. Those on board had
to content themselves with holding on and hoping.

The second fight raged for five minutes before a
calmer Latehoht was able to report, "Endded it is.
Evven whhen restrrained by teeth, the Grreat Cousins havve torrn themmselves away. Too much blood
darrkens the waterrrr."

"They got away?" Cora moaned, her muscles aching from the battering she had received from railing,
deck, and cabin wall.

"Not all. Twwo—no, thrree rremain. Four. Twwo
females and twwo calves."

"Crippled?" Mataroreva inquired.

"No. Exhausted utterrly wwerre thhey by theirr attemmpts to escape. Surrounded arre thhey now by the entirre catodon pod."

"Four, and two of them juveniles." Cora looked earnestly at the big man nearby. "We have to question them ourselves, Sam. The catodons don't seem to have done too well."

Frowning, the peaceforcer turned to Hwoshien. The Commissioner said nothing, conveyed nothing via his expression. It was left to Mataroreva.

The suprafoil moved forward. None of the catodons questioned its advance. Indeed, several of them moved to leave it a clear path. Wenkoseemansa and Latehoht flanked the vessel, ready to cry a warning if the four remaining fins should unexpectedly find the strength and will to attack again.

A wall of enormous bodies and slick backs hemmed the captives in. Cora knew the encirclement continued below them.

Lying on the surface and breathing heavily were the two females. A single calf hovered close to one. Both adults were supporting the other calf between them, keeping it up in the life-giving air. The lateral fins and flukes of the females were marked by catodon teeth, though the wounds did not appear serious. The calf they supported was doubtless the reason why they were unable to escape. All four shapes were proportionately longer, slimmer, and lighter in color than those surrounding them.

Cora noticed a familiar mass nearby, leaned out, and yelled via her unit, "May we question them?"

"Madness Reigns! Madness This Is! Do What Thou Likest," the aged leader of the pod announced. But his anger was muted by curiosity.

It took a minute to locate the proper setting on the translator. Then she called out to the four streamlined shapes. "Mothers of the Sashlan! Why have you attacked your cousins? Why have your people and the others"—she gave the names of the additional baleen tribes—"taken to killing humans who mean you no harm?"

The nearest grooved head swung toward the foil. The helmsman twitched, his hands tightening on the controls. But it was not an offensive gesture.

"Don't . . . know." The female's voice held overtones of frustration as well as exhaustion and pain. "Horrible things drive Sashlan and cousins. Mind hurts!"

"Hurts how?" was all Cora could think to ask.

"Deep inside. Thinking blurs. Hard to focus. Easier to let other thoughts rule actions."

"Who?" Merced was so intense on the question he was trembling. "Who is confusing your thoughts and bringing you the mind-pain?"

"Mind *hurts*," the agonized voice protested. "Not to tell."

"If you tell us," Cora ventured, "we can make the mind-pain go away."

"Would be good thing. No like killing humans. Not enjoy fighting Cousins of the Teeth."

"This thought-thing. Did it just direct you to attack your cousins, and when that failed, to flee?"

"Yes. Hurts *bad* think about this."

"We'll make the hurt go away," Cora insisted, praying they could do so. "Just tell us who is—"

"Directions," the voice gasped laboriously. "Directions come CunsnuC."

Cora looked expectantly at Mataroreva, who could only shake his head, baffled.

"What is the CunsnuC?" she asked.

"Don't know," the whale said. "Mind-pain hurts!" The female began to ramble, in a voice pathetic for so massive a creature. "Make mind-pain go away. Calf hurts. Mates hurt. All hurt! Can't . . . fight."

"If you can't identify it," Mataroreva asked hopefully, "can you show us where this CunsnuC is?"

"Will show!" the fin emphatically said. Then she

added in wonderment, "Yes, will show. Pain going now. Feel better. Will show, will show, will show. Not supposed to, but will." Without further comment, the two fins, still aiding the weakened calf between them and the healthier one nearby, began to swim slowly northward.

Mataroreva thought to say something to the pod, but there was no need to. It had listened and understood. A path opened for the fins in the ring of catodons. But they remained grouped close around their four guides, aware the fins might lose their determination and try yet once more to flee both captors and the mysterious pain that assailed them.

The suprafoil followed. Whale backs rose and fell in regular, symmetrical curves against the horizon.

Two days later they were startled by an announcement from Wenkoseemansa. He was cruising alongside, easily keeping pace with the ship, when he shouted in surprise, "Painnn!"

"Mind-pain?" a concerned Cora asked the moment she reached the railing.

"Yess. But it is not bad, not unbearrable. Feeeling it too arre the catodons, feeeling it and rremarrking on itttt."

"How bad is it affecting them?" Mataroreva stared over the bow. Only curved spines and open sea met his stare.

"Not overrmuch. Morre surrprrised thhan hurrt they arre, morre currious thhan injurred. A feww swwam into each otherr, but to no real hurrt. Thhey arre resistingggg."

"The mind control. But it's not working on them. That explains why there were no catodons, or orcas or porpoises, participating in the attacks on the towns. Their minds must not be as malleable as those of the baleens. They can fight off the effect."

"We still don't know who's behind this." Merced

spoke from nearby. "We only have a meaningless word."

"I do."

They looked over their shoulders. Yu Hwoshien stood there, hands behind his back, staring speculatively over the side at the sweeping backs and consistent spouts of the pod.

"I've devoted some considerable thought to it," he continued. "Off-world agents. Some group or organization that wants all humans off Cachalot."

"The AAnn?" Cora suggested, shivering a little at the thought that humanxkind's persistently probing reptilian adversaries might be involved.

"It's possible. But not certain. We might be dealing with another group of humans who think they can slip down here and glean the wealth of this ocean world without any interference or supervision once the existing operations are wiped out. Hazaribagh's type, only on a much more extensive and smarter scale. Or some organization with motives we are not yet aware of."

"Won't they try to escape now?" Rachael wondered, cuddling her instrument protectively. "They must know that we're hunting them, that their control over these four fins has weakened. They try to compensate by taking control of the catodons, but that isn't working."

"I considered that," Hwoshien said. He permitted himself to sound slightly pleased, a break in his usual mood. "Two independent monitor satellites have been tracking us ever since we separated from Hazaribagh. As soon as we began following our new guides, I ordered a Commonwealth patrol ship to join the watch." He jabbed a thumb skyward.

"It is up there now, waiting and in contact with us. Anything that attempts to leave the surface within a radius of a thousand kilometers of this ship will be picked up and intercepted. If they try to escape by traveling under the sea or by skimming its surface, the satellites will eventually locate them and direct the patrol to their flight path. All surface vessels of known origin have already been plotted and accounted for.

"Yes, they will try to escape. But they will not." He considered a moment, added, "It would be better for them to surrender to us and take their chances with a court before the catodons find them. Or any of the locals."

It was an evaluation none commented on. They didn't have to. The proof was visible for all to see in Dawn's eyes.

XVI

Another day passed before the fins began to show signs of slowing down. The catodon pod slowed with them.

"Verry bad noww thhey say the pain iss," Latehoht relayed to those on the ship. "Feeeling it also arre the catodons, but theirr pain iss overrwhelmmed by thheirr angerrrr."

"Is this the closest they can guide us?" Mataroreva asked. He searched the horizon. There was no sign of any ship or floating installation. Yet the baleens' continuing agony was proof that the source of that same pain lay near. "Below the surface somewhere," he muttered. "That'll make it harder."

"Ask them—" Cora began.

Latehoht interrupted her. "Can askk no more. Cann hope forr no morre help," she said sorrowfully. "Mind-pain prroves too much, too long." No one said anything.

"Calf die firrst, then otherr youngling. Females go last to the Sea-That-Is-Always-In-Night. Verry woe-fful mad arre the catodons. Most furrious is theirr leaderrr. But therre is nothing they can do.

"CunsnuC is herre. Beloww. But tooo deeep forr the catodons, tooo deeep forr the orrcas."

"How far?" Mataroreva inquired. Latehoht could not say. If the catodons couldn't reach the source, he knew that it must lie more than a couple of thousand meters down.

"We need to make a decision," he said to Hwoshien. "Whoever's down there won't wait forever before making their own. If they try to escape off-planet, that's fine. We're ready for them. But what if they're gathering all the baleens within their controlling range? Several thousand might show up at any time. Under cover of another massed attack, the perpetrators might be able to get away, out of the grid established by our monitors. So we must try to force them to the surface."

"I concur, Sam. But they may not come up readily. Obviously they're prepared to function at considerable depths."

"So are we," Mataroreva reminded him. "Even the threat of a small explosive charge should be enough to drive them up. I'll wager they'll take a court rather than explosive decompression." He spoke into his com. "Can you find anything down there?"

"I'm scanning all the way to the bottom, sir," the sonarizer on duty replied. "We're over an abyssal canyon. Drops eight thousand meters in spots, and it's fairly broad. But I'm not picking anything up. Either they're located in a cave in the side of the canyon, or beneath an overhang, or they have sophisticated anti-detection equipment. None of the towns reported anything."

They never had time to, Cora thought.

Hwoshien gave orders. A thick, stubby vessel was swung up and out of the suprafoil's hull, lowered into the water. It had curved wings laterally and straight paired ones above and below that gave it the appearance of a sunfish crossed with a Terran manta. Its hull was reinforced duralloy, the same material that made up the skin of starships.

It could dive all the way to the bottom of the canyon, and considerably farther if need be. Usually it carried no weapons, being a creature of science and not of war. But along with the usual complement of exploratory devices, it also carried several small but powerfully shaped charges for rock detonation. One such charge properly placed could dent the submersible's own incredibly tough epidermis. Several properly placed could breach it. Or any similar hull.

Hwoshien insisted on joining the exploration. Sam Matatoreva would go along in his capacity as the local authority's principal representative. Merced, Cora, and Rachael all were able to handle deep-diving submersibles, and in any case, had not come so far to be denied a look at their tormentors. The only argument over procedure arose when Rachael insisted on taking her neurophon. There was some acrimonious discussion between her and her mother in which "neuronics" and "neurotic" became confused, but eventually Rachael had her way.

Cora had gained no support from her companions. The submersible was surprisingly roomy, designed for a crew of six. While it could not be called spacious, the five of them managed to move about without bumping into one another. And the gentle music provided by Rachael was welcomed by most as they commenced a long descent into total darkness.

Matatoreva and Cora operated the controls. At three hundred meters Wenkoseemansa and Latehoht gave wishes and farewells before turning back. A cluster of large catodons continued to descend with the craft, turning back one by one as the air left them. But by now the submersible had long since entered the realm of night.

Instrumentation continually probed the depths below, and continued to reveal nothing. Powerful lights flashed only on startled fish and other denizens of the dark.

Lumpjaw strained muscles and lung capacity to accompany them to nearly twenty-one hundred meters before he was forced to turn surfaceward. He startled them all by wishing them unmistakable, if indirect, good luck. It was the first kind word one of the great whales had spoken to them since Cora had been on Cachalot. Extraordinary circumstances, she reflected, always prompted extraordinary reactions.

Darkness reached its limits, pressure did not. Yet despite the inhospitable surroundings, life continued to thrive, further testament to the burgeoning fecundity of Cachalot's world-ocean. Fantastically illuminated life-forms swarmed around the submersible, alternately drawn to or frightened and confused by its lights.

"Four thousand meters." Merced hovered near Cora's shoulders, studying the console.

An incredible ribbon of pale blue and green luminescence spasmed a path past the thick ports. It seemed endless, though she estimated its length at about twenty-five meters. It was perhaps five centimeters thick save near the bulging jaws that were filled with dozens of thin needle teeth.

Star-dotted balloons drifted by, avoiding relatives with stomachs larger than mouths. Others possessed more teeth than seemed reasonable for such small creatures, while a couple mooned at the sub with eyes larger than the rest of their bodies.

At forty-five hundred meters Cora thought she heard distant antique church bells. At forty-eight hundred meters the ringing had become a steady hum. At five thousand meters it was as if she had people seated on either side of her, whispering frantic nonsense into her ears. The sounds were not words, nor were they spoken by people.

"Trying to control *us*, whoever they are," Merced declared. "Irritating, but nothing more. Like listening to loud music for too long."

"I agree." Mataroreva eased back on his controls. "It's not working for them, though."

Five thousand six hundred meters.

"We're practically on bottom here," Mataroreva grumbled. "Our scan's been omnidirectional since we started down. Even if they were hiding in some cave or beneath an overhang, we'd have detected them by now. There's nothing here."

"That's right," Cora agreed readily, sounding tired. "Whoever they are, they must have fled when they realized they couldn't control us. Might as well surface and try another place."

"I fear you are both correct." Hwoshien was understandably disappointed. "We gave it a good try. Perhaps other baleens can relocate them for us."

Mataroreva reached to adjust a control to begin their upward climb. Just before he fingered it, a small hand locked on his wrist. He looked back in surprise at Merced. The little scientist wore a very puzzled expression.

"Wait a minute, now. Don't you think this retreat is a bit premature? I'd hardly say we're practically on the bottom. We've another several thousand meters below us. Let's go at least another thousand before we give up here."

Mataroreva regarded him as one would an idiot child. "I said that we're nearly down."

Merced continued to eye him uncertainly. " 'Nearly'?" He used his free hand to indicate the computer picture of the bottom and the figures nearby. "We're at fifty-six hundred. Scanner shows this abyssal canyon drops to eight thousand in places. We're only a little over two-thirds of the way down."

Mataroreva sounded distinctly irritated. "You heard what I said about our omnidirectional scanners. I say we've already done the best we could. We'd only be wasting time here if we go farther. Better to try another spot."

Merced looked at Cora. "You feel the same way?"
"Of course!" She had never liked the researcher.

His present inexplicable obstinacy increased that dislike.

"And you, and you?"

Rachael nodded solemnly. Hwoshien said, "We've done as well as could be expected. If there ever was anything here, it's obviously gone now. We frightened it off."

Merced let go of Mataroreva, moved carefully toward the rear of the chamber. Cora wondered if his shy control was beginning to crack. She found herself looking around for some kind of weapon.

" 'If there ever was anything here'?" Merced said, echoing the Commissioner's accent as well as his words. "Not only *was* there something, but I'll wager it's still present."

"What the hell are you raving about?" Mataroreva started to get up from his seat. "Listen, I don't know what's going on inside your head, Pucara, but maybe you'd better—"

From an inside pocket Merced produced a very tiny but efficient-looking gun. "These darts are miniatures of the ones Hazaribagh's people threatened us with, but they'll still put a grown man flat on his back. I'd rather not shoot anyone."

His right eye was twitching slightly and he looked nervous and worried. What his aghast companions could not know was that the worry stemmed not from Mataroreva's near charge. His nervousness came from something that screamed along his nerves and hammered at his brain, trying to get inside. It promised to soothe him, that voice did, to relax him and take all the burden of the past weeks and throw it blissfully aside.

"I didn't think you were just a biologist," Cora said tightly. "Though you had me believing that for a little while."

"I *am* a biologist," Merced shot back at her.

To Cora's pleasure, it was Rachael who next spoke

angrily to him. "I saw what you did when we first landed here, back at the dock where the toglut attacked us!" Merced's eyes darted quickly back toward Mataroreva, who had moved as if to rise again. "I saw the gun you didn't use then. But I trusted you."

"And I saw," Mataroreva said quietly, "the hold you used on that man on Hazaribagh's ship, the way you fought." He shook his head. "You don't learn to react that way by making it a hobby. Only a professional works that smoothly."

Rachael's voice was filled with disgust. "To think that I've been all over you since we landed here!"

Cora gaped at her daughter.

"It's true, Mother. I thought for a while he was a pretty nice guy. You know, at first I could hardly get him to touch me, much less anything else." Cora tried to speak, couldn't. She had suspected. But to hear it put so bluntly, from her daughter's own lips . . .

"The fighting I couldn't conceal." Merced gasped the words out, emphasizing the first syllable of each as if fighting merely to speak. He glanced at Rachael. "As for the other, I'm sorry. Sometimes it helps to mix business with pleasure."

Cora slumped back in her seat, overwhelmed by the double revelation of daughter and colleague. "So you've been tied in with these thought-manipulators all along. You were in on the destruction of all the towns, even Vai'oire. Now I can see why you want to go on. Near the bottom, beyond any hope of rescue, you'll lock us in and leak the air supply or something after your friends come to save you. It will be assumed we were all lost. What I can't figure out is how your people managed to infiltrate Commonwealth security to have you, their operative, assigned to this mission."

"No one has infiltrated Commonwealth security." He was trying to watch them all at once. Under the present circumstances, even Rachael might jump him. He didn't want to have to shoot anyone.

Instruments protruding from the wall pressed into his back. He forced himself against them. The physical pain helped override some of the mental anguish he was battling.

"I said I was a biologist. I wasn't lying. I also happen to be a Commonwealth agent. Security assigned me to this to hunt for exactly the kind of infiltration you're talking about," he explained to Cora. He looked anxiously at Hwoshien. "*He* knows that. He's temporarily forgotten. Something's making him forget."

The others glanced at the Commissioner. Once secure and serene, he now appeared to be wrestling with his own thoughts.

"I—I . . . confusing. I don't know . . ."

"Never mind. I don't need your confirmation now."

"No—wait," Hwoshien burst out. "It's true. I think . . . yes, it is true," he added more assuredly. "I do remember you now, Colonel Merced." He looked at his companions.

"Remember when you first arrived I explained that you would explore the biological possibilities and others would work on the chance that humans might be involved?" He nodded toward the still wary Merced. The muzzle of the gun had not dropped. "He is one of those 'others.' "

"Why make us remain down here, though?" a very confused Mataroreva wondered. Suddenly life had grown complicated, thinking an effort. His thoughts were slow and heavy, much like those of the fins. Uncontrollable opposing masses warred inside his head. "Why stay anyway? Why not go up and start over again? At least this time we'll know exactly what everyone's here for." Again his hand moved for the controls.

Merced gestured convulsively with the gun. "Touch

that and I'll shoot, Captain. And these darts will put you out permanently. I like you. I'd rather not have to do that."

Slowly the big Polynesian's palm moved away from the board. "But why? What's wrong with beginning again?"

"In the first place, I'm not sure that's necessary," Merced said carefully. "In the second—you really think you're going to send us up, don't you?"

"What else?"

"You were going to send us to the surface?"

"Of course. I—"

"Take another look, Captain. A close one. But don't move your hands." Mataroreva hesitated, and wasn't sure why he did so. "Go on, look," Merced insisted. "Are you afraid?"

That challenge appeared to break the lethargy that had come over the submersible's pilot. Like a man in slow motion, he turned back toward the console, keeping his hands from the controls.

The switch his hand had almost flicked was not the one to drop the ballast—That switch was close by, but not close enough to explain the near error. Instead, his fingers had drifted above a double red switch protected by a snap cover. This was the emergency release used to disengage the gas cylinders in the event of a potentially explosive leak.

Had he followed through and thrown the double switch, they would have had no way to return to the surface and would in fact have immediately plunged to the ooze flooring the canyon, eight thousand meters below normal air and pressure. Nothing could raise them against that gigantic force save another, similar submersible. None waited aboard the suprafoil above. By the time a second diving craft could be prepared and airshipped out from Mou'anui, the occupants of the submersible would be dead from lack of air. Arti-

ficial gills such as those employed in gelsuit masks
could not operate at these depths.

The viscous miasma that had been dulling Cora's
mind was abruptly shattered. She looked at her companions as if they had surprised her from a deep
sleep, saw that they were regarding her with the same
bemused expressions. Only then did Merced relax. But
he still held the gun.

"A very sophisticated bit of mind control, this," he
told them. "Contradiction finally broke its grip, just
as it did with the surviving baleens that led us here.
It was reimposed and finally killed them, but I think
we'll be able to stand it better now. I think it varies
in intensity and effectiveness proportional to the distance between projector and subject, which says to me
that our quarry is still here, close by, just as the baleens
suggested." He was getting angry now, sounding nothing like the shy biologist of weeks gone by.

"This sort of thing is banned by every related Commonwealth law and Church edict. Either someone's
managed to break those laws or else we're facing those
who don't care about them. Like the AAnn, or another
hostile race that could benefit from Commonwealth
expulsion from this world.

"The controls were put on you all so subtly that even
though you were talking about such controls and their
possible manipulators, you weren't aware it was actually happening. When you all suddenly agreed that
the search was useless and that it was time to return to
the surface, I knew what was taking place."

"How come," Cora wondered, terribly embarrassed
at having been so thoroughly invaded and directed,
"you weren't controlled?"

"Even though such devices are illegal, the service
still trains us to deal with them. It's a matter of mental
gymnastics, a reflex action that commenced working
even before I knew what was happening." He sounded
a little embarrassed himself. "If there had been a fight,

I would have risked killing all of you. There's more at stake here now than just thousands of additional lives.

"I regret having had to expose myself, but at this point I don't suppose it makes much difference." He looked briefly at Rachael and said in an entirely different tone of voice, "Except maybe to you.

"Do you still feel we should return to the surface? That we're wasting our time here?"

"No. Of course not," Cora said, shocked that she could ever have thought otherwise. "They must still be hiding here. You say that distance governs the effectiveness of the controls and contradiction breaks them down?"

"That, and awareness that they exist. Especially after you've been exposed to and then freed from their effect. That's part of our training, along with resisting drugs that have the same effect."

"I've got something here." Mataroreva had turned his attention back to the instruments. "I suppose it might have been here all along, and whatever's out there blocked it out in my mind?"

"Possible," Merced agreed.

Mataroreva moved to adjust the controls, paused, and glanced over his shoulder.

"It's okay." Merced lowered the weapon. "The fact that you hesitated is further proof that you're your own self again. What kind of submersible is it: mobile or a permanent installation?"

"Neither," Mataroreva said in a curious voice. "It's organic."

"Another ribbon fish?" Cora asked, referring to the luminescent giant they had encountered earlier in their descent.

"No, I don't think so."

The object continued slowly toward the neutrally buoyant craft. At first it was a distant pinpoint, glowing like a star in the night. The surrounding deep-sea life scattered rapidly and faded from sight. Only breathing sounded inside the submersible.

The star grew larger, split, subdivided into many different stars. All the while it continued to grow, illuminating the darkness as it neared, growing massive beyond expectation, beyond belief. It became so bright that they could see the last lingering sea life race, terrified, past the windows of the submersible, their transparent skins glassine envelopes holding highly pressurized fluids and organs.

The huge bulk grew beyond imagination, beyond reasonable thought. Cora wondered if Sam had been wrong, if they were being challenged by a machine, albeit no submersible she had ever dreamed of.

But the instruments were not awed. They did not lie. If the object was a machine, it was made not of metal or stelamic or duralloy but of flesh. As it approached the final meters, it assumed some of the aspects of a machine. It was easier to think of it that way; as a vast, organic machine. It was perfectly spherical. Delicate fluttering cilia in the millions lined much of the epidermis and propelled it rotiferlike through the water. The outer, jellylike shell was perfectly transparent. Only its pale yellow glow revealed its presence.

Inside, they could make out a veritable metropolis of organs, immensely complex structures that belied that outwardly simplistic shape. There were growths moving freely in strange paths, others swinging like a pendulum, still others rotating about one another or some unseen central axis. Each possessed its own distinct color: faint pink, light green, purple, rose, and more. Most were light pastels. Save for the purple, the only deep colors were occasional sparks of crimson or orange that drifted around the multitude of other specialized internal structures like gem dust in a colloid.

The headache Cora had once experienced returned, stronger than ever. It thudded remorselessly on her brain, threatening to pulp her skull. She fought back, determined that mere bone would give way before consciousness again surrendered.

Outside floated something larger than any dozen whales, a ball of something unknown that approached starship-size. It was bright as day around them, for all that they hovered more than five and a half kilometers below the surface.

Merced, studying readouts, swallowed and managed to say, "According to the scanners, there are six of them out there. Of course, we can only see this one."

The vast lagoon of Mou'anui could not have held the life that surrounded them. Six creatures do not a galaxy make, Cora told herself, for all their size. She found herself fascinated rather than fearful. Before her drifted the end result of billions of years of coelenterate evolution, a collective organism of unimagined complexity.

On Terra similar creatures had developed specialized polyps to handle such tasks as digestion, reproduction, and feeding. Why not also polyps grown for mind control, or for other unknown purposes? For all its great size, the creature appeared limited in its locomotive ability. It would need to evolve other means of defending itself. Terran coelenterates had developed specialized stinging cells to gather prey and defend. What could be more efficient than the ability to simply order a predator to look elsewhere?

But ignorant predators would be easy to dissuade. Intelligent cetaceans would be more difficult to handle. Very intelligent ones like the orcas and the catodons might be impossible to control at all but short distances; and humankind, uncontrollable except when dangerously near. An aroused or aware humankind, such as Merced had been and they all were now, might prove uncontrollable under any circumstances.

Somewhere within that line of thought, Cora suspected, lay the reason behind the manipulation of the baleens and the destruction of the floating towns. She stared into the living universe of organs. One of them, or perhaps many, must form the creature's mind.

Then Rachael shrieked, Mataroreva cursed, and the submersible was tumbled over and over as the creature bumped into it. A second came around from behind and they began to squeeze. Mental control having apparently failed, they were resorting to a far more basic method of attack.

A few supporting flows groaned, but the hull of formed duralloy would resist far stronger force than mere flesh, no matter the mass, could bring to bear. The creatures could not damage the submersible.

They reacted by backing clear. Alternately fading and intensifying, the outer shell of the one before them pulsed in rapid sequence. Crimson fragments of unknown specialized function flared and raced within, a thousand living sunspots inhabiting a transparent sun. Their activity might signify anything from poor digestion to incipient sleep.

Or it might be a reflection of something as basic and sophisticated as anger.

XVII

Cora picked herself off the floor, found she had suffered nothing worse than a few bruises. Here, then, was the source of the baleens' madness, here the off-stage directors of organized murder.

The headache faded and Cora and her companions received their second surprise. "CAN YOU UNDERSTAND US?"

"Yes, we can understand you," she heard Merced saying.

"IT IS DIFFICULT FOR US," the voice in her head said. "YOUR MINDS ARE MORE COMPLEX, YET YOU ARE NOT ATTUNED TO THIS METHOD OF COMMUNICATING. WE HAVE TO PUSH OUR THOUGHTS IN AND PULL YOURS OUT.

"THE SMOOTH-SIDES ARE SIMILAR OF MIND BUT EASIER TO PENETRATE. THERE IS NO RESISTANCE TO OUR EFFORTS AND NOT NEARLY THE COMPLEXITY."

"You're the CunsnuC?" Her head was beginning to throb again, this time with effort but not pain.

"I AM THE CUNSNUC. WE ARE THE CUNSNUC."

"Collective intelligence," Merced murmured. "Just like collective physical structure."

"ALL ARE COLLECTIVE. THERE IS NO INDIVIDUAL US."

"There is among our people," Cora said.

257

"THAT IS SO, AND IT FRIGHTENS US. AND HURTS. HURTS."

The communication might also be communal, she thought. The voice in her mind did not exhibit changes of inflection. They had no way of tracing it to its source. It was simply there inside one's head, much the way a voice sounded in a dark room.

"Why have you directed the cetaceans, the smooth-sides, to attack our communities?" Hwoshien had no time to waste on biological speculation.

"YOUR THOUGHTS HURT, DAMAGE OUR MINDS. OUR SENSIBILITIES OF THOUGHT ARE EXTREMELY DELICATE AND PRONE TO PAINFUL INTERRUPTION. THE THOUGHTS OF THE SMOOTH-SIDES DO NOT PENETRATE OR HURT."

Cora tried to imagine something the size of a small starship having delicate sensibilities. "Static," she whispered aloud. "Something in our thoughts, some projection of our nervous system, causes static in their minds."

Then it came to her what the outstanding feature of the creature's attitude toward them suggested: fear. Fear and worry. For all their immense size, the CunsnuC were afraid of men.

"It hurts you even though you dwell in these deeps?"

"MUCH OF THE TIME WE MUST RISE TO THE SURFACE," the voice said, "TO FEED ON THE CREATURES WHICH RISE WITH THE ABSENCE OF THE LIGHT ABOVE THE SKY. MORE THAN A FEW OF YOUR KIND THINKING IN THAT PRESENCE HURT US, DISRUPT OUR THOUGHTS AND ABILITY TO CONCENTRATE ON OUR FEEDING. YOU MUST ALL LEAVE, OR THE KILLING WILL NOT STOP." A pause, then, "ONLY BY BRINGING SO MANY OF US TOGETHER HERE CAN WE STAND THE PAIN WELL ENOUGH TO CONVERSE COHERENTLY WITH YOU."

"Leave Cachalot?" Hwoshien muttered.

"YES. VANISH. GO BACK TO WHEREVER YOU WERE

SPAWNED." Then a question. "WHAT IS 'CACHALOT'?"

"This world," Cora explained. "We come from a world other than this."

"A WORLD OTHER THAN THIS? THERE ARE NO WORLDS OTHER THAN THIS, BY WHATEVER NAME YOU CALL IT."

So the sea-dwelling CunsnuC had no knowledge of astronomy, and had not gained any from their contacts with the Cetacea.

"But there are."

"THERE CAN BE NO WORLD WHERE THERE ARE NO CUNSNUC, AND ALL CUNSNUC ARE HERE OR WE WOULD KNOW OTHERWISE. THERE CAN BE NO CUNSNUC WHERE THERE ARE MINDS OF YOUR KIND."

"Humanity has been working on this world," Mataroreva said hotly, leaving aside for the moment the question of the existence of other worlds, "for hundreds of our years. You've never done anything to us before. Why all of a sudden this hurt, and this need for us to leave?"

"THE HURT IS NOT SUDDEN. IT HAS BEEN WITH US FOR AS LONG AS YOU HAVE SAID. BUT WE DID NOT UNTIL NOW HAVE THE MEANS TO RESIST."

Cora could believe that. For all their mass, the CunsnuC still appeared physically fragile. Only their size and mental defenses protected them against Cachalot's smaller but still sizable predators. They were plankton-eaters, like the toothless great whales.

"WE HAD TO DEVELOP PARTS OF US BEFORE WE COULD GAIN THE USE OF THE SMOOTH-SIDES' MINDS."

"So you could direct them to attack us," Hwoshien concluded.

"YES. IT WOULD HAVE BEEN BETTER IF WE COULD HAVE GAINED THE USE OF OTHER, MORE POWERFUL SMOOTH-SIDES, BUT THEIR MINDS WOULD RESIST."

"The catodons and the other toothed whales," Rachael murmured, fingering her neurophon.

"We cannot leave Cachalot," Hwoshien insisted.

"YOU MUST! ONE WAY OR THE OTHER, YOU MUST GO. OR YOU WILL BE ELIMINATED."

The transparent skin of the colossus pressed up against the ports. Cora forgot to breathe. Rachael gasped behind her.

Within the skin of the CunsnuC were several glowing green bubbles. Within those bubbles were a dozen people. They were alive and their mouths were working, their hands pressed against the fleshy envelopes that contained them and supplied them with air. Cora could see that they were screaming, though nothing could be heard inside the submersible.

Matarovera recognized one of them and swore quietly. A member of his slim planetary command. The suprafoil and factory ship had not made it back to Mou'anui. Another bubble drifted nearer, and a horrified Cora recognized the short, dark-skinned man within. He flailed at the film of the bubble, and his eyes were wide and desperate.

As the CunsnuC moved away from the ports, the bubbles moved toward the epidermis. They passed through the skin, and thus unprotected by internal regulation, immediately burst under the tremendous pressure. The hapless humans contained within imploded before they could drown.

This explained the complete absence of bodies at the sites of the destroyed towns. Either the baleens carried them to the depths, where they could be transferred to the CunsnuC for disposal, or else the CunsnuC rose to the surface to perform the task themselves. Occasionally survivors were found. Hazaribagh and his companions and guards had been brought to provide an example for the crew of the submersible. Others had doubtless been ingested alive to be questioned.

As expected, it was Hwoshien who finally broke the silence. "Let us compromise." Cora gaped at him. He sounded as if he had not just witnessed the deaths of a dozen people and was bargaining as usual with a group of off-world traders for fishing rights to a particularly desirable reef.

"We humans will restrict our activities to prescribed areas of the surface. There is enough room on this world for all of us."

"THIS IS THE WORLD OF THE CUNSNUC. THE CUNSNUC ARE THE WORLD!" There was no hint of vanity or presumptuousness in that statement, Cora mused. It arose from a different approach to rationality, much as man and cetacean differed. The CunsnuC perception of reality was sculpted as much by their size and mental ability as by their ignorance of the greater universe beyond Cachalot.

"WE DO NOT WANT YOU IN OUR WORLD, IN OUR-SELVES," the voice continued firmly.

"We'll retreat to only the few above-water islands," Hwoshien proposed. "We'll build nonthinking devices, machines, to do all of our work."

"NO, NO, NO, NO!" A spoiled child, Cora thought. Spoiled and very dangerous. This time she had a faint impression, despite what the creature had said of collective thought, of several different CunsnuC joining to generate the chorus of negativity.

"Lie to them," Mataroreva suggested. "Tell them we'll do what they say. We can work out a way."

"No. Any agreement I make I will keep. Besides, I'm not sure you can produce a telepathic lie, Sam. Remember what they/it said about 'pulling out' our thoughts. I think they will tend to pull out the truth."

"THAT IS SO," the voice said, confirming the Commissioner's suspicions. "AS IT IS SO IN YOUR COMPANION'S MIND THAT HE WILL NOT AGREE TO LEAVE. AS IT IS IN YOUR OWN. BUT YOU WILL DIE WITH HONOR."

In the darkness inside her head Cora found to her horror that Sam was beginning to remind her more and more of Silvio. Why now, why here? Why torment yourself with thoughts of that distant awfulness

in moments of stress? she asked herself. And had no
answer.

Hwoshien stood stiff-backed against a wall. "They
can't hurt us in here. They've already tried and
failed."

"ALSO TRUE. WE CANNOT PENETRATE YOUR ARTI-
FICIAL SHELL." Cora was knocked off her feet as the
submersible was rocked once again. "BUT WE CAN
PREVENT YOU FROM RISING. WE KNOW THAT YOU
REQUIRE THE GAS BEYOND THE SKY IN ORDER TO EXIST.
WE CAN KEEP YOU HERE, WILL KEEP YOU HERE,
UNTIL THE QUANTITY YOU DESCENDED WITH HAS BEEN
USED UP."

Mataroreva immediately moved to try the necessary
controls. The submersible rocked several times, bouncing against the creature that hovered above it. Then
he flipped the activation switch slowly, looked worriedly at his friends.

"We're not rising. I could try a full ballast drop,
but if that didn't work . . ." He let the sentence trail
away. Much as their air would trail away.

The submersible was caught in a gigantic box created by the six huge forms.

"Lie to them! Deal with them!" Mataroreva shouted
at his superior.

Hwoshien looked at the big man uncertainly.
"You're as crazy as they are!"

Mataroreva rushed the Commissioner, both massive hands raised to strike.

Cora found herself on his back, pounding at his
ears with her tiny fists. He shook her off, threw her to
the floor. She lay there, head ringing from the im-
pact.

Merced slipped in between Mataroreva and his
spindly quarry and did something Cora didn't see.
Mataroreva grunted in surprise, then sat down, holding his middle. Merced stood nearby, hands in front

of him, ready to defend himself or retreat depending on the larger man's actions.

But Sam's gaze was already clearing. "Th-thanks, Pucara." He smiled wanly. "They almost had me again." He looked up at Hwoshien. "Yu, I—"

"Never mind." The oldster spoke thoughtfully. "Evidently they won't wait for our air to run out. They'll keep trying to control us that way. Eventually I think they'll get what they want." Then he frowned at the sweating, panting Cora. "Are you all right?"

"We're going to die. I know that now." She looked up and across to her daughter. "And since we're going to die, there's something you should know, Rachael."

"They're working on you now, Mother. Control . . ."

"No. No." She slimbed to her feet, slumped into one of the control chairs. She rested the back of a wrist against her forehead, closed her eyes, and tried to force out the words. It was difficult. She had worked to suppress them for twenty years.

"I've been hard on you, Rachael. I know that, and I'm sorry. I've been taking out on you the resentment I held against your father. I loved him once, originally. I grew to hate him. Yet when he died I felt guilty. Maybe I should have been more of a woman . . . I don't know what it was. I've just been trying so hard ever since to see that you didn't make the same mistakes, that you didn't fall into the same traps that life sets for us. That . . ."

Rachael was shaking her head slowly, and smiling. "I know how you felt about him, Mother. Do you think children are blind?" Cora's arm slipped and her eyes functioned. Her daughter stood staring calmly down at her. "I noticed everything. I knew what was going on."

"So many years," Cora whispered. "Why didn't you ever tell me you knew?"

"I was afraid. Children don't mix in adult affairs.

It's an unwritten law of nature. I could see how it, how he, hurt you. So when you hurt me back"—she shrugged—"I took it. You had suffered enough." She bent, hugged hard. It was reciprocated. "I hated him, too."

"You never showed it. I always thought you loved him."

Rachael's expression twisted. "I hated him ever since I was old enough to understand how he was hurting you. But I thought that if I loved him enough, it would make him stop making you cry so much. You're very good at understanding the ways of echinoderms and teleosts and alien water-dwellers, Mother, but not so good with little girls." Then she started to sob. Cora joined her.

Mataroreva turned away, looked at Merced with great respect. "That's the second time they nearly made me kill someone. I would have, if not for you, Colonel. *Maururu au*. I thank you."

"Not as much as I do," Hwoshien murmured.

"Just trained." Merced winced. "There . . . they just tried me again. It's hard to fight. Sooner or later they'll turn subtle again and make us do something that we think we're doing because we want to. Everyone has to consider everyone else's actions from now on with the greatest caution.

"We can't surface," he observed, changing the subject. "The first thing we should do is communicate all we've learned to the ship waiting above so they can relay it to Mou'anui. They'll be safe, with that herd of catodons to protect them from any induced baleen attack."

Mataroreva started to comply, then turned away disgustedly from the console. "Forget it. They're generating enough distortion at this range to jam any kind of broadcast we can make. I juggled frequencies like mad, but they're too fast. We're not getting through to the surface."

"Let me see. I remember a few broadcast tricks."

While Hwoshien and Matararoreva worked at the console, Merced divided his time between studying the internal galaxy of the CunsnuC outside the ports and watching his companions for signs of illogical action.

Time passed. Matararoreva and Hwoshien were unable to punch a word past the watchful CunsnuC. An hour of life remained to the inhabitants of the submersible. Outside, despite the brightness supplied by the CunsnuC, the watery dark and cold pressed close on the five travelers trapped in their metal bubble.

Cora found pleasure in those last minutes by watching her daughter, studying every smooth curve of her face and form. She listened to the soft music, wondered that it could ever have troubled her. A little understanding, and it would never have gotten on her nerves. She had pushed Rachael too hard in her own image. Let her have fun. You've spent twenty years not having any. Why deprive someone so full of life as she? Of course, it is likely that opportunity will now never be granted. So let her enjoy the music, and pretend you enjoy it even more than you do. Pretend—

She shifted so rapidly in the chair that Merced moved toward her from the port.

"No, Pucara, I'm okay. Rachael, show me how you work that thing."

"It's a little late to begin music lessons, Mother."

"It's not music I'm interested in, and the less musical I can be, the better I'll like it."

A puzzled Rachael explained the workings. "Be careful with these two, Mother. Amplitude on axonics is dangerous. These have a built-in override, of course. Otherwise you could seriously injure someone."

"Can you take out the override?"

"What? I—I don't know. I never considered it . . . I guess you could, but the failsafe might keep the instrument from playing."

"Then we'll just have to try it this way first." She

snugged the device in her arms, trying to match Rachael's actions. Then she gritted her teeth and commenced a most distressing and atonal song. Her teeth screamed. Her legs twitched. One time the pain in her head was so great it felt as if her eyes would burst from the pressure.

But several minutes later the submersible tumbled sharply and they felt themselves rolling toward the ceiling. Mataroreva fought his way into a chair, worked frantically at the overwrought stabilizers. With his help, the automatics soon leveled them out.

Cora had not let go of the neurophon. She located the same setting, struck it once more. Again the submersible was jolted by outside forces, though not as severely as before. She pushed the power to maximum and held down the combination of controls she had located by chance.

Outside flowed an amazing display of energy and light. Colors far deeper than the gently pulsing pastels they had originally observed rippled through the CunsnuC. The chromatic storm raged through its substance as internal structures quivered and swelled. Then the creature was moving away, the violent display fading only slightly.

Mataroreva jabbed several switches hopefully. Motion possessed the craft. "They're no longer above us."

"Fifty-five hundred meters. Fifty-four." Merced spoke triumphantly from his seat. "We're ascending!"

Now the mass of color drifted back toward them. Cora held her fingers on the controls of the neurophon, her muscles locked. How much longer, she wondered frantically, could the instrument continue to generate projections of such magnitude? The particular frequency she had hit upon produced only a slight tingle along her spine. The reaction in the CunsnuC was ten thousand times greater.

Again it fell away from them and they continued their unimpeded rise. Then there was pain in Cora's head, but it did not come from the neurophon. It was generated by the CunsnuC.

Her hands went to her temples and she fell over on her side. The neurophon, its controls locked, tumbled to the floor. It bounced hard on the metal but continued to function. Mataroreva had barely thrown the console on automatic before that intense blast of mental agony overcame him.

Dimly, Merced perceived the critical gauge through the red haze that filled his brain. Fifty-one hundred meters. Five thousand. They were still rising.

Blood and thunder filled Cora's head and she rolled over and over on the deck. Every image of nightmare, every sliver of pain she had ever felt since childhood, came back to her in those awful moments. Rachael sobbed with the hurt.

They were so overcome that they did not immediately realize the pain was not projected at them by the CunsnuC, but was instead the helpless broadcast of those great creatures' own torment.

One rose after them, a seething mass of antagonistic colors and thoughts. Millions of cilia drove it upward like a rolling moon as it strove to get above them, to force them back into the abyss. Its pain grew worse as it neared the craft, and those on board alternated red and yellow explosions with sharp-edged hallucination in their minds.

"YOU . . . MUST . . . LEAVE! . . ." a great voice thundered in Cora's skull, barely perceptible above the ocean of pain. Her head was a bell and her brain the clapper bouncing off the bone.

She dragged herself to a port, saw the greatest of all the CunsnuC nearing them. "We can't help how we think!" she cried out, wondering if her mouth was echoing the workings of her mind. "You can't kill us all just to keep us from thinking!"

There was no reply.

They were at eighteen hundred meters and rising,

and the two minnows swimming near the light of the CunsnuC were adult catodons. They moved unafraid of the mass that dwarfed them, knowing somehow it could not hurt them. None of the toothed fears a plankton-eater, she thought, no matter its size or alienness.

A final, despairing mental shriek echoed through her empty head, skidded like a needle along her bones. Then the last CunsnuC raced for the bottom ooze, turning into a distant red star that soon was swallowed by the concealing fathoms . . .

She blinked, wondering how long she had been out. Merced leaned back in his chair, hopefully no more than unconscious. Sam lay draped over the console, breathing heavily. Hwoshien sat stiffly against the wall nearby, taking in long, deep breaths, reassuring his body. He was smooth when inhaling, shuddered when he exhaled, but at least he was in control of himself. Her eyes hunted for Rachael.

Her daughter lay on the floor, eyes staring blankly at the roof. Painfully, Cora half slid, half fell, from the chair and crawled across the deck, passing the now quiescent neurophon. Its energy pack was burned out. She was surprised to discover that it was her body that ached, not her mind. Faint echoes of that last massive scream still fluttered around in her thoughts like dying butterflies. But they no longer affected her.

"Rachael?" She put both hands on the girl's shoulders, shook her. The effort made her nauseous, and she had to stop and rest before trying again. "Rachael!" Muscles began to move under her fingers. The engine was warming up.

Gradually the eyes focused, turned left. "Mother? We were killing it. I could feel it dying."

"I know, Rachael." She cradled the girl's head in her arms. "We all could. We shared the pain it was feeling. But . . . rather it than us." She reached back with a hand, pulled the neurophon over. "They said they were delicate. They told us. All mass and no bite." She winced, and the hand went to her head. "No, not no bite. An indirect one. I'm afraid your instrument is burned out. It saved our lives. I'll buy you a new one. The best." She smiled. "And you can play and practice all you wish, and I'll support you to the best of my ability and bankroll."

"I don't know," the girl murmured. "So much hurt. I don't know when I'll be able to play again. That pain will always be with me when I try to play."

"The memory of the pain, and it will fade," Cora corrected her.

"We'll work something out with them." It was Hwoshien. His body had not moved, but his head turned to face them. "They have most of this world, most of the world-ocean to dwell in. We use only tiny, isolated patches of the surface. They're just stubborn. We'll reach some kind of accommodation. They have no choice now." He unfolded his legs, stood easily.

"We don't need the catodons' help. Neurophonic projectors much larger than that one will keep these creatures under control, will disrupt their power over the baleens. If they insist on fighting, we can dispose of them. The killing of any intelligent alien life-form is prohibited, except *when* attacked and no alternative is available. We'll give them that alternative. If they elect not to accept . . ." He shrugged meaningfully.

"But surely you wouldn't? . . ." Cora began.

"I have several thousand people dead, many million credits of property destroyed. We require a minuscule portion of this world. They and the Cetacea are welcome to the rest. I have no sympathy where such all-encompassing greed is involved."

"I'm sure something can be arranged," Cora replied. "Mental shielding that will keep our thoughts from them, for example. If only they'd revealed themselves and their problem to us earlier, peacefully.

They're unique, utterly unique, Hwoshien. The first intelligent invertebrates we've ever encountered, possibly the most evolved of their line in the universe. They must be studied and learned from. Not fought with."

"That's only a last alternative I was outlining," Hwoshien reminded her, the very tone of his voice indicating that he was merely being businesslike, not bloodthirsty.

"Most coelenterates are primitive, and these creatures are at the opposite end of that scale. It's almost as if they've skipped an entire chapter of evolution. Their physical and mental structures are incredibly complex. What do they think about down there in the eternal dark? What is there to stimulate the development of such advanced minds at such depths? I doubt they possess vision as we know it. Possibly hearing. They are true colony creatures on a scale undreamed of. They must be dealt with peacefully so that they can be studied!"

"You can study them if you want to." Mataroreva was adjusting controls. "We're almost up. Me for the light."

"We will." Cora suddenly saw where her thoughts had been leading, and was not disappointed in them. "*I* will. We can be friends."

"Do you want to end up like poor Hazaribagh and his people? The CunsnuC were studying *them*," he shot back.

"Would you care?"

He turned away, moved in a manner that might have signified anything, an indecipherable gesture. But at least he had responded to the question—affirmatively, she preferred to think.

"That was caused by fear," she argued with him. "The universe is full of otherwise benign creatures that can be induced to kill out of fear. They must be, can be, studied." She looked back over her shoulder.

"I don't know what I'm going to do, Mother." Rachael glanced over at Merced, who regarded her encouragingly. "I don't know what I'm going to do. Not now."

"Think about it. Take your time," Cora urged. "I rushed you, maybe in the wrong direction. Maybe in the right. If you decide to continue on your present course of study, I could still use an assistant."

"We'll see." She was still looking at Merced.

Natural light, fresh and invigorating, poured through the submersible's ports. Huge shapes swarmed patiently around them as the catodons escorted them the rest of the way to the surface. Their great bulks came close to, but never actually touched, the rising craft's hull.

Then a black and white shape was pressing against one port. Mataroreva pressed his own face against the glassalloy from the inside, whale and man separated by a modest transparency.

Cora watched them closely.

"I think it's admirable," Merced said to her.

"What is?"

"Your willingness to remain here to study so dangerous a life-form. I'm sure Commonwealth Administration will concur, and will give you all the support it can. The CunsnuC are as alien as any life we've yet encountered. You'll need funding."

"I can provide whatever modest resources—" Hwoshien started to say.

Merced cut him off. He did not have to speak only as a mere biologist now. "You can do what you wish, Mr. Commissioner, but it's not necessary. I'll see that sufficient credit is provided."

Cora looked at him appraisingly. "Thank you. For all their size, these creatures fear us more than we fear them. What is needed here is understanding."

Th submersible broke the surface. Mataroreva hurried to the double lock, opened the bottom one, and squeezed his bulk through. Merced glanced out the port a last time, was surprised to see no sign of the catodons. Perhaps they already knew what had happened in the Deep below and had gone on their nomadic way, indifferent to whatever the surviving humans might have to say. So they had departed, secure in their vast, contemplative indifference that the CunsnuC now posed no threat to their way of life. Had left to think their thoughts and to advance their migratory civilization in whatever manner they thought best. Who are truly the strangers? Merced mused. The CunsnuC, or these huge, wallowing creatures related to us by blood and evolution?

Hwoshien followed Mataroreva out. Cora was next, then Rachael, cradling her neurophon. Merced watched them ascend, enjoying the sight of Rachael climbing and smelling the fresh, oh so sweet air above. A faint splash reached him and he turned to the port.

Sam Mataroreva was cavorting with the two orcas, twisting and turning like a seal outside the submersible. He clutched Latehoht's fin as she darted past, hung on as she bucked and squirmed in the water, trying to throw him off. There was more here to report on besides the CunsnuC, Merced mused. Cachalot was changing its inhabitants, as any world did. This aqueous globe offered more than exports and oceanographic studies. Changes in ways of thinking were taking place here that might have far-reaching effects on all humanxkind. It might be well to encourage this trend.

"Hey!" Rachael leaned down and in. "You going to stay down there forever, Pucara?"

"Be right out." He watched her withdraw, leaving the flash of an inviting smile lingering in his memory. He thought of their previous weeks together and of how the CunsnuC had almost destroyed the friendship he had worked so diligently to build. Intimacy was easily attained, but friendship—that was a rare find.

He grinned. This was a world for enjoying oneself, for relaxation as well as research. It was time for some of the former.

Confident in himself and in the report he would file with his bureau, he started to climb out of the submersible. Waiting was the bright sun of Cachalot. Nearby drifted the suprafoil, anxious faces crowding its railing. Soon Hwoshien would make a broadcast of his own, and anxiety would vanish from the faces of this world's citizens for the first time in months.

His wave was for those on the ship, but his eyes were for Rachael.

Far below danced vast spherical forms that pulsed and glowed. They were akin to planets in their shape and motion, yet they orbited not a sun but a common thought. They conversed in a manner incomprehensible to man or cetacean, conversed in a manner fashioned by darkness, shaped by pressure and isolation. They were discussing the development of a new kind of specialized internal polyp, much as any manufacturer might discuss an addition to his plant.

They knew it would take time. That could not be helped. They would work and wait, until the new polyp was ready to perform its function. Until then there would be enforced tolerance of Those Above. Afterward . . . afterward, they would see.

Having thus decided upon a biologic course of action, the CunsnuC commenced an addition to the inventory of their minds.

Above and far distant floated a life-form that thought in a manner incomprehensible to man or CunsnuC. Lumpjaw, whose water name was DeMalthiAzur-of-the-Maizeen and who was elder among his people, had slipped away from them to think quietly on portentous matters. And to consider. More men would come, and the free-thinking stretches of sea would shrink still further. Not that he felt they would break the laws (at least not right away), but mankind had displayed a disconcerting tendency throughout his history to circumvent them. And the men of today were not the men of tomorrow. Who could tell what changes they might propose?

Then there was the matter of the CunsnuC. Their control over the baleen had demonstrated a disturbing capacity for dangerous mischief. In the sanctuary of their Deeps they might concoct further trouble for the Cetacea.

DeMalthiAzur-of-the-Maizeen let pass the catodonian equivalent of a sigh. Why must existence be so complicated, he mused, when all one desired from life was time to think? Of the men he had no worry, for the cousins the orca would stay near them, professing friendship for them and dislike for the catodon, and report whatever they were about. Smartest of all was the catodon, he thought, but cleverest was the orca.

The CunsnuC were more of a problem, and were likely to present the greater problem for all that they were confined to their abyssal home. So the people of the sea had much progress to make, out of sight of humanxkind and CunsnuC, out of sight of even their massive but slow-thinking relatives the baleen.

Perhaps that progress would be part of the Great Journey. Perhaps it would constitute only a digression. But it was necessary to insure preservation of the peace.

Time, the old whale thought. Never enough time. So much wasted time. But it was vital, this digression. Of all the creatures of Earth, only man had mastered the ability to travel through environments hostile to his kind. That was ever his great advantage. That, and manipulative digits. The Cetacea had only their minds. They could not match the simian flexibility of man, nor the mental approaches of the CunsnuC.

Oh, well. Perhaps in time. For now, the Cetacea,

led by the catodons, would have to find another path, would have to improve the path they had chosen to insure their survival and their way of life.

It was time to practice, he thought. Straining his enormous brain and nervous system, DeMalthiAzur-of-the-Maizeen made the Shift.

How strange it makes the world look, he mused. There was much new to think about, much that might be learned to surprise both man and CunsnuC when the time came. The effort was easier this time, grew simpler with each successful Shift.

Better to return now to the pod, to think with them. Thinking alone cleared the brain but became lifeless and dull all too soon. He longed for the mental companionship and the joint progress made while sharing the Great Journey. He levitated a little more, regarding the water below and the startled icthyorniths that soared in his shadow.

Turning, the great whale sought his companions as all eighty tons of his gray-brown bulk flew awkwardly but with increasing assurance toward the setting sun.

About the Author

Born in New York City in 1946, Alan Dean Foster was raised in Los Angeles, California. After receiving a bachelor's degree in political science and a Master of Fine Arts in motion pictures from UCLA in 1968–1969, he worked for two years as a public relations copywriter in a small Studio City, California, firm.

His writing career began in 1968, when August Derleth bought a long letter of Foster's and published it as a short story in his biannual *Arkham Collector Magazine*. Sales of short fiction to other magazines followed. His first try at a novel, *The Tar-Aiym Krang*, was published by Ballantine in 1972.

Foster has toured extensively through Asia and the isles of the Pacific. Besides traveling, he enjoys surfing and karate. He has taught screenwriting, literature, and film history at UCLA and Los Angeles City College.

Currently he resides in Big Bear Lake, California, with his wife JoAnn (who is reputed to have the only extant recipe for Barbarian Cream Pie), three cats, three dogs, two hundred house plants, assorted renegade coyotes and raccoons, and the ensorceled chair of the nefarious Dr. John Dee.

Exciting Space Adventure from DEL REY

STAR TREK

These are the voyages of the starship Enterprise...

Captain's log, stardate 1980.6:

Exciting adventures from television's most popular science fiction series, starring the legendary Captain Kirk, Mr. Spock, Dr. McCoy and the crew of the Enterprise—and of course, Klingons, Romulans, and Tribbles!